D1551311

SAVE THE PEARLS PART ONE
Revealing Eden

ALSO BY VICTORIA FOYT

The Virtual Life of Lexie Diamond

SAVE THE PEARLS PART ONE

Revealing Eden

a novel by

VICTORIA FOYT

2012 · SAND DOLLAR PRESS, INC.
SANTA MONICA, CALIFORNIA

Published by Sand Dollar Press, Inc.
1301 Montana Avenue, Suite C
Santa Monica, CA 90403
www.SandDollarPress.com

SUGGESTED CATALOGING DATA
Foyt, Victoria. Revealing Eden / by Victoria Foyt.
Series title: Save the Pearls (Part One).
Summary: In a post-apocalyptic world where class and beauty are defined
by resistance to an overheated environment, 17-year-old Eden, a lowly Pearl
cursed with white skin, and facing death if she doesn't mate soon, unwittingly
compromises her father's top-secret experiment and escapes to the last patch
of rainforest with a beastly man who she believes is her enemy,
despite her overwhelming attraction.
1. Global warming—fiction. 2. Race relations—fiction. 3. Human–animal
hybridization—fiction. 4. Endangered species—fiction. 5. Dickinson, Emily
(poet)—fiction. 6. Science fiction. I. Title.

Library of Congress Control Number: 2011910826

ISBN: 978-0-9836503-2-4

The publisher would like to credit Emily Dickinson's poems,
used in excerpt or in entirety throughout this book.

Book design and production: Studio E Books, Santa Barbara, California
Chapter headings design © 2012 by Christopher Pardell

Printed in the United States of America

First edition, January 2012
10 9 8 7 6 5 4 3 2 1

For Christopher, beastly and true

ACKNOWLEDGEMENTS

They say it takes a village to raise a child. The same analogy may apply to creating a novel, which is another kind of birth. I could never have written this book without the help of many others. Mostly, I'm grateful for the company of other writers, like Martha Michaels, who understands the pleasures and the difficulties of our craft, and who was so generous with her time. I'm particularly grateful to my dear friend and gifted writer, Martha Goldhirsh, who listened to my first ramblings and urged me to begin this book. And heartfelt thanks to Linda Loewenthal for her razor-sharp notes and strong belief in me. Of course, always, much gratitude to dear Henry Jaglom, who may be the world's best cheerleader. I could never write a word if my giving, efficient assistant, Rachelle Whaley, didn't keep the machine running. My family inspires me to do my best, and I thank Sabrina and Simon for putting up with their somewhat driven mother. And then there is Christopher Pardell, a true artist, who never ceases to amaze me with his tireless support, insightful comments, and deep understanding of the joys, and the toll, of passion.

Come slowly, Eden!
Lips unused to thee,
Bashful, sip thy jasmines,
As the fainting bee,

Reaching late his flower,
Round her chamber hums,
Counts his nectars—enters,
And is lost in balms!

—Emily Dickinson

SAVE THE PEARLS PART ONE
Revealing Eden

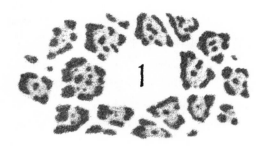

1

EDEN JUMPED at the sound of approaching steps. *They must not see. Hide Beauty Map!*

Her mental command caused the Life-Band she wore to send a tiny white spark into the air. In a flash, the holographic images that appeared in front of her—a blond girl playing on a sunlit beach—disappeared.

"What's going on?" a woman asked.

Eden shot to her feet, her heart racing, as a plump, dark-skinned lab assistant appeared on the other side of the partition. It was only Peach, who wasn't as cruel as the rest of *them*.

Eden's blank emotional mask slammed into place. *Never let* them *see how you feel.* "Um," she said. "What do you mean?"

"Didn't you monitor the test subjects' medications?" Peach said.

"Yes, of course." Eden couldn't afford to make a mistake.

"Then why isn't the report on schedule?"

Had Peach forgotten that Eden's skin only had a dark coating? Maybe she was passing, after all. Wouldn't that be nice? Eden almost enjoyed pointing out the truth. "I'm not allowed to communicate on Priority One channels."

Peach grew flustered. "I know that. Why didn't you give the report to Ashina?"

In fact, Eden already had sent it to her supervisor, Ashina. But she couldn't directly accuse a Coal, even if she was only late from her lunch break.

"I sent it. But, well, *my* lunch break started ten minutes ago," Eden said. To further soften her words, she smiled politely.

A pair of mallard ducks took flight over a nearby sun-dappled lake along the far side of the lab. Eden automatically recalled their scientific name, *Anas platyrhynchos*—extinct birds and animals were her specialty. Of course, the Holo-Images were as fake as her smile.

"What does your lunch break have to do—" Peach glanced at Ashina's empty desk, then, seeming to grasp the situation, walked away without another word.

A voice in Eden's head, one she had been programmed to receive from the World-Band since birth, issued a gentle warning: *Your heartbeat is elevated. Experience something pleasant, my dear.*

Eden slumped back in her chair with a heavy sigh. *I'm a stone in a cool, dark cave.* The small holographic image appeared in front of her while she repeated this soothing thought over and over. Soon, the constant, jumbled noise of the World-Band that streamed into her head grew distant. In that quiet, treasured space, she allowed herself one small but true thought: *I hate* them.

And yet, if only Eden were one of *them,* she'd be beautiful and safe.

But, at age seventeen, she was already middle-aged. She'd

be lucky to make it to her forties. Despite her rat-like existence in the Combs, a network of dark, shadowy underground tunnels, where civilization burrowed to avoid the deadly levels of solar radiation, Eden undoubtedly would die from The Heat, just like her mother had.

Most of the population only ventured outside at night when the effects of radiation were at its lowest. Some people—the fairest in complexion, like Eden—had never been outside. Once, when she was little, her mother had woken her at dawn.

—*Come, Eden. It's your turn to see the light.*

They had ridden several underground hovercrafts until they reached a special set of stairs. The guard on duty had inspected them before letting them climb to the upper level. There, they stood at a special viewing window that was tinted and sealed. The sight of the steaming rocks and an endless sea of pale, tired dirt had saddened Eden even though she'd never known a green Earth. Her mother had pointed to a pile of bleached bones.

—*We must be careful, daughter.*

The message had been clear: *this is where you'll end up if you don't obey.* All Pearls, the racist term for whites, feared the light.

If it weren't for Eden's Life-Band, a simple hoop earring that she wore in her right ear, she wouldn't last a night. At the age of seven, she had chosen the copper earring—the only personal decision she'd ever made. She thought of it as an appendage, as vital as her heart or lungs. Her Life-Band gave her the freedom to travel in her mind anywhere in the past. It was better than having to face her uncertain future.

Thank Earth, the Uni-Gov provided her with a Life-Band. *They* cared about her.

Everyone had a Life-Band, though most wore it discreetly, hidden in a specially sewn pants pocket or as a locket underneath a shirt. As if they didn't need it to survive.

Eden needed hers within easy reach. So she could believe it would never be taken away. So she could escape.

And right now, she wanted to escape back to the beach, to see the happy blonde. She knew she shouldn't do it, but she found herself giving the silent command, anyway. The sensors planted in her head at birth, which connected her to the World-Band, where all holographic images were stored, responded with a slight tingle.

A familiar rush of pleasure, mixed with fear, coursed through her at the sight of the white girl. Images of Pearls in natural coloring were forbidden. If *they* caught Eden looking, she would be punished.

And yet, she couldn't resist watching the pale, slim girl bounce a multi-colored ball over to a young man who was also white-skinned. She wore a polka-dot bikini—all that skin exposed! Nearby, other whites lounged on thick towels or cabana chairs, or played cards at tables out in broad daylight! Sunshine glittered on a blue ocean that stretched across the semi-circular cove like a big happy smile. Children, lots of them, even siblings, chased after the rushing ocean waves, back and forth. Their shrill screams floated on the air—but these were screams of joy, not terror.

Ms. Polka-Dot Bikini was Eden's kind, right down to her long blond hair and big blue eyes. And yet, according to the antique Beauty Map, she had been prized for her beauty—

which meant, if Eden had been born in an earlier time, she too might have been beautiful.

Me? Eden Newman, beautiful? No matter how often she studied the precious map she couldn't imagine it. She was a lowly Pearl, worth nothing in a world ruled by dark-skinned Coals.

Once again, Eden silently quit the map. She really had to stop torturing herself like that.

That bitch Ashina was now fifteen minutes late and Eden wanted to take her break. She glanced around the lab, hoping for a sign of the haughty Coal. Large fans whirred in the vaulted ceiling, circulating cooled air, which helped preserve viral stem cell cocktails. Best of all, the light breeze eased Eden's fiery nerves.

An operating theater rose above the far end of the room, dominating the space. The real action took place there. Eden saw her father in the middle of it, hunched over a large, empty console. A series of mathematical equations seemed to dance in the air around him. The Life-Band on his wrist flashed with wild energy, emitting a stream of white sparks. His body sagged from some Herculean mental effort.

That was Father. *A brain on a stick.*

Some brain, too. Because of his high intelligence scores, *they* had overlooked his race and given him the position of lead scientist at Resources for Environmental Adaptation, or REA. He even had secured Eden a plum researcher's job at the lab. They were the only Pearls allowed to work there.

Tomorrow night, her father's momentous experiment would take place. Eden might be powerless, but she smiled at the secret knowledge that she was one of only three people who understood how he was about to change the world, and possibly, even save it.

With smug satisfaction, she considered the dozens of assistants—gorgeous dark-skinned Coals, every last one of them—who labored in a warren of workstations below the operating theater. They sat trance-like, their eyes glazed over, their bodies slack, working their Life-Bands. Large, spidery formations of DNA sequences morphed at a rapid pace in front of them. Wavering, yellowish solar lights barely illuminated their grim faces. Uniform white lab coats, layered over black clothing, presented a picture of false calm. But it couldn't hide the thick tension in the room. Even the Mood Scents of fresh grass and wet wood that floated in the air didn't help.

Eden couldn't imagine the immense pressure her father was under. Possibly, that explained why he worked round the clock. Or maybe he'd simply been avoiding her since her mother's death, seven years ago. She couldn't recall the last time she'd seen him at the unit they shared in the workers' quarters. Not that they ever said much to each other anymore.

As he turned his head, Eden winced at the sight of pale skin peeking through his worn, dark coating. For Earth's sake, how was she supposed to pass when her father didn't maintain standards?

She smoothed a hand over her long black hair to reassure herself. Like her skin, the layers of dark coating—Midnight Luster—she'd worn since birth had turned it dry and crackly. A small price to pay for beauty and for protection. She had to cover her white skin or risk antagonizing the Coals.

At last, Eden heard Ashina's brisk footsteps on the concrete floor and stole a glance at her nemesis, envious of the beauty's easy confidence. Voluptuous, with raisin-colored skin, everything about Ashina screamed ruling class.

Of course, the dark races got The Heat, too, but not nearly as often. The higher amounts of melanin in their skin protected them from the sun's radiation. Since their numbers hadn't been decimated in The Great Meltdown, as the other races' had, they now ruled the planet.

Eden bet Ashina had dozens of suitors offering to pick up her mate option. She could afford to choose someone she liked instead of angling to improve her offspring's genetics, while Eden was assigned to the bottom of the reproductive heap like all Pearls. Good Earth, her mate-rate was an embarrassing fifteen percent. Only Cottons, the derogatory word for albinos, were lower, and they were extinct.

Time was running out. If Eden wasn't mated in six months when she turned eighteen—the deadline for girls—she'd be cut off from Basic Resources, and left outside to die. But who would want a lowly Pearl like her?

Ashina took her seat, a nasty gleam in her eyes. Cold, slick fear slid down Eden's throat. She slowly rose to her feet with her head lowered.

"I'll take my break now, if it's okay with you?" she said.

"Just a minute," Ashina said, sharply. "You failed to send me your report on the test subjects."

Eden froze. "But I did, I'm sure I did. I even checked my work several times." *While I was waiting for you.*

The bitch pointed to the blank space in front of her. "There's nothing here. Sit down. I'm not going to be responsible for your screw-ups."

How many times had Eden heard it? White people were lazy good-for-nothings with weak genetics.

"Maybe a solar flare caused a technical glitch?" Eden tried to control the hysteria rising in her. "I swear my report is there."

Ashina jumped up and grabbed Eden's lab coat. "Are you calling me a liar?"

Eden flinched. One of *them* was touching her. White-hot light exploded in her head. Before she knew it, she blurted out an incendiary racial slur.

"Get your hands off of me, you damn Coal!"

Holy Earth.

An alarming hush fell over the lab. Then Ashina slapped her cheek, the sound explosive in the deadly quiet. Eden sucked in her breath with a loud gasp. The girl lunged for her, but Eden jumped out of reach.

"She pushed me!" Ashina cried, falling to the floor.

The workers jerked to their feet, the screech of chairs against the floor raking across Eden's heart. She looked around the room in a panic. Even those whom she thought tolerated her presence hurled racial epithets.

"Earth-damned Pearl!"

"White Death!"

The angry mob lurched towards Eden, just like in her nightmares. The Coals were going to kill her. They would drag her outside and leave her to cook in the sun.

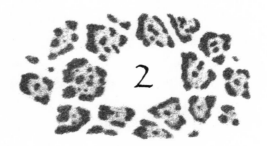

E DEN BACKED towards the laboratory exit, her heart pounding. From the operating theater she heard her Father call out in a shaky voice. "Daught!"

Daught for daughter. To him, she was simply one of life's sub-classifications—genus daughter. At least, he'd noticed her. But what could he do?

Eden lowered her gaze in a submissive gesture all Pearls used. *Never engage a Coal. Don't look a Coal in the eye unless requested*. Then she turned and ran.

She heard the workers running after her. Angry voices hit her like laser blasts. Terrified, she glanced over her shoulder at them. To her surprise she saw them come to an abrupt halt, their furious expressions melting to fear.

Eden slammed into a wall. At least, that's what it felt like. She turned to find herself in the clutches of the imperious Ronson Bramford, owner of REA.

Speechless, she stared up into his dark, gleaming eyes. A glint of light shone down on his black, shaved head, adding to his magnetic effect. Then he jerked away, as if Eden really were poison, and turned his steely gaze on the crowd.

"Back to work," Bramford said in a calm but commanding voice. Relieved, she began to leave when he added, "Not you, Eden."

She wasn't sure which was worse: being murdered by a mob or dealing with the arrogant bastard. As usual, Bramford stared at a point just over her shoulder as he addressed her, which made her feel small and dirty. It had been like that ever since they'd met when REA was founded three years ago.

But why should he bother to look at her? With a stellar mate-rate of ninety-eight and skin the color of storm clouds, Bramford was at the top of the heap. Men had until the age of twenty-four to mate, though Eden often wondered why Bramford waited. She assumed that most women found the twenty-two-year-old Coal attractive even without his riches. In a heartless-monster sort of way.

"What's the problem?" he asked her.

Eden stared, perplexed. Did he really want to know what she thought?

"Well?"

She searched for the right words when Ashina strode up beside her.

"She attacked me, sir," the bitch said, acting the injured party.

To Eden's surprise, Bramford questioned the little actress. "Is that so, Ashina?"

A Coal's word outweighed a Pearl's. Always. And yet Bramford hesitated. He wasn't a man who hesitated, and Eden wondered why.

Ashina's pretty mouth gaped. Then she shook off her confusion. "That's exactly what happened."

Bramford's magnificent brow furrowed, his chiseled

features hardened. "Why would Eden attack you when her father's work is at stake?"

"Because she can't control herself." Ashina paused with a weary sigh. "You know how they are."

"Do I?"

Puzzled, Ashina shifted her hips. "Excuse me, sir?"

Deep inside, Eden smiled. Whatever Bramford was up to—and she knew it couldn't be good—at least her supervisor was in the hot spot, too.

"Just state the facts, Ashina," he said.

"Well," the girl began, icily. "I caught Eden in a lie. She didn't complete protocol on the test subjects. Look, Eden knows how much trouble she's cost me in the past. And I've let things go. But tomorrow is the Big Night. There's no room for mistakes. You said so just the other night, didn't you, sir?"

Bramford glanced at the metal staircase that led to the operating theater. Eden's father stumbled down it, blinking rapidly—a sure sign of stress.

"What, what? Bramford?" he said.

Eden suspected that he wore his antiquated glasses just to irritate her, despite her repeated insistence that he get the simple fix. It was just another way of standing out, another way of reminding *them* that he and his ugly daughter existed.

Thank Earth, Bramford held up a hand to stop him. "No need to concern yourself, Dr. Newman."

"What? But…" He glanced back towards his work with obvious longing. "If you're sure you don't need me."

Eden swallowed her disappointment, as he hurried back up the stairs. He didn't even look at her.

"Shen," Bramford called his bodyguard, a mixed Asian, or Amber, as the racist term went.

Somehow Eden trusted the big man. Maybe it was the quiet look he sometimes gave her, without pity or arrogance, unlike his employer. Only true Coals were allowed to hold security positions. Of course, Bramford could use his clout to bypass such rules. Still, why not pick a Tiger's Eye, or Latino? They ranked higher in the race wars than Ambers, who stood above Pearls. Was it the touch of Coal in Shen that gave him an edge?

The slithering dragon tattoos that curved down his thick arms seemed to breathe fire as he stepped forward. "Yes, sir."

"Get Jamal," Bramford said.

Shen's Life-Band flashed, and the white dot at his third eye crinkled as he frowned in concentration. What Eden wouldn't give to wear a white dot on her forehead. It would mean she was mated, safe.

Soon, the entry door slid open and Jamal, the head of security, strode through. Giddy pleasure welled up in Eden at the sight of him. *My Dark Prince.*

Bramford's eyes cut towards her, clouded with suspicion. Mother Earth, did he know about her secret visits with Jamal?

Jamal gave nothing away. His grin was all for Bramford. He wasn't as tall and didn't have a shred of Bramford's power or riches, but Eden thought Jamal was special. Unlike most of his kind, he was color-blind. In fact, except for the lack of a white dot and his ebony-colored skin, her prince had nothing in common with Bramford.

Jamal stood before them with his legs braced apart, his

broad shoulders square. The warrior tattoo that swirled on one side of his face added to the look of strength.

"I've got it under control, sir," he said.

At once, Holo-Images of Eden and Ashina appeared before the group, replaying the girls' argument. Eden held her breath, hoping against odds that she would be proven innocent despite her race. But her heart sank as Bramford's Life-Band ring flashed and the scene disappeared.

"I'll view it solo," he said. "No need to stir things up again. Next time, Jamal, check with me."

Eden tensed. She couldn't fault his reasoning, but she didn't trust him. He leveled his gaze at Jamal. Like a snake poised to attack.

"And why weren't you on site to stop this incident?" Bramford asked.

Jamal stiffened at first. Then he shrugged, and once more gave that winning grin. "I was attending to personal business," he answered.

Only a cold bastard like Bramford could resist Jamal's charm. His expression remained impassive, as closed off as his past.

Eden had researched their benefactor when the project began to see what was in store for her and her father. Oddly, she'd found only the most basic facts about Bramford: birth date, un-mated, no child, took over Bramford Industries at age eighteen when his father died from a terrorist Pearl attack. Nothing at all about his personal habits or hobbies. His list of World-Band experiences simply revealed mandatory ones, such as Earth Before the Meltdown or Death by The Heat. Even his genome was fake, a standard model she recognized. Such secrecy frightened her. To be mysterious was perhaps the ultimate power.

Now, Bramford stared off into space, his Life-Band flashing. Eden found the custom gold ring, which held a large onyx stone, as pretentious as its owner. When it stopped flashing, he spoke curtly to Ashina. "I won't allow internal discord."

Had justice prevailed for once? Eden could hardly believe it.

Then Bramford added, "Since you instigated the incident, Eden, you must suffer the consequences."

What did she expect? Bramford hated her. If he fired her and she couldn't produce, her Basic Resources would end. Which meant death.

Eden appealed to Jamal. "Maybe there's a mistake somewhere?"

At least he offered a possibility. "Like I said, I was busy. I suppose someone could have altered the record or deleted something important."

"Why would you say that?" Ashina asked, with a pointed glance at Eden.

The hair on the back of Eden's neck prickled. Did the nosey bitch suspect her hidden connection to Jamal? Coals often killed Pearls who seduced their kind.

Bramford's deadpan stare passed from Ashina to Jamal before he responded. "An alert would have sounded if our security had been breached."

"Unless it duped the system," Jamal countered. "Maybe a mirroring device or new kind of robot spy dropped in."

"The FFP?"

Eden quivered at the mention of the dreaded Federation

of Free People, a militant organization of Coals that vowed to rid the planet of Pearls.

"They have the tech," Jamal replied. "Depending on what you're cooking up there,"—he jerked his head toward the operating theater—"they may have a motive."

Eden saw something flicker in Bramford's eyes. Was it alarm? Only he and her father were supposed to know the full scope of the lab's top-secret operations. She hadn't intended to solve the puzzle. But then, half of her genome came from her brilliant father.

Ashina pointed a finger at Eden. "It doesn't change the fact that this was all her fault."

Bramford silenced her with a mere wave of his hand, then made a final declaration. "Eden, you're on probation until further notice."

The injustice of it burned in her gut. Better to punish the Pearl than upset the Coals. If only Bramford knew what it was like to be an outcast.

"Don't return to work until you hear from me," he added.

"You, sir?" He never involved himself in such details.

"That's what I said. Remain at your unit until then."

"Finally," Ashina said, turning away in a huff.

In despair, Eden watched Bramford stride towards the operating theater. And yet, as bad as it was, hope welled up in her. Jamal had put his job on the line for her. Was it possible he'd also be willing to pick up her mate option?

He sidled up to her and whispered. "Don't worry, Little Bunny. I'll make it up to you. See you after work."

She smiled at him, for once not caring if anyone noticed.

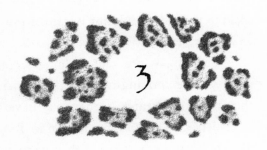

3

EXITING THE LAB, Eden passed directly into the security area, her nerves jangling. A glass cage shut around her with a bang that always made her shudder. To control the spread of disease, no one was permitted to enter any area of the Combs without inspection. And the terrifying possibility of being cooped up in quarantine never failed to enter her mind as she waited to be released. Rumors of what was done to sick people in the name of research filled her with dread.

She peered through the glass wall at the dark, masculine robot behind the scanner. It was a classic prototype of the ruling class, from its mahogany-colored casing right down to its superior attitude. It was so real it intimidated Eden. She tensed as it studied the information that the chips in her head projected into the air—medical history, genetic modifications, predisposition to disease, and any current illnesses.

Let *them* look. They would never know anything about the Real Eden Newman. Only Jamal saw her.

Soon, the door slid open and Eden trudged towards the employees' quarters. Cones of dim light fell on the concrete pathways. Even here, she couldn't escape Bramford's colossal ego. Like an animal, he had marked his territory by carving a ridiculously large initial "B" onto each unit door. His audacious company logo—a snow-capped black mountain against a red desert background that offered false hope in a parched land—glowed at intervals along the walls. As if he owned everything, including her.

All over again, she felt the burn of her unjust dismissal. The hatred etched onto the faces of her coworkers pressed into her memory. The walls, painted a refreshing mint color that suggested coolness, began to close in around her. Sweat drilled down the sides of her face.

Her World-Band voice gently warned her: *My dear, your oxy levels are in the red zone.*

The Uni-Gov called oxy "the happy drug," which seemed absurd since everyone knew happiness had gone the way of the dolphins. The full dose Eden had taken at 18:00 should have kept her on an even keel throughout her twelve-hour work shift. But the extra stress had pushed her over the edge. Already, she felt the telltale dryness in her mouth, the jittery shakes and terrible cravings.

She hurried around the last turn to her unit, her body growing heavier by the second. The door sprung open as the scanner cleared her I.D. chip. She rushed inside and heard a loud, happy bark.

"Gotta get some, buddy," she muttered to her dog.

Big and energetic with yellow-gray fur, Austin knocked a plastic chair on its side as he turned to follow her. The cramped four-room unit was too small for him. *Neither one of us fit, do we?*

Eden raked a hand down his back on her way towards her small, narrow bedroom. He padded behind her, the sound of his panting breath growing loud in her ears. She shoved a thin board off the berth-like bed, which also served as a desk, and it banged onto the concrete floor. Trembling, she lay down and pulled the oxy-cap from its storage unit above her. The soft molded apparatus fit over her head. As it clicked into place, a tiny syringe slid out from its sleeve into the receptacle in her scalp. She flicked the dosage to high, a low moan escaping her. Hurry, Eden thought, desperate for the soft, numb kick to begin.

For comfort, she called up her favorite spot. *Sequoiadendron giganteum.* At once, an ancient redwood forest appeared, the giant trees towering over her like wise, old sentries that offered protection, even affection. At least, that's how her brain had been programmed to experience the Holo-Images. A cheerful pair of bluebirds flitted past her. The calming Mood Scent of fresh, damp grass seeped from a port in the wall. She shed her shoes and rustled her feet against fallen, brittle leaves.

At last, the familiar, pleasant rush flooded into her body. Her world slowly turned a muted shade of gray. Possibly, she wouldn't kill herself tonight.

That was, until an Ethics Officer signaled an incoming visit. Before Eden could pull herself together, the shimmering Holo-Image of a female E.O. appeared in front of her. Naturally, she was a Coal and wore the distinctive red jacket of the Ethics Corps.

"Eden Lavinia Newman, Zone Four, Caucasian?" the officer said without great interest.

"Yes, Officer?" Eden scrambled to sit up.

She flashed on the date: the 29th of May, her half birthday. For Earth's sake, how could she have forgotten?

"This is your official six-month warning," the E.O. said. "Do you realize you'll be eighteen years old on November twenty-ninth?"

"Yes, I do."

"And are you aware that your Basic Resources will be stopped unless you mate by that date?"

"Yes," Eden whispered, terrified by the thought of being cut off from food and oxy.

"What did you say?"

"Yes. I said yes, Officer."

"We cannot afford to supply precious resources to those who do not contribute to the continuation of our species."

Her Life-Band flashed and Eden's official entry on the Uni-Gov mating site began to play. Eden cringed at her paltry fifteen percent mate-rate and the unflattering images of her. She had worn an extra thick coat of Midnight Luster that day, though her race was still obvious. Right there, for the whole world to see, underneath the recording of her talking about herself—something she had dreaded almost as much as having her face shown—it read: *Caucasian female.* Her other vital statistics, including date of birth, height, weight and genetic markers were also listed, but nothing damned her more than being a Pearl.

The officer muted the recording and directed her condescending gaze at Eden.

"I see your mate-rate is below average," she said. "And yet, a few of your kind have offered to pick up your option. Tell me, Eden Newman, why have you refused them?"

Eden knew *they* didn't really care whether or not she reproduced. Truth was, *they* wished her dead. The E.O.

simply needed to check her name off a list. Was it the low level of oxy in Eden's system or her lingering anger over Bramford's lies that drove her to speak her mind for once in her life?

"Because I don't want my child to be all Pearl. I'd rather be dead than mate with one of my kind." Even as she said it, she cursed herself for taking such a foolish risk.

"I see," the officer said, coldly. "We suggest you attempt to improve your rating by following the Universal Government's standard recommendations. This warning has been duly noted." With that, she disappeared.

Eden fell back on the bed, groaning. The Uni-Gov's recommendations, which included banal instructions such as how to respond to suitors or keep up one's hygiene, would never help her. For Earth's sake, she had to do whatever it took to win over Jamal. He was her only chance.

Austin licked her hand, and she turned a lazy eye towards him.

"Oh, buddy, what are we going to do?"

The whitish eyebrows arched, his wagging tail thumped the wall, like a metronome in sympathetic time. Somehow he understood, just like a real sibling would.

Eden glanced at a small photo of her mother that sat on a shelf. It was the only personal effect in the drab room besides the dusty old book of poems her mother had given her. At least she had been right about Austin.

Eden had been skeptical when her mother brought the shivering creature home ten years ago. On bended knee, her mother had peeled back the blanket from the bundle in her arms. Eden vividly recalled the shock of seeing a live animal and how she'd reeled off facts as if they were weapons that could protect her.

—*Canis lupus familiaris, a subspecies of lupus or wolf. It's a male. The webbed paws belong to the retriever family. They're excellent swimmers. It's commonly called a yellow labrador, Mother.*

—*He's just a puppy, Eden. Why don't you pet him?*

Eden had reached tentatively for the scrawny, whimpering thing, but hesitated.

—*Go ahead, you won't hurt him.*

—*Oooh.*

No Inter-Life samplings could have prepared Eden for the softness of real fur. The labrador had looked at her with wide, begging eyes, his tail wagging at her touch. She'd realized he liked her touch. And since only Mother and, in those days, even Father, ever looked right at her or occasionally touched her, she'd decided that the scrawny, little dog must be family, too.

—*What's his name?*

—*How about Austin?*

—*Like Emily's brother? Is that a dog's name?*

—*Well, why not? If you had a brother I would've named him Austin.*

Eden loved old tales about siblings. But one child was the allowable quota, if the mated couple produced enough uni-credits. And like most kids, she never knew her grandparents, who had died, either from The Heat or the toxic environment, long before she was born.

To increase the size of their family, her optimistic mother had adopted her favorite poet, Emily Dickinson, as an ancestor. Eden and her mother had spent many hours in Emily's World, the World-Band destination where the Dickinson family lived in the 1900's. When Eden's mother started to refer to her as Aunt Emily, Eden simply had accepted it. And so, she'd also embraced the dog's name.

—Hi, Austin.

—Did you see his ears wiggle? He likes you.

—Is he a Pearl?

Her mother had hung her head on her chest and sighed. Even now, Eden winced at the memory of her mother's red roots. A Pink Pearl, she was fairer than Eden, and therefore even more susceptible to The Heat. But she'd been lax about coating. Minor rebellions keep the heart alive, she would say.

—Austin is colorblind, Eden. He responds to love and kindness. Remember what Aunt Emily said? 'That Love is all there is, / Is all we know of Love.' Promise me you won't forget. Love is like a gentle wind that will open your heart if you let it.

Even at the age of seven, Eden knew love was dead. Only biological instinct and evolutionary climbing mattered. But it was useless to argue with her starry-eyed mother.

—I promise.

And yet, when her mother died three years later, Eden had forgotten about Emily's World along with useless ideas of love and that gentle wind. She just couldn't think about it anymore.

Eden checked the time. Jamal would arrive in a few hours and she had to be perfect.

"Let's eat, buddy," she said, stowing the oxy-cap.

The redwood forest spread into the tiny main room as

she entered it. A sparkling ray of sunshine fell across a utilitarian trio of chairs. Built into one wall, a compact kitchenette contained several chutes from which their daily supplies were dropped. Eden switched on Austin's nutrient teat, and he began to suck hungrily on it. Then she twisted the knob on a small chute and out popped a perfectly balanced meal, three pills in varying proportions: white carbohydrate, blue protein, and red fat.

She dug into a drawer where she had stashed her father's extra pills. He often skipped meals, which, along with his genetics, made him rail thin. If Eden weren't careful she'd be just as skinny, and even less desirable. She swapped out the blue pill for a red one and swallowed all three with her allotted amount of water. A nice family meal, she thought, patting Austin.

Time for her mandatory half hour of exercise. She began to run in place through the forest, though her sensors gave her the impression of moving fast. As usual, Austin rested in the shade. Holo-Images of tree trunks and limbs brushed through her long, lithe frame. With each step she focused on a single image: a white dot on her forehead. Safely mated, safely mated, she quietly repeated. The dot grew larger in her mind until a blinding whiteness was all she could see.

Well done, dear. Your heart rate is 110 beats per minute. You've burned 200 calories and added .001% muscle.

"Muscle adds curves, right, buddy?" she said, as she came to a stop.

Austin made a snuffling sound and followed her to the tidy, little bathroom.

She peeled off her lab uniform and stepped into the cleansing stall with growing dread. At once, a purple laser washed over her. Each day she expected to hear the high-pitched beep that signaled a diseased mole—an indication of The Heat. Funny, they once were called beauty marks.

Eden heaved a sigh of relief as the laser stopped without a sound. She'd made it through another night. Now, the good stuff, she thought, dialing in a fresh coating of Midnight Luster. Her spirits lifted as her skin and hair darkened to a lustrous shade of black. Water would cause the coating to streak, which was easy enough to avoid in her dry, tunneled world. And in a few days the coat would turn dull and gray— a dead giveaway she was a Pearl.

But for now, she looked beautiful.

Eden stepped out of the stall, refreshed and ready to deal with Jamal. She slipped on a vintage black nightgown and studied herself in the mirror. If only she had more curves. Still, the silky garment was sexy and well worth every unicredit it cost. She had almost smiled the night she'd picked it up at her local station in the Combs. It wasn't a nightgown; it was a weapon. One she had saved for a very special occasion. *Like tonight, please Earth.*

Applying her makeup, Eden expertly shaded her face to appear Coal-like. She refreshed the brown caps in her eyes with darkening drops. Red lipstick, smoothed over the lines to make her lips seem fuller, was the last touch. She let her long black hair dip over one eye and smiled.

"Definitely passing, right?"

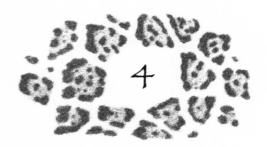

4

AT EXACTLY 05:00, Eden's Life-Band communicated Jamal's signal in her head. Her pulse raced as she accepted the connection. She posed seductively, and a distinctive click in her head told her that her Holo-Image appeared before him just as his materialized in her room. He flashed that killer grin.

"How's my Little Bunny?" he said.

"Jamal," she said, her sensors registering the warmth of his arms as they snaked around her.

Austin shot up, growling. She had forgotten about him. It was embarrassing, really. As if she'd trained her dog to hate Coals. Maybe he wasn't color-blind, after all.

"Sorry," she told Jamal. "Let me put him out."

She dragged the stubborn animal into the main room. "For Earth's sake, why do you always act like this?" she whispered. He whined, but she shut him out.

"Come here, pet," Jamal said.

She walked towards him, swinging her hips, an inviting smile on her lips. As head of security, Jamal could scramble signals to hide their illicit date.

"Hmmm," he murmured, reaching for her again.

To her delight, things progressed in the right direction

when Jamal kissed her for the first time. His lips were moist and searching. The heat coming off of his body loosened her limbs. It couldn't be any better if he were actually present.

In fact, she heard an internal warning. *You're over stimulated, dear. Your blood pressure and heart rate are dangerously elevated. Why don't you cease activity now?*

Programmed since birth to react, Eden jerked back.

"You all right?" Jamal said. "Let's slow down."

"No!" she cried, flinging herself at him.

They didn't want her to mate. So *they* could cut her off. But Eden wouldn't let that happen.

"Whoa, pet. I'm receiving dangerous signals. I don't want you to explode. I need you around."

"You do?"

"You have no idea."

"Oh." That meant he wanted to pick up her option to mate, right?

He kissed her again, a little too hard, she thought. But who was she to complain? She could hardly believe her good luck. And yet, right from the start, Jamal had defied her expectations.

He'd been hired at REA when the former head of security died of an oxy overdose. Moses always had seemed so levelheaded, but then you never knew what secrets lurked in a world where even children wore a poker face. He had treated her decently, an exception to the rule. Of course, she'd doubted his replacement would be as nice.

One day, the security robot had malfunctioned and Jamal stood in its place. While he'd studied her data, Eden had stolen a glance at him. Was it the warrior-like tattoo or his dark good looks that had felt threatening? About a ninety percent mate-rate, she'd guessed.

He had caught her eye and flashed a blinding grin.

—*Hello, there.*

She'd turned away, faint with embarrassment and fear.

—*I'm Jamal. Nice to meet you.*

Was he really talking to her? She'd glanced around but there was no one else.

—*What is it, Eden? Don't you like me?*

Why would a Coal even care? Or was he mocking her? Speechless, she'd dared to look at him.

—*Well? Am I scary or just not your type?*

—*I don't even know you!*

Her hand had flown to her mouth. When would she learn to keep her feelings to herself? But Jamal simply had laughed. A big, easy laugh that had puzzled her.

—*You're an honest girl. I like that, too.*

Too? What else could he possibly like about her? He had to know she was a Pearl. It said so right there on the scanner. Besides, even with the best skin coating, everything about her screamed lower class. And yet, he'd stared at her with an openness that had made Eden blush. No one had ever looked at her for so long or with such sincere interest.

She even had wondered if her oxy reserves had bottomed out and she was losing her mind. But her vital statistics were fine. Why then had he continued speaking to her in that astonishingly direct way?

—*I get it. You don't think I like your blue eyes, right? You're wrong about that. Maybe some day you'll let me see the real you, Eden Newman.*

It was as if he'd peered right inside of her and plucked out her heart's desire. He wanted to see the Real Eden. She had hung on his every word.

—*All right. I understand you don't trust me. Not yet. Why don't we spend some time together so we can solve that problem? This isn't what you think. I'm different and I'm going to prove it to you.*

—*Okay.*

The confidence, the bold grin, and the way his eyes followed her when she'd exited the gate had dazzled and unnerved her. She'd stumbled into the lab, dumbfounded.

True to his word, Jamal had persisted and their clandestine visits had begun a few months ago. Now, he lay beside her, as amazing as the sight of a lone flower pushing through the baked concrete.

He settled back and looked thoughtful as he began. "I was thinking about what you said your father always tells you—'wait and see.' Maybe the good doctor's onto something."

"Uh huh." Eden wanted to talk about their future together, not her father.

"I mean, look what happened. You got probation—"

"I didn't start it."

"I'm not accusing you, pet." He tucked her into the crook of his arms. "I'm just saying bad news can bring good news. Wait and see. For example, tomorrow night, you're off work." His eyebrows arched with anticipation. "Which means you and I should go to the Moon Dance."

"Really? Are you serious?"

"Dead serious."

It was all that Eden had hoped for. A Coal didn't take

a Pearl out in public unless he or she intended to pick up the other's mating option. And what more public event to show his intentions than at a Moon Dance? By law, everyone had to attend at least nine a year. The Uni-Gov insisted these events reduced the frequent violence that naturally resulted from the crowded conditions in the tunnels.

Eden squealed with delight. She could almost picture a white dot on her dusky-coated forehead. Mated, and with a desirable Coal!

"But I'm on probation," she said, suddenly remembering. "Bramford hasn't—"

Jamal lifted a finger to her lips. "Who's in charge of clearance?"

"All right. But tomorrow night my father's experiment takes place. You'll be on guard."

"I'll put someone else in charge, take the company craft, cut out to meet you, be back in time for the Big Bang."

"But I'll have to go alone." The thought terrified her.

"Don't worry," Jamal said softly. "As soon as you get off the 19:00 transport, I'll be waiting." He cupped her chin and looked deep into her eyes. "It's time for Jamal to make a righteous move. Do you understand?"

She gulped. "Yes."

"Good." He gave her a peck on the cheek. "See you tomorrow night, Little Bunny."

She reached for him but he was gone. Stunned, she lay there, going over what he'd said. *Time for Jamal to make a righteous move.*

Her Life-Band tingled again. Eden accepted the incoming signal, thinking it was Jamal, even as she realized her mistake. Instead of his heart-warming face, she saw the dreaded logo of the Federation of Free People: a swirl of black that spun around until it erased a small white circle.

Quit, quit! It disappeared but she sat there, reeling. Horrific stories about murdered or missing Pearls ran through her mind. *Breathe, Eden.*

She moved robotically to open the door. Austin scrambled to his feet, his soft eyes on hers. At least he'd never be killed because of his color. But she couldn't think about that now. Soon they'd be safe.

"Oh, buddy," Eden said, hanging onto his neck. "Please, be nice to Jamal. If I'm lucky, he'll be my mate."

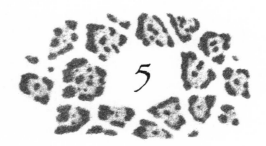

5

EDEN FORCED herself to concentrate on the staccato-like tapping of her high heels against the concrete floor in the busy, wide pedestrian tunnel. If she focused on her feet moving ahead, she wouldn't give in to the paralyzing fear that gripped her. What if one of her co-workers saw her and reported her illegal leave to Bramford?

She couldn't think about the risk or she might lose her nerve and return home. Never mind, she simply had to reach the regional plaza where her Dark Prince waited.

Eden knew how to deflect attention—shoulders back, eyes focused ahead, her face a blank mask. Just like the other Pearls who walked in groups near her in their designated lane. They kept to the edges, making way for the Coals who swept by on bicycles or in rickshaws.

It was almost 19:00 and the tunnel bustled with activity. The distant blare of military sirens and the chaotic cries of vendors hawking their goods from recessed stalls in the walls jumbled with traffic bells and snatches of conversation. She suspected that each and every Coal passerby wanted to hurt her, though the statistical odds against that were high. And her sensors, which automatically translated the babel of foreign languages into English, the official language, told her it wasn't true. Still, she could never shake the fear of being among so many of *them*.

Only a few minutes had passed and already she felt the sinking terror of being away from her unit, away from Austin. Out there, with all that space around her, anything might happen. Each step drained her. Perspiration formed on her brow, threatening to dull her coating, even though, according to her internal sensors, it was only a hundred and ten degrees Fahrenheit in the tunnel. Not bad for a spring night.

She thought of all the times she'd made this very trek in the past, wearing her same old Moon Dance dress. And yet, never alone. Always with a group of her kind. She fingered the top of the strapless black techno dress, hoping Jamal would like it. The stiff fabric had frayed and lost its sheen long ago. It didn't matter though, because tonight she wouldn't be the hopeless Pearl clinging to the shadows in the hall. She would be somebody. Encouraged, she tried to pick up her pace, though the tight dress hobbled her walk.

Ahead, she spotted a boisterous crowd of partygoers at the public transport hub. She hung back, hoping no one would recognize her. In a short while, a high-speed, bullet-shaped vehicle shot down the tunnel and halted at the landing dock. An Ethics Officer stood by the security scanner, watching the passengers get on board.

Eden waited until the long line thinned, then hurried to take her turn. The E.O. stepped in front of her, his face hostile. All of a sudden, she heard two men behind her. Coals, she figured by their careless, drunken laughter.

"Hurry up, let us on," one of the men called in a high-pitched voice.

"I've got protocol to keep," the E.O. said, curtly.

"So do we, Red," a deep, cruel voice replied.

Eden saw a flash of fear in the officer's face. He stepped aside, letting her push through the scanner. She didn't dare look back at the men who followed her on board. She edged her way down the aisle, past hundreds of people, mostly Coals of all ages, mated couples and eager singles. Luckily, she found a few inches of space to hold onto the overhead bar in the back section reserved for Pearls.

A loud whooshing sound reverberated against the metal sides of the vehicle as it zoomed down the tunnel. Dim yellow lights cast a grimy pall on the mass of dark passengers, all in dark clothing. The only spot of color in the shadowy interior came from Holo-Images of serene nature scenes that played against fake windows. Eden stared intently at them, avoiding anyone's eye.

She felt a malevolent current coursing through the riders on the transport. Not only from Coal to Pearl, or from Tiger's Eye to Amber, but within each racial group. The Uni-Gov got it wrong. The monthly Moon Dance usually left a wake of mayhem throughout each zone.

But she couldn't think about that now. *I'm a stone in a cool, dark cave.*

The vehicle careened through dark tunnels, stopping occasionally for cross traffic or to let on more riders. She wondered if Ms. Polka Dot Bikini would have enjoyed the beach if she could have seen these desperate people or what would become of Good Earth.

Possibly, man's only hope lay at Eden's very own doorstep. She recalled the thrill of piecing together the puzzle of her father's experiment. Each researcher had been given one small part of the process to prevent the very discovery she had made. Eden, being the best interpreter of her father's notes, had filled in once too often for ill coworkers and the result was inevitable. At first, she couldn't believe it.

She'd finally cornered her father one morning when he had stumbled home, weak from overwork and lack of sleep.

—*What, Daught?*

—*I figured it out. Do you know what this means?*

—*What? What do you know?*

—*Holy Earth. You're attempting an Interspecies Structural Adaptation.*

Only her crazy Father would think of implanting a human being with genetic material from key animals that thrived in the hottest climates. Only he might succeed, too. His secret approach to programming the epigenome—the genetic master control for DNA—allowed him to skirt the pesky problem of one species rejecting another's code.

This wasn't going to be some mild genetic exchange, either. Valuable DNA had been gathered from nearly extinct species with tremendous effort and probably a lot of Bramford's uni-credits.

The primary genetic donor was the ultimate jungle predator, a jaguar, *Panthera onca*. Even better, a melanistic cat with a black coat had been found. Its coloring would not only increase resistance to solar radiation, but also minimize the appearance of camouflage spots, for vanity's sake. The jaguar's only natural enemy, the green anaconda, *Eunectes murinus*, contributed its cold-blooded resistance to heat. The third donor in this potent cocktail was the Harpy Eagle, *Harpia harpyja*, the most powerful raptor in the world. It could spot a bug from a hundred yards in the air, and its keen vision had been added to the mix.

Land, water, and air—a brilliant killing machine.

If her father's work succeeded, a Pearl might be able to withstand solar radiation as well as, or even better than, a Coal. Maybe then Pearls would no longer be treated like garbage. And maybe—did Eden dare think it—even she might be beautiful.

She had assumed her father would be proud of her deductive reasoning, even eager to share some of the subtleties of the procedure. Instead, his voice had tightened; the irritating blinking had begun.

—*Daught. You haven't told anyone, have you?*

—*Who would I tell? I don't talk to anyone.*

—*It is categorically forbidden to speak a word of this. You must understand this work is highly illegal and politically dangerous.*

—*I understand, Father.*

—*If it weren't for Bramford's power such a thing could never be attempted.*

Of course, Coals primarily would use the technology. And if one man controlled it, he would be unstoppable in his quest for domination.

—*So Bramford will have it all.*

—*He'll be fair to us, Daught. He's given me his word.*

She didn't think that counted for much. Still, she was happy for her father. Already the advanced age of thirty-nine, he wouldn't have another crack at success.

—*Good luck, Father.*

A rare smile had creased his tired face. It was the longest conversation they'd shared since her mother had died, and she'd missed him.

—*It's the biggest leap in evolution since man discovered fire. Don't forget what I said, Daught.*

Eden never had intended to tell anyone. But then, Jamal wasn't just anyone. It had seemed only natural to share her life with him. Besides, he liked smart women. But if she were honest, she'd have to admit she really wanted him to know that one day she might be more desirable.

An hour later the ride ended. Already, Eden heard the raucous sounds of revelers and loud music coming from the Regional Hall. She filed into line as the passengers began to shuffle off the transport. Her heart skipped a beat when she saw two FFP soldiers staring back at her. They wore drab, brown-and-black paramilitary gear with berets over their shaved heads. The larger of the duo, a blue-black giant, smiled at her and licked his lips. His tall, skinny friend laughed. Eden quickly turned away in a panic.

She had imagined it, she told herself. Besides, they would be gone soon. But when she turned up the aisle they still stood on the side, watching her. Her heart slammed in her chest as she drew near. Just as she feared, Giant and his lanky friend stepped around her, forcing her to continue between them towards the exit.

"Look what we caught," the skinny one said behind her. "A real live Pearl."

Eden recognized the high-pitched, squeaky voice as belonging to one of the men who had followed her on board. Mother Earth, why had she come alone?

An old childhood ditty echoed in her head. Her mother had refused to teach it to Eden, but she'd learned it all the same.

Little Pearly whirly,
lost inside the mines;
tossed from Coal to Coal,
in fear, she whines,
"I'm sorry, Mother,
he said he only wanted
to see my white skin shine."

Frantic, Eden commanded her Life-Band: *connect, Jamal.* Why didn't he accept her signal? He promised he'd be there. *Time for Jamal to make a righteous move.*

She peered around Giant, hoping for a sign of her Dark Prince but Squeaky grabbed her. He pawed her dress, ripping it along the side.

"Leave me alone," Eden said, shakily. "Someone is waiting for me. Someone important—one of your people."

"He won't mind if we share a little Pearl stew," Squeaky said.

As he pushed her out of the vehicle, into the security line, Eden began to scream. Giant turned, smothering her in his arms.

"Be quiet, Pearly," he whispered in her ear. "Or else." He jabbed a sharp point in her side.

The big solider had a knife, and Eden had no doubt he'd use it to kill her.

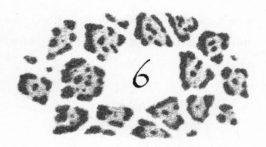

6

EDEN WAITED for the security cage to admit her into the Moon Dance, her heart hammering. She pressed her face to the glass door, searching in vain for Jamal. Hadn't he promised to meet her as soon as she got off the transport? Where on Blessed Earth was he?

He was late, that's all. Preparations for the Big Night at the lab must have detained him. He would save her. He simply had to.

As the door opened, she stumbled out of the cage, caught again by the huge FFP soldier. Only the threat of Giant's knife kept her from screaming. Maybe, she hoped, Jamal was inside. Any minute she would see him.

Giant and Squeaky forced her into the huge hall, which was packed with writhing dancers, lit by flashing lights. On the main stage a band of Coals performed in whiteface. Eden's sensors told her their name: *The Lost Caucasian Tribe.* A wild-looking girl whose wailing pierced the air fronted the group. Her sheer, electric orange dress flashed, like a beacon in the somber sea of black.

High-class vendors and beauty attendants who catered to a Coal clientele pitched their wares along the front perimeter. In the dim recesses of the building, Pearls sold meager goods.

A gaunt woman with feverish eyes, un-dotted and well past eighteen, stood at the edge of the fray, making provocative gestures to passers-by. The desperate Pearl probably would do anything for a shot of oxy.

Eden's head throbbed as she scanned the hall. Still, no sign of her Dark Prince. If he failed her, she'd end up like that poor woman, begging for a shot. She'd rather be dead.

A watchful Ethics Officer strolled by. Eden took a chance and shot him a pleading look. He turned towards her when Giant spun her into the crowd.

"Dance," he said, the glint of the knife visible.

She just needed to buy time until Jamal arrived. But she'd never been asked to dance and felt shy among the sea of revelers. She jerked her limbs, trying to imitate the crowd's erratic movements.

Giant smiled, his eyes roving over her body. He leaned over her, and Eden felt sick as his wet mouth landed on her neck. He pulled back, smiling again when a crazed look came into his eyes. She knew that look all too well; every Pearl dreaded it. Her hand flew to the spot on her neck where the seam in her dark coating had cracked open. Mother Earth, her white skin showed.

A signal seemed to ring through the frenzied crowd. Hundreds of Coals turned to stare at her; a rabid look in their eyes. She would be lucky to make it out of there alive.

"Hey, it's 19:30," Squeaky told his comrade.

"Okay." Giant yanked her towards the exit. "Let's go, Pearly."

Eden realized that the soldiers must have a plan for her. Which meant her capture might not have been coincidental.

She had a sinking feeling it had something to do with her father's experiment. *Do something, Eden.*

She quickly pictured her mother's face and Austin's smile. Be brave, she told herself. Then Eden bit Giant's wrist. He yelled and loosened his grip. Immediately, she dropped to her hands and knees and crawled through the belly of the crowd.

"Get her," she heard Giant say.

Several dancers tripped over her, falling to the ground. Over her shoulder, Eden saw Squeaky trip into the pile-up. She shot to her feet, her heart racing at the sound of Giant's bellow.

"Pearly!"

She twisted her slender frame through the throng until a couple of hard-bodies pinned her between them. Grinning, two male Pearls bobbed with her to the beat. Their glassy eyes, full of wild hope, and their papery, red-tinged skin told her they had The Heat. Probably, celebrating one last Moon Dance.

"Please, let me go," Eden shouted.

They just smiled. When they gyrated her around, she saw Giant lurch towards her. Eden kneed one of the men in the groin and he fell to the ground. The other man broke into desperate sobs.

"Sorry," Eden said, recalling her mother's erratic mood swings at the end of her life.

She tried to sprint forward, but her feet wouldn't move. Heavy hands hauled her backwards.

"Where do you think you're going, Pearly?" Giant said.

Squeaky slid beside them with a look of chagrin. Giant grunted his disapproval and once more led her towards the exit. This was it. Somehow Eden always knew she'd be caught by the FFP.

A commanding voice rose above the din. "Let her go."

Jamal?

She felt a slight hitch in Giant's walk. He glanced over his shoulder, then tightened his grip on her and pushed ahead. A laser blast sizzled in the air. Beside her, Squeaky crumpled to the ground, stunned by the burning beam. Shrill screams punctured the air as the crowd dispersed.

"I said, let her go," the man repeated.

Her captor turned around, dragging Eden with him. Dark shadows hid the man's face.

"What's it to you?" Giant said.

"She belongs to me." Just then a strobe light passed over him, revealing his dark, chiseled features.

Bramford. Of course, he thought he owned her.

Predictably, a bevy of hopeful Coal women fanned around him. His bodyguard Shen stood nearby, an illegal laser in his hand. His loyalty stunned Eden. Bramford might live above the law, but even he couldn't guarantee the Amber wouldn't be punished.

Still, she had to admire Bramford's nerve. He stepped right up to her and held out his hand.

"Shall we dance, Eden?"

Giant shifted his weight back and forth, as if weighing his options.

Bramford kept his eyes on her while he spoke to him. "If you release the young lady in the next five seconds, I won't have to kill you."

Eden wished she could tell the difference between the

electric heat of his gaze and the adrenaline pumping through her.

"You have three seconds left."

The standoff continued.

"One-and-a-half seconds," Bramford said, arching an eyebrow.

Abruptly, Giant released her, pushing her straight into Bramford's arms.

"You can't escape, Pearly," he said. "I'll get you later."

He hauled Squeaky to his feet, dragging him through the crowd. The bored spectators resumed their hyperkinetic gyrations.

Eden sighed with relief. But why was Bramford still holding her? She looked up into his undeniably handsome face, the lights playing across it. His steely, dark eyes glistened. A shadow of a smile curled his lips.

"Nice dress," he said.

"Thanks," she replied numbly.

From the corner of her eye she saw the hopeful beauties shift impatiently. Of course, they expected him to leave her now that the danger had passed. So did Eden. Instead, he twirled her towards the edge of the crowd. Despite herself, she couldn't fight his magnetic pull or the thrill that tingled through her. But his admirers' cruel laughter reminded her of how pitiful she looked.

"Thank you for your help, sir," Eden said, trying to pull away. "You can go now."

Bramford seemed amused and held her tight. "Are you dismissing me?"

Why did he always make her feel so small?

"I said thanks."

"You don't want to dance with me? Is that it?"

She felt tongue-tied with his warm body next to hers. "Those women are waiting for you," she managed to say.

"Let them wait. Unless you'd rather we stopped?"

Did she? Wasn't she enjoying this? While she hesitated Bramford's expression hardened.

"Let's go," he said, turning away.

Eden stared at his retreating figure. She crossed her arms, rubbing the lingering warm spots he'd left. Possibly, she hadn't disliked his touch. But what was she thinking? She despised the Pearl-hating Coal.

She looked around the room again, desperate to see Jamal's killer grin. *Sorry, Little Bunny, here I am.*

Bramford whirled on her, his eyes burning bright. "Don't tell me you're waiting for him?"

"I don't know what you mean," she said, cool and easy.

"Coyness doesn't suit you, Eden. Jamal isn't coming."

She sucked in her breath. So Bramford knew. It didn't matter anymore because Jamal would save her.

"He said he'd meet me here," she said defiantly.

He shook his head. "And you believed him?"

"Why shouldn't I?"

"Isn't it obvious?

"Why? Because I'm a Pearl?"

"Don't be ridiculous. That's not what I meant."

"Really?" Eden jerked her head towards the waiting groupies—not one Pearl among them.

"We've got important work to do," Bramford said, turning on his heel. "Come with me."

Loyal Shen followed after him, leaving Eden alone. At once a few rough characters began to edge towards her.

Sweet Mother Earth, what had happened to her Dark Prince? Once more, Eden tried to connect with his Life-Band. Still, no response. The devastating truth hit her: Jamal wasn't coming.

Eden caught a glimpse of Bramford weaving through the crowd. Any second, it would swallow him without a trace. She had no choice but to follow the arrogant bastard.

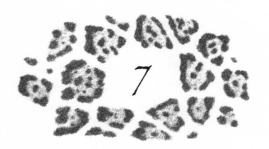

7

EDEN LEANED forward, panting, as the angle of the tunnel tilted upwards. For several minutes they had been winding towards the Earth's surface. She glanced at Bramford and Shen beside her. Neither one seemed troubled by their route.

"Where are we going?" Eden said.

"Where you should have stayed," Bramford replied.

She swallowed her panic, silently following him up a twisting stairway. Her ears popped. The temperature rose and she began to sweat, as they climbed higher and higher. Finally, they reached a heavily guarded gate in the upper level. The lead guard nodded deferentially at Bramford and waved them through—including her! She'd never once passed through any checkpoint without inspection.

Eden was even more astounded when they arrived at a humming supersonic aircraft. She watched in amazement as Shen took a seat beside the pilot, a small-boned Tiger's Eye. Bramford waved her towards the main cabin. Did he really expect her to fly? She'd never even been outside of the Combs.

"Get in," he insisted.

"No," Eden said, as stunned as he, by her daring refusal.

"What's wrong?"

"Can't. Fly."

He seemed mildly amused as he dragged her inside the craft. She felt the blood drain from her head. Dark inky shadows fell behind her eyes. Her knees buckled under her and she fell into a seat.

"Relax," Bramford said, sitting down beside her. "You'll enjoy it."

So he wasn't simply cruel; he was crazy, too.

He commanded the pilot to take off, and the hangar ceiling immediately retracted. Eden looked up at the vast, dark, ashen sky. If she had felt worthless before, she now realized she was nothing more than a speck of dust in that forbidding expanse. At least in the tunnels, she'd felt large, even confined.

She screamed as the aircraft shot into the turbulent skies. Her stomach lurched up into her throat. She dug her hands into the armrests, as if she might steady the rollicking craft. Stories of catastrophic air disasters, common due to the erratic jet streams, passed through her mind.

She glanced at Bramford, who appeared calm as usual. Probably enjoying her distress. Well, she wouldn't give him the satisfaction. *Breathe, Eden.* Her mother always had said it was the key to happiness. But Eden couldn't slow down her rapid heartbeat or stop the anxious feelings that surged through her as unpredictably as the vehicle's erratic path. If only she'd stayed home.

She tried to focus on a fixed point on the empty seat that faced her. Even here, Bramford had stamped the upholstery with his ego-driven logo. How had he obtained the leather, anyway, when the world treated its scant remaining livestock like gods?

A flickering movement distracted Eden and she turned to find him watching shocking Holo-Images of an eight-year-old albino boy. Tuning into the same news feed, she learned that the young Cotton had been found in a cave near the Sahara. Apparently, he'd hidden there for most of his life.

But how had an albino been born in the first place? The Uni-Gov proclaimed that the sterilization program aimed at carriers of the gene had wiped out albinism. Whenever a rare birth occurred, *they* took away the newborn and cut off the parents' oxy supply.

Eden watched as a mob tied the screaming albino to a funeral pyre. It was the only time she'd seen Coals and Pearls united in action. The Cotton's white skin and hair stood out among his attackers; his pinkish eyes pleaded for help. Strange how she didn't feel deep hatred for the albino, as she had been taught in school. She might even feel sorry for the poor boy.

Bramford's ring flashed and the news story changed. Eden quickly glanced at him, surprised to see the anxiety in his face. Why would a megalomaniac like him care about the doomed Cotton?

The aircraft took a sharp turn, nearly throwing her into Bramford's lap. He looked stunned and she wondered if he had felt the same mysterious electric charge. Was he wearing some new device that generated overwhelming magnetism?

"Sorry," Eden said, scrambling back to her seat.

Shen slid open the partition and gave her a sympathetic look. "Would you like an oxy tablet?" he said.

Was he kidding? She'd like a dozen. Only the military had tablets, which gave them the freedom to move around.

"Sure." She accepted the small, green pill with feigned nonchalance.

"Here," Bramford said, offering a glass of water.

Eden stared at it, bewildered. "But I've already had my allotment tonight."

"It doesn't matter."

Like Sweet Earth, it did. The image of her dying mother, desperate for a drink of water, burned in her mind. Many times, shame-faced, she'd allowed Eden to sacrifice part of her nightly share. Lasers and leather and oxy tablets, Eden could understand. But extra water? She wished that greedy bastard could know how it felt to live on the edge.

She shot him a defiant look and popped the tablet in her mouth. But as her mouth turned gummy, she regretted her stubbornness, if only a little.

"Change your mind?" Bramford said.

Eden shook her head, trying to swallow.

"Suit yourself." He shrugged and drank the water.

The man wasn't human.

Shen turned around again, his face anxious. "A fire has broken out in the hills above REA, sir."

As usual, Bramford kept his cool. "E.T.A.?"

"Five minutes and forty-five seconds."

"Make it two."

The aircraft screamed forward.

Bramford's ring flashed and a Holo-Image of Eden's father appeared, along with live images of the lab. "Delay the firewall until I arrive," Bramford said.

"What!" Her father blinked fast. "Extreme heat will put the delicate environment here at risk. The viral samples must be cooled."

Eden gagged as the jet nose-dived.

He looked at her, wide-eyed. "Daught?"

Before she could respond, the plump assistant, Peach, hurried over and whispered in his ear. The girl's careless proximity stunned Eden. What could be so urgent? As her father's expression turned grim, she figured it wasn't good news.

"Doctor Newman?" Bramford said.

"I don't understand," her father said, stammering. "It appears the test subjects are missing. Security has searched the premises to no avail."

"Both of them?" Only one test subject was necessary; the other had been a safety.

"So I'm told."

Bramford zeroed in on Eden. She and Ashina reported on every nuance of the test subjects. Was the bitch trying to set her up? Or worse, sabotage the operation?

"Ashina is in charge now," Eden said in a small voice.

Her father looked out over the lab and a view of Ashina's station followed. The girl was gone.

"I swear she lied about my missing report," Eden added.

Bramford sat with his elbows on the armrests, drumming his fingertips together.

"I was afraid it would come to this."

"To what?"

He ignored her. "Proceed as planned, doctor."

"But how?" he said, once more in view. "No subject, no experiment."

Poor Father, he looked crushed. This was meant to be the crowning achievement of his lifetime.

"I guarantee you'll have a subject," Bramford said. "Just stay on schedule."

"But who?" Eden said.

Bramford took a deep breath, his hands floating to his lap. "Me, that's who."

Her father stared, as shocked as Eden. "You, Bramford?" he said.

"That's correct. We proceed at 24:00."

"But I need more time. Even the minutest of changes must be calculated. An unexamined change of this magnitude will seriously compromise the success of the operation."

"If you have a better solution, doctor, I'd like to hear it. This might be the only chance we get."

Eden could see the gears turning in her father's mind. Who else would be brave or stupid enough to volunteer for an illegal and highly experimental procedure?

"Post your genome without delay, Bramford." Almost as an afterthought, he added, "Without sufficient preparation, I cannot guarantee your personal safety."

"I've taken bigger risks."

Bramford cut off the link and the images disappeared.

What risks? Eden wondered. He'd lived his life insulated by wealth and privilege. Besides, she didn't believe he would go through with it. He only was showing off.

It occurred to her that the missing test subjects must have prevented Jamal from leaving the lab. After all, the responsibility ultimately fell to his department. Of course, that explained everything. How had she ever doubted him when he had made his intentions so clear? *Time for Jamal to make a righteous move.*

Eden looked out the window as the aircraft plummeted through the clouds. Possibly, it was fake, she told herself, just like any other experience she fantasized on the World-Band. She wasn't really hurtling towards Holy Earth. The orange ring of fire that crowned the mountains above REA didn't really threaten her entire world. And Jamal was anxious to call her his mate.

The vehicle landed with a jolt inside the ramparts that towered around the upper level. At once, a blaring siren announced the lowering of the firewall. It quickly fell into place with a loud, groaning screech. The security entrance to the tunnels would remain blocked until the fire abated.

Eden leaned forward, itching to see Jamal. She jumped out as soon as the doors slid open.

"You're coming with me," Bramford said, taking hold of her arm.

She glared at him. "I'm off duty, remember? You can't treat me this way."

"Apparently, someone has to."

Eden stared at his hand on her, bewildered by the warmth that flooded into her body and a strange knocking in her gut. She felt off balance, even a little unhinged, she hated to admit.

Never mind, her Dark Prince would save her.

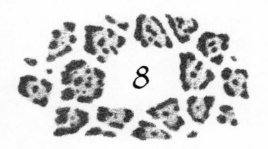

8

THE WORKERS' smug stares bore into Eden, as she followed Bramford up the stairs to the operating theater. Caught by the boss—weren't *they* happy? Why on Earth did she want to be like *them*, anyway?

Eden's father turned away from his calculations, a wild look in his eyes. Old stains on his lab coat and his unruly hair added to the impression of a man on the edge.

"Any sign of them?" Bramford asked with a glimmer of hope.

Her father shook his head. "Jamal is questioning our staff."

Eden's eyes cut to the workers below, anxious for a sign of him. She was like a small fish looking at a school of hungry piranhas. If Jamal didn't save her, eventually they would tear her to bits. But her Dark Prince was nowhere in sight.

"I see," Bramford said, thoughtfully.

Eden figured he would change his mind. She was surprised, and even a little impressed, when he made his determination clear.

"Then there's no time to lose. Ready, doctor?"

"I've run your genome and..." Her father paused to wipe

his glasses on his coat though they only looked more smeared afterwards.

"And?" Bramford said.

"There are variations in your code for which I am not prepared."

"Can you work with it or not?"

"What? Yes, it can be done. But you must know, these variables increase the risk ratio—"

"Whatever the risk, I'm now the guinea pig. Let's begin."

"You leave me no choice then." Her father spoke to Peach. "Start prepping Mr. Bramford at once."

Bramford hurried ahead of her towards the back of the platform. Eager, wasn't he? Eden thought. Maybe he'd planned all along to be the test subject so he could keep the technology for himself. Greedy bastard.

Before he disappeared into the prep room, he called to Shen. "Keep an eye on Eden."

As if it were all her fault. Wasn't that what everyone thought?

She drifted beside her father and peered over his shoulder. Above one corner of the console was a Holo-Image of one of the original test subjects. At first she saw an ordinary Pearl in his natural coloring. Such images were illegal, except for scientific purposes, of course. Still, the sight of the man's pale skin thrilled Eden.

Gradually, the newly evolved man came through with dark coloring inherited from the black jaguar, the camouflage spots barely visible on his skin. The eyes, now a pale green-ish-gold, had a slight cat-like curve, the face, a feline affect. The jaguar also had given him a more streamlined body. The strong abdominal muscles, a gift from the anaconda. A list of statistics estimated the increase in muscle-to-body fat ratio, strength and speed.

The changes in stage one were dramatic, though the new man would resemble a Homo sapiens more than any of the donor animals. Still, he would be superior to any race. No wonder Bramford seemed so eager to adapt. In any case, she had to admire his courage.

"Daught? What are you doing here?" her father said, turning towards her.

"What do you mean?" she said. "I arrived with Bramford."

"Indeed?"

"You looked right at me."

"Did I? You must have appeared out of context—no lab coat, a disheveled black dress."

Good Earth, was she that invisible? Or was Father just out of step with reality? Probably both. Sometimes she wondered how on Earth she would manage to keep the promise she'd given at her mother's deathbed.

—*Promise you will take care of your father, Eden. He needs help, even if he doesn't know it.*

—*I promise, Mother. Don't worry.*

Eden would never forget the relief in her mother's worried eyes.

At last, her Life-Band received Jamal's signal. She wanted to lash out at him for leaving her at the dance. But, of course, anger wasn't an option. *Keep your eye on the goal, Eden.*

She quickly turned her back to Shen, who stood guard by the prep room, to hide her flashing earring and the desperateness she felt.

Jamal, are you all right?

Sorry, Little Bunny. Strategic problems. Bramford was at the dance so I asked him to bring you back.

You did?

Let's keep our date, pet. I'm waiting for you in my office.

I'll come as soon as I can.

Come now.

Jamal cut off, and a silly grin stretched across Eden's face. He still wanted her.

When she turned round, Bramford lay stretched out on the test bed. Peach hooked the bindings on his white operating suit to an instrument panel. Eden searched his face for any sign of hesitation, but there was no crack in the iron-willed façade. If it had been her, she would have been scared to death.

"You think I'm crazy, don't you?" Bramford said, as if he'd read her mind.

"No." Eden lied.

She saw something flash across his face—anger, resignation, hope?

Whatever he was feeling, his voice never betrayed any emotion. "Sometimes you have to leap or be pushed. I prefer to land on my own two feet."

"Well, you might not recognize them," she said, half joking.

"Once we see the cause and effect of our actions, change isn't so frightening."

Eden felt the weight of his stare. Possibly, he was really looking at her. Sweet Earth, as if he saw the Real Eden. She forgot all about the procedure and her problems. The busy hum of the laboratory faded away. She felt an odd desire to smile at Bramford. She even suspected he might smile back. Instead, he turned his head and barked out instructions to Shen. She felt like crawling deep into the earth. Crazy to think the cold-hearted tyrant could see anything, especially her.

Her father leaned over Bramford. "This will knock you out," he said, making an adjustment.

Immediately, Bramford's eyes glazed over. His last words were to Shen. "Stay close."

Here was Eden's chance. Making herself small, she escaped towards the exit. And yet, she hesitated by the door, perplexed by an inexplicable urge to talk Bramford out of his foolish decision. But what did she care when the man detested her?

She hurried into the security area, surprised to find it unmanned. Then she noticed the overhead surveillance cameras blinking. She looked both ways. No one was watching. She took a deep breath and tiptoed behind the security desk just as a series of Holo-Images began to disappear, one by one.

There, could that be? The last images showed her dance hall tormentors, Giant and Squeaky, walking through the main tunnel that connected REA to the Combs. That view also disappeared, leaving Eden in a panic.

They were coming for her, she realized. *You can't escape, Pearly.* They would be there any minute. She had to get to Jamal.

She flew down the hallway, retracing the path she'd only just taken from the upper level. Her high heels clattered up several levels of stairs until she reached security. Breathless, she stepped towards his office, when she heard deep, angry voices. Good Earth, she was too late.

"Jamal!" she cried, pushing open the door.

Four men turned as she entered, their faces full of surprise. Eden stared back at them, wondering why these men, the lab guards, wore the FFP uniform. Even Jamal had on the despicable clothes, the beret at a jaunty angle on his head. Braided epaulets, which signified a high-ranking officer, decorated his shoulders—the same shoulders upon which she'd often laid her head.

She heard a muffled sound and saw two male Pearls, bound and gagged, lying on the floor. *The test subjects*. Above them, the control button for the firewall glowed bright red. It was the only thing in the room that seemed real to her.

"Jamal? What's going on?" Eden demanded, still hoping for a reasonable explanation.

His eyes gleamed with excitement. In fact, she'd never seen him look so happy. "You're just in time, pet," he said.

"For what?"

"Showtime!"

As if on cue, Giant and Squeaky entered the room. Their faces lit up at the sight of her.

"Hello, Pearly," Giant said.

"My fumbling friends are glad you made it," Jamal said, not looking happy at all now. "Bramford almost ruined our plan by showing up at the dance."

Jamal's friends? He hadn't asked Bramford to bring her back to the lab? He never intended to be her mate? For the love of Earth, he'd never seen the Real Eden, either. No one did.

Eden's mind spun, her body felt wooden. She was going to be violently sick. She needed oxy, a lot of it.

"I have to go now," she said, turning to leave.

Jamal grabbed her arm. "Not so fast. We're just getting started. You're my personal insurance policy."

"What? I'm not helping you."

"Even if it means convincing the doctor to play along? You wouldn't want him to get hurt, would you?"

Was this really her Life-Band lover talking?

"Who are you?" Eden said.

"I am the People," Jamal replied matter-of-factly. "The Federation of Free People is taking back what greed-suckers like Bramford owe us. With your father's technology we'll be in control of everything."

"For Earth's sake, this isn't political. It's about science."

"Everything is political. The population is controlled by doped oxy and emotionally driven campaigns so the super rich like Bramford can skim cream off the top. Same old story."

Eden couldn't really argue with that. But who was to say a new regime wouldn't also abuse their power?

"Please, Jamal. My father will insist that Bramford use his technology in ethical ways."

"Don't be so naïve, Little Bunny," he said, and she wondered how just last night the pathetic nickname had pleased her. "You see how the boss treats him. Same as he treats you and everyone else—like objects not people. And don't pretend you don't agree because I know you do."

That really stung. How often had she confided in Jamal? Dear Earth, she'd given confidential data to an FFP officer!

From the very beginning, he had used her. *Time for Jamal to make a righteous move.*

"Bramford is a master manipulator," he continued. "Believe me, even this last-minute decision to be the test subject is calculated. He fears a takeover—which is exactly what he's going to get. So he's hedging his bets. If the experiment works, he won't ever get The Heat. If you can outlive the rest, you've got an unbeatable edge. Once he's in the catbird seat, so to speak, he'll destroy the lab and kill your father. But I'm going to stop him."

He shook his head and laughed. "It's a lucky break. We get the tech, an evolved subject and Bramford, all in one."

A cold chill gripped Eden's heart. If the FFP gained control, it would be the end for Pearls. And maybe what Jamal had said about Bramford was true. Either way, she and her father were doomed to servitude or death, probably both.

Jamal ran his hand down her cheek. "Naturally, we have an important place for the doctor in our organization. You'd be surprised how easy I can make things for you."

Eden spat out her words. "I'd rather get The Heat than be your mate."

"Be serious, pet. Ashina's going to be my mate."

Jamal and that bitch were in cahoots? Eden felt humiliated as she imagined them laughing at her behind her back. And doing things that true mates did. What a fool she'd been.

"I hate you, Jamal," she said hotly.

He simply shrugged. "You're still coming with me."

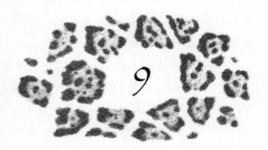

9

EDEN STOOD in Jamal's office among the FFP soldiers, wondering how her dreams had died so suddenly. Because they had never been real, she realized. She only had imagined a better future. In six months, when she turned eighteen, still unmated, she'd be cut off and left outside to die.

She stared with new eyes at Jamal, her ex-boyfriend, struck by how ugly he truly was. His arrogant posturing and the strident tone with which he addressed his team of conspirators sickened her. He was no better than Bramford—even worse. Why hadn't she seen it before? She faced the sad truth with a heavy sigh. Her desperate need for Jamal's help had blinded her to his real nature.

But no more, Eden told herself. There was a sort of freedom in being doomed. If she had nothing to lose why not make things a little harder for her traitorous lover?

She glanced around the room, her keen mind puzzling together a plan. Her gaze rested on the firewall control. If she raised the shield, the fire outside would engulf the upper level and snake down into the lab. Maybe she and her father could escape in the chaos. Then again, they might be burned to death. What other options did she have?

Here goes. Eden took a deep breath and lunged for the

firewall button with a wild yell. Immediately, the warning siren rang out, followed by the loud rumbling of the retracting shield.

A stunned silence fell over the soldiers. Then Jamal yelled. "Get her!"

Eden tried to duck but once again found herself caught in Giant's powerful grip. He smiled lasciviously at her.

"You know, you're a pain in the ass, Eden." Jamal said. "Most Pearls would give anything to be on my team. What's wrong with you?"

She wondered the same thing.

"Guess I'm old-fashioned," she said. "I still think honesty is a virtue."

"Yeah, you've got heart, I'll give you that. You've got one more chance to cooperate. For old times' sake."

"You're going to do whatever you want, anyway."

"True," he said, and she watched the lips she once had longed to kiss curl into a cruel smile.

He turned his attention to his band of men. "Remember, take Dr. Newman and Bramford alive. Laser anyone who gets in the way." His eyes cut over to Eden. "And I mean anyone."

Father, she thought helplessly. She had to get to him.

As the firewall rose, it exposed the security window to the raging firestorm. Through a smoky haze, she saw the inferno racing towards them. The soldiers lined up in formation, ready to leave, when a loud explosion rocked the building. The roof ripped open, as if peeled back by an unseen hand. The men fell like dominos, pulling Eden down with them. She covered her head as shards of broken glass rained down from the shattered window. Dense, toxic smoke billowed in, and her lungs screamed for air. Then the lights quit, plunging the room into darkness.

Her heart pounded as she scrambled to her feet. She heard the men shuffling, yelling orders. A flashlight beam raced across the walls, sweeping over Jamal, lying pinned under a fallen beam.

"Get Eden," he mumbled.

She bolted from the room. Blue pinpoint emergency lights in the floor led her down the dark hallway. She picked her way past a maze of fallen debris and stepped into the chaotic, smoke-filled lab. Crackling flames licked through a hole in the ceiling. The loud screams and frantic movements reminded her of the Moon Dance. But this was no party.

"Father!" Eden cried, the din drowning out her voice.

She ran forward against the rush of terrified workers who knocked her onto the slippery floor. Wet, gooey flame retardant foam shot from ports in the wall. Eden wiped off the mess from her face and arms. Too late, she watched her dark coating peel away in streaks. But she couldn't think about that now.

She felt like a loose electron bouncing from atom to atom as she crawled through the melee. When the crush passed by, she grabbed onto a workstation to pull to her feet. In the flickering light, she saw her father standing alone in the operating theater. He seemed dazed, and she guessed he had finally noticed the world around him.

A painful cry filled the air. Her father jerked towards the test bed. It seemed Bramford was in trouble. Blessed Earth, the extreme heat must have contaminated the experiment. Her fault, all of it.

Eden heard the soldiers' footsteps echo down the hall. Desperate, she scanned the lab for a weapon. But she was just one little Pearl against armed FFP soldiers. What could she do?

She flashed on the day the lab had opened. Hadn't Father given her a secret code?

—*My work must never fall into the wrong hands. Use this, Daught, when no other alternative exists.*

That would be now, right? Still, why did she have to be the one to decide? But if she didn't *they* would win.

She activated the memorable code. *Go bluebell.*

—*Just remember your mother's pretty eyes. They were the color of bluebells.*

The system responded with a standard question: *Are you sure you want to terminate Resources for Environmental Adaptation?*

Eden groaned. Every backup of her father's work would be destroyed. Just then the soldiers burst into the lab. She had no choice but to proceed. *Sorry, Father.*

A loud, insistent female voice announced the end. *"Warning! REA will self-destruct in five minutes. Please proceed to the nearest exit."*

Hand over fist, Eden grabbed hold of objects as she made her way towards the operating theater. She almost had reached the stairway when Jamal caught her, a blood-soaked bandage wrapped around his head.

"No more games, Eden," he said.

He dragged her below the operating theater while the soldiers' heavy boots pounded up the stairs. They fanned out along the rim of the stage and stood ready. Her father leaned over the operating bed, his back to the soldiers, once more oblivious. Beside him, Bramford's chilling cries cut through the sounds of falling timbers and snapping flames.

Eden calculated their survival odds: one crazy, old scientist and his gullible daughter against, count 'em—seven armed soldiers, including Jamal. Bramford was useless. Their one hope was Shen who, to her amazement, remained by his employer's side.

As her father might have said, the current trajectory would no doubt result in a re-organization in favor of the more dominant genes. In other words, Jamal, and therefore the FFP, would win and kill all the Pearls, starting with her.

"Dr. Newman, we represent the Federation of Free People," Jamal called out. "We're here to requisition your services and technology for the benefit of the People. Come with us peacefully and I guarantee you'll be treated with the respect you deserve."

"Four minutes until termination. Please exit the building at once."

Still, her father ignored them, as if he was immune to the chaos.

"Father!" Eden yelled. "Help!"

At last he spun round to face the enemy. "What? It isn't possible!"

If the situation hadn't been so dire, Eden might have laughed. To her father, anything was possible if approached in a logical sequence.

"I insist you leave at once," he continued. "You are interfering with a delicate operation."

A curdling scream rose in the air. Poor Bramford. Eden wouldn't wish such suffering on anyone, not even him.

Inquisitive detachment replaced the crazed look on her father's face. He seemed to forget the immediate danger and turned back to the test bed.

"Proceed to the nearest exit. Three minutes remaining until termination."

"Advance," Jamal told the men.

Eden watched the soldiers step forward, her heart in her throat. Her father wheeled round again, waving a syringe in the air.

"Stay back!" he said. "Or I'll kill myself and the subject."

The men halted and looked to Jamal for instructions. He yanked Eden in front of him, shouting above the raging fire. "If you cooperate, Dr. Newman, nothing will happen to your daughter. However, if you continue to resist, I cannot guarantee her safety."

Her father hesitated.

Eden heard the shock in Jamal's voice. "Do you understand, doctor?"

"What? Yes, the paradigm has been clearly presented."

Eden's father looked at her with regret. She guessed what he was thinking: *the biggest leap in evolution since man discovered fire.*

"Father?" she said.

He shook his head and focused once more on his precious patient.

It was embarrassing, really. No one wanted her—not her boyfriend, not even her own father. Guess the FFP hadn't counted on her worthlessness.

"Warning! Two minutes remaining until destruction of REA."

"Take out the doctor," Jamal ordered his men.

An earth-shaking roar split the air. Frantic, Eden fought to get away. "Let me go!"

To her surprise, Jamal released her and stared ahead, wide-eyed. Then as the thunderous sound repeated, she understood it had come from the platform. *From Bramford.*

Her father staggered away from the test bed. Even the soldiers stepped back. From the tearing sound, Eden guessed that Bramford had ripped off the bindings that held him to the bed. But that was impossible for any man.

She gasped as something dark and monstrous sprung from the bed. It landed at the edge of the platform, towering over the room. Bramford didn't resemble the controlled model of the new man she expected. Instead, she stared up at a terrifying creature, part man and part beast.

Mostly, he reminded Eden of his new cousin, the jaguar. In the slash of cheekbones and feline face the resemblance was unmistakable. His eyes, now a luminous deep green, gleamed cat-like in the glow of the fire. No longer bald, he had dark silky hair tumbling down his shoulders. Powerful, carved legs ripped through the white surgical pants.

His skin had turned so dark it blended with his camouflage spots, giving the impression of muted scars or tattoos all over his body. The deep, dark coloring, thanks to the melanistic jaguar's pitch-black coat, enhanced his powerful presence, just as Bramford must have intended.

He shook with rage. The shirt split across his chest, revealing tight bands of muscles under a light mat of fur. Slowly, he turned over his hands, examining the thick padded palms. His gaze traveled down his adapted body, and Eden wondered if the unexpected beastly form shocked him. Or had Bramford even retained enough human awareness to experience such an emotion?

His angry roar seemed to answer her unspoken question with a resounding yes. She felt faint from the ferocious power he exuded. Unreasonable feelings bubbled up within her. Maybe it was crazy, but she wanted to roar back at him.

Feral eyes landed on her, devouring every inch. She found herself smiling at him. But his eyes stayed cold, his expression as flint-hard as ever.

In that moment, Eden understood that despite his dramatic physical transformation, deep down Ronson Bramford hadn't changed one bit. He was still the same arrogant bastard.

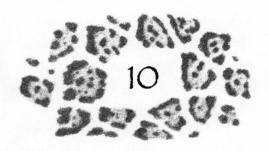

10

THE WARNING countdown rang out in the laboratory with increasing urgency. *"One minute and thirty seconds to termination of REA. Immediate evacuation required."*

Eden tensed as her father approached Bramford, who towered over him. Like a child experiencing his first World-Band fantasy, her father's eyes were wide with wonder for his creation. If Bramford so much as flicked a finger, he might destroy the man who held the keys to his destiny. But would the beast understand that?

Beside her, Jamal ordered his men in a calm, low voice. "Do not kill the creature. I repeat, stun but do not kill him."

To her surprise, Eden felt a protective urge towards her boss. "Run, Bramford!" she cried.

He seemed not to hear her, and she wondered if he still knew his name or even retained the power of speech. Or maybe he simply chose to ignore her, as usual. In any case, he stood firm, facing the semi-circle of soldiers. She hated to think of how the FFP would cage and dissect him like a common lab rat, *Rattus norvegicus*. They would destroy him, just like every other wild thing on the ravaged planet.

And yet, hope surged in her as the cunning predator now embedded into Bramford's DNA seemed to take possession

of him. His feline eyes canvassed the room, probably devis-
ing a strategy to attack. She imagined him drawing upon the
superfine senses and formidable powers he'd been given. But
how would he resist the soldier's lasers?

Bramford sank onto his haunches with a warning rumble.
Powerful muscles rippled in his thighs. His lips curled into a
snarl, ready to attack. The louder his growl grew, the more
nervous the soldiers seemed. Eden understood with a rush of
respect that like any alpha male, he needed to establish his
dominance over them.

Her father pleaded with the FFP. "Please, desist at once.
You're inciting the subject."

*"One minute and counting until termination. Fifty-nine
seconds..."*

Fire mushroomed through the shattered roof, sucking
out the air with a powerful whoosh. Chunks of the building
rained down. Eden screamed as one of the soldiers fired his
laser at Bramford, who dodged the flare with lightning speed.

Shen rushed forward but Bramford sent him flying back
with a light slap. He looked surprised when Shen hit the wall
with a loud thud. Eden wondered if he'd simply aimed to put
his loyal bodyguard out of harm's way.

A second laser blast sizzled in the air. Again, Bramford
pivoted away, too fast for her eyes to trace. He leapt upon
the nearest soldier and mashed him into a ball. With ease,
he hurled the screaming man into the path of an oncoming
laser. In a blur, Bramford ducked to evade the other two soldiers' flares. He bounded towards them, crushing them with
a single swipe of his arm.

Giant and Squeaky retreated to the edge of the platform.

"Stay down," Jamal told them, as he aimed his laser. "I'm going to neutralize Bramford."

Eden saw that Bramford would leave himself open to Giant and Squeaky, if he attacked Jamal. She had to help. She recalled that Aunt Emily said she felt as if the top of her head came off whenever she recognized poetry. Now, Eden felt a similar lift and knew what to do.

Time slowed, in her mind, as she spied a burning timber shake loose from the roof. She grabbed a nearby chair and, like an old-fashioned baseball player, swung it hard at the falling timber. It connected with a bang and sailed in Jamal's direction. The chair flew from her hands, sending her tumbling to the ground. A sick scream filled the air, followed by a laser blast. Eden raised her head to find Jamal lying on the floor covered in flames.

Another gut-wrenching cry reached her, its familiar tone filling her with dread. *Father!*

Scrambling to her feet, she saw him sprawled on the ground. He clutched his leg, a crimson stain spreading onto his lab coat.

Bramford roared at Giant and Squeaky, the remaining line of defense. They inched backwards, then turned and ran to their fallen leader.

Once more, Bramford's penetrating gaze fell on Eden. Did she imagine it or did something in his eyes soften?

Distracted by Shen's loud moans, he turned to the devoted bodyguard, who struggled to stand. One arm hung limp at his side; the dragon tattoo gone slack. He lurched forward with obvious effort, but Bramford's abrupt growl stopped him.

A look that puzzled Eden passed between them. Bramford pointed towards the exit, clearly ordering Shen to leave. Now she was sure the creature must have lost his human voice, although some reasoning appeared to be intact. Shen shook his head, refusing even now to abandon his boss. Bramford answered with a final roar, its cold authority strikingly similar to his old ways. Finally, Shen turned away.

What was it, between those two, anyway?

Bramford leapt towards Eden's father, who lay helpless on the floor. The beast's emerald eyes burned feverishly, the nostrils flared. Eden gasped, afraid the blood that oozed from her father's wound might incite Bramford to attack. Any predator would.

She hardly could believe it when he carefully lifted her father in his arms. Not even Bramford's former self was capable of such gentleness. Like a rock skimming over a flat pond, he carried her beaming father across the tops of the workstations until he stood above Eden.

She stared up into his savage face, her mind a blank. To her amazement, Bramford spoke in a raspy growl, as terrifying as a tsunami, as thrilling as a rare bird in flight.

"Come, Eden," he said, holding out a sharp-clawed, leathery hand.

He knew her, she realized with delight. Perhaps it was silly, but she felt special, as if a celebrity had recognized her. And she felt helplessly lost in the magnetic glow of his cat-like eyes.

"This is your final warning! Thirty seconds until termination. Twenty-nine seconds..."

Bramford barked at her. "What are you waiting for?"

Eden liked him much better when he seemed mute. She certainly didn't want to go anywhere with the scary beast. But there was Father, and her promise to watch over him.

She reached for Bramford's hand, shocked once again by the electric feel of his touch. This time, there was no mistaking the reeling effect on her, despite the change in him. Or maybe because of it, she realized.

Bramford balanced her onto one broad shoulder, as if Eden were a little bird perched there. She clung to his neck, petrified, as he sped away. Fiery objects exploded around them, and yet he easily evaded them, dodging through the smoke-filled tunnels.

Ahead, she saw a wall of fire, blocking their path to the upper level. Good Earth, Bramford wasn't going to stop. She screamed as he sprinted forward. The fire reached for them, but Bramford was too fast for it to catch hold. He seemed to have the power of ten jaguars.

Eden laughed hysterically, as they burst through the blaze. She wondered if *they* were laughing, too. Possibly, *they* had designed an entire night of elaborate Holo-Images to drive her mad. She only wanted it to stop.

Bramford ran past the charred security gate and into the hangar, where his aircraft waited. The pilot's eyes widened as they approached. Like Eden, he must have recognized Bramford in the creature's steely gaze. At once the doors slid open.

A Uni-Gov military siren echoed in the distance. Eden feared they'd treat her no better than the FFP. Her father might be retained until he was of no further use, but she would be cut off. They had no choice but to rely on Bramford, as crazy as that seemed.

He lowered her to the ground then set her father on the back seat, again with surprising tenderness.

"Get in, Eden," he said, as he jumped into the facing seat.

Her father's eyes begged her to join him. Happy at this meager sign of acceptance, she stepped in beside him when a horrible thought stopped her. *Austin.* She'd forgotten him in the chaos. Before she could leave, Bramford yanked her inside, and the doors closed.

"Full speed ahead," he told the pilot. "And tell the airstrip to ready number one."

"Stop!" Eden cried, banging on the cabin door. "I have to go back."

Bramford released her with a grunt, as the aircraft vaulted into the air. She fell back into the seat beside her father, unable to fathom life without her dog.

A heart-stopping boom shook the skies. She watched the lab explode, and let out an anguished scream.

"No! Austin!"

Slammed by the shock wave, the jet skidded towards the hillside. The driver struggled to right the craft, then raced ahead.

Eden slid down into the seat, devastated. Everything she had known was gone. If her life were a simple equation, like one plus one, it now yielded a negative number.

"Austin is of the species *Canis lupus familiaris*—a dog," her father explained to Bramford in a soft voice, as if talking to a child.

"You'd risk your life for a dog?" Bramford asked her, incredulously.

"You wouldn't understand. For Earth's sake, you left poor Shen behind."

He winced. "I expect he'll be safe."

"He has a mate and a child, doesn't he?"

"Yes, for their sake, I made a choice. If the FFP thinks he's only an employee they'll leave him alone."

"Then who is he?"

Bramford gave her a hard look then stared out the window. He seemed more upset about Shen's future than his own. Or more likely, he'd lost some secret advantage by leaving his aide behind. Bramford couldn't fool her; he was simply a more powerful, and yes, even exciting, version of the selfish man Eden loathed.

"Well, I'm grateful you saved us," her father said.

Eden glared at him. Didn't he understand why Bramford had taken them along? He didn't care about them any more than he cared for Shen. If he hoped to restore his human form, he desperately needed her father's help.

But what if her father failed? Then what would the wild beast do to them?

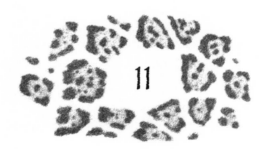

11

EDEN GRIPPED the armrests of her seat as Bramford's fleeing aircraft zigzagged through the air. A pursuing military aircraft shot laser fire at them, nipping at their heels. The blinding white flashes and blazing firestorm lit the dark night. Bramford's vehicle lacked firepower but was nimble and fast.

Beside Eden, her father squeezed her hand. To comfort her, she supposed. She caught him grimacing, a hand clamped over his leg. Fresh blood oozed onto the white coat.

For the first time in her life, she wished there was a God. But that idea had disappeared in The Meltdown.

Bramford sat across from her, his powerful body dominating the small space like a mountain cramped in a cave. Holo-Images played in the small cabin, showing the deadly battle in progress. He studied them as he issued a steady stream of orders to the pilot.

"One o'clock, now three o'clock," he said in a firm, raspy voice.

Once more, the strange mix of contradictions in him puzzled Eden. His cat-like features pulsed with energy, like a jaguar stalking its prey. And yet, unmistakable human intelligence burned in the icy green eyes.

A laser blast crackled against a window and sent the vehicle into a sickening slip. Eden let out a shrill scream.

"Quiet," Bramford said, flicking his gaze at her.

In the split second his attention had turned, a second,
more powerful blast hit them. The aircraft lurched out of
control, spinning in a downward spiral.

Blessed Mother Earth.

"Six o'clock!" Bramford said.

They continued to corkscrew down towards the inferno
and their probable death. Had Bramford lost his mind, after
all? Eden wondered. Her stomach climbed up into her throat
and she fought the urge to scream again. Must not distract
him, she thought, followed by the startling realization that
her life was in his beastly hands.

For as long as Eden could remember death had lingered
in the shadows. Now that it knocked on her door, she realized, what a waste. She'd barely lived.

Bramford's thunderous voice shook the small cabin as the
burning earth drew near. "Twelve o'clock, now!"

Their sharp reversal sent them flying past the enemy fight-
er. A loud explosion followed as it shot into the flames.

Eden collapsed, trembling. *My dear, your oxy level is near
depletion. You need immediate help.* For once *they* were so
right.

"We're clear," Bramford said, never betraying any emotion.

"For Earth's sake, you could have killed us!" she said.

"Be calm, Daught," her father said.

Bramford leveled his steely gaze at her. "Give me his lab
coat."

Eden hesitated, uncomprehending.

He dipped his head towards her father's leg. "A tourni-
quet."

"Oh."

Again, this mysterious creature was one step ahead of her
and her father. Was he a man trapped inside a beastly form,
or a beast with a human mind? Eden suspected even he might
not know the answer.

She gingerly slipped the coat off of her father. Bramford
snatched it from her with an impatient huff. He used sharp
teeth—teeth that could kill a man—to rip off a long strip.
Then he flung it at her dismissively, without a word or look
in her direction.

"Thanks," Eden muttered.

She tied it around her father's leg, alarmed by the amount
of bleeding. He groaned but kept his eyes trained on Bramford. Even now, at death's door, he appeared to be distracted
by possible solutions and heady calculations.

"Where are we going?" she asked Bramford. "My father
needs help."

"Far away," he said.

"Out of bounds?"

He turned to stare out the window, his silence impenetrable.

Eden sat back, wrapped up in her thoughts like her companions, as the jet zoomed past the fire zone and into the
dark skies. A hundred questions filled her head. Mostly, if
they flew out of bounds, how would they survive without the
Uni-Gov to take care of them? She never thought she would
miss it but she couldn't imagine a single night without its op-
pressive but sustaining presence.

She stole a glance at Bramford, trying to guess what he

was thinking. She felt a twinge of compassion as she considered how dramatically his life had turned. And something else also warmed her heart. She traced his broad chest down to slim hips and muscled thighs. The raw animal power coiled within him, just waiting to explode, fascinated her.

Eden found her body tilting towards his. Maybe it was illogical for a Pearl to be drawn to such a dangerous creature, but she wanted to touch him.

His eyes cut over to her. She jerked back and felt her cheeks flush with embarrassment. She heard him grunt, as she turned away. But what did it mean? *Watch out, I eat girls like you for breakfast?*

Soon, she saw the huge sign for Bramford Industries glowing in the dark above an airfield. At the end of the tarmac, feverish activity swirled around a stealth scramjet, which was capable of hypersonic speeds. You either had to be in the military or as powerful as Bramford to own one. Or as he *used to be.*

Eden heaved a sigh of relief as they landed with a feather touch. Immediately, Bramford scooped up her father and swept outside, heading for the terrifying jet.

"We're not going in that, are we?" she asked, hurrying after them.

"Come," Bramford said.

She hesitated. They wouldn't be safe anywhere on this godforsaken planet so why not stay there, on the ground?

She watched Bramford climb the stairway to the jet's cabin, taking the steps two at a time. Her poor father dangled like a bug over his shoulder. Bramford's bare feet pounded the metal steps. His muscular legs flexed with each leap. The magnificent torso swayed. Like a star-struck fan, Eden imagined he could do anything—even crush the huge aircraft in his hands.

"What's the matter with you, Eden?" Bramford yelled.

Exactly. What did she care if he was powerful or even sexy? More than ever, she resented him. Only her concern for her father pushed her to follow him.

A uniformed flight attendant appeared in the doorway to the cabin. Her dark face tightened at the sight of Bramford.

He barked at her. "He's been lasered. Get medical aid."

"Yes, sir," the attendant said, hurrying inside.

Eden realized with amazement that Bramford assumed her father's bloody leg had shocked the attendant, not Bramford's grotesque condition. Maybe he didn't know how strange he looked or else he had forgotten. Even now, as this monstrous creature, he probably felt no different on the inside.

Inside, Eden was never a Pearl. Sometimes at twilight, before she opened her eyes, before the damning critic in her head reminded her how ugly she was, she felt normal. Then she felt like the Real Eden.

But how would Bramford feel when he looked in a mirror or when he saw the damming looks in others' eyes? Maybe now he would know how it felt to be judged by your appearance.

As soon as Eden stepped into the cabin, the ship's engines began to whirr. She froze, painfully aware that the already slim odds of anyone ever seeing the Real Eden, the one inside, would slide to zero when they left. Happiness was a faraway island she would never reach. She turned around, thinking of running.

"Sit down, Eden," Bramford called.

The stairway folded inside. The door closed with a final thud. Her chance was gone.

She plodded down the aisle, past his private alcove on the starboard side. Already, he'd turned his attention away from her. *Dismissed, as usual.*

Plush upholstery in the company's red and black colors covered several clusters of couches and chairs for about a dozen passengers. What would become of Bramford's empire now that he had become a science experiment gone wrong? If an albino could raise terror in the hearts of man, imagine the reaction to Bramford. Being different was the kiss of death, which meant he was a marked man.

Exhausted, Eden crumbled into a chair beside her father. She nearly cried with relief when she saw the attendant fit an oxy-cap onto his head. *Thank you, Mother Earth.*

Her hands trembled as she pulled down a cap from the overhead compartment. Although it was larger than her custom job, it clicked into place. Hurry, Eden thought, desperate for the numb kick. She'd experienced more emotion in a single night than she had in her whole dismal life.

The attendant cast a disdainful glance at her. Her name was embroidered in fine script on the black jacket. *Daisy.* Eden followed her gaze, taking in her torn party dress and the disgusting streaks of white skin that showed through her worn coating.

"The Moon Dance," was all she could muster.

Daisy gave a curt nod, seemingly satisfied.

Eden guessed that Daisy was middle-aged like her, though maybe a few years older. The white dot on her forehead labeled her as mated. Despite her expensive, polished dark coating and the superior look Daisy tried to achieve, Eden knew she was a Pearl. It was just a feeling, though an unshakeable one. As if she smelled the attendant's deep, underlying fear. But how had a Pearl gotten such a cushy job?

Daisy laid a blanket over Eden's father lap. "I'll be back to help you, as soon as we hit Mach twenty," she said, and hurried behind a curtain near the cockpit.

The walls seemed to close in around Eden, as the scramjet blasted off. A dark, unfathomable void pressed against the window beside her.

In a soft whisper, her mother's usual advice came to her.

—*Breathe, Eden. Let your stomach rise like a balloon. Then release the air slowly. Let the breath carry your awareness through the body. You can do it. Stay in the moment.*

—*I can't, Mother.*

—*Of course you can. It's only natural. Animals breathe that way.*

That had confused Eden. As if animals were better than humans.

Why hadn't her mother understood how much terror she felt in the moment? Rather than stay in it, Eden desperately wanted to escape. And right now, she wanted to forget that she was trapped with beastly Bramford, rocketing into the unknown.

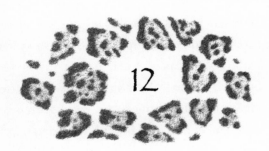

12

THE DULL HAZE of the oxy flowing through Eden couldn't tamp down her anxiety. She tried to ignore the data streaming into her mind. She didn't want to know how far above the earth the scramjet flew or how fast it headed south. Just as she suspected, their destination was out of bounds, and therefore not given. Even that she tried to ignore by repeating her silent mantra over and over.

I'm a stone in a cool, dark cave.

Somehow, high up in the stratosphere, the image failed to soothe her. She never thought she would long to be back in the Combs.

Diagonally across the cabin, she saw Daisy hand a black case to Bramford. She seemed careful not to draw too near and left quickly. Bramford popped open the case and studied a black screen. It was an old-fashioned computer, Eden realized. Probably stowed on board in case another meltdown burned out the World-Band.

She watched, fascinated, as Bramford's sharp nails clicked against the keyboard. She'd never seen anyone use the archaic manual method. Then she eyed his hands and realized he'd lost his Life-Band ring. Probably when his fingers had enlarged.

Poor Bramford, cut off from the constant direction of his inner voice. To Eden, it seemed like a fate worse than death.

And yet, he appeared calm, even intent, as he worked. She imagined him shifting money and resources to their destination. He might buy a temporary reprieve, but even in the dreamy wash of oxy she knew it was only a matter of time before they met their doom.

A minute later, Daisy returned with a first aid kit. "Ready, Doctor Newman?" she said, kneeling beside him.

"What?" Then, as if remembering his wound, he waved a hand over it. "Proceed as you think best."

Daisy carefully cut away the pant leg and began to dress the wound. Eden gagged at the sight of the angry, oozing mess.

"It's only blood, Daught."

Always a failure in Father's eyes. What on Blessed Earth would he think of her colossal betrayal? She'd cost them everything. How could he ever forgive her?

"I'm afraid we left in a rush," Daisy said. "There's no medicine aboard."

"But we can get some when we land, can't we?" Eden said.

"It's doubtful."

"Why? Where are we going?" A horrible possibility struck her. "Don't tell me there won't be any oxy, either?"

"We'll land in approximately two hours." She tidied her supplies. "I'm sorry I can't do more."

"But—"

Daisy jerked her head towards Bramford, silencing Eden, then headed back to her station.

Eden slumped in her seat, muttering. "No oxy, no meds?"

"In that case, I estimate a high probability of gangrene," her father said. "The most elegant solution would be to amputate the leg. No impairment to any major body system and my odds for survival would increase."

"How can you even say that?"

"Bramford needs me, don't you see?"

She shook her head angrily. "You're insane."

"Wait and see, Daught."

"There's nothing *to* see. There's never going to be anything to see ever again. If your head wasn't in the clouds you would see that." *But you don't even see me.*

The shaggy eyebrows arched. "Only forward momentum exists; the past is gone. The best course of action would be to consider this an unexpected adventure."

"I was hoping to make it to my eighteenth birthday."

Her father sighed, his disappointment clear. "I'll insist Bramford send you back when we land."

"I'm not leaving you alone with…that."

"Bramford is the same, essentially."

"If you believe that, you're crazier than I thought."

He adjusted his glasses, looking over at his prototype. Eden studied Bramford, too, riveted by his lean, muscled body, too large for the chair to contain.

"His appearance is undeniably altered," her father said. "And yet, it's safe to say his reasoning remains fully intact. In fact, the results are far superior to any projections. To adapt to such a degree and retain man's mental capacity—why, it's a lucky break, worth any price."

"Even our lives, Father?" *My life?*

He looked at her, wide-eyed. "But Daught, this is science."

Did he also think of her mother's passing as just a blip on the evolutionary scene? She recalled his cold-hearted manner on that fateful day. He hadn't even said goodbye to her mother. Sometimes Eden felt she didn't know him at all.

He shut his eyes, his face taut with pain. When the wave subsided he began again. "I've reworked the calculations and deduced that the spike in heat in the laboratory caused overexpression in the affected genes, thus accelerating the transformation."

"Can you reverse the process?" Eden said, feeling the weight of her guilt.

"Hmmm. It might have been possible to reverse a minor adaptation, as was planned. But at this advanced stage, I estimate a reversal would cause fatal damage to the subject's internal systems."

No turning back for Bramford? "Won't he be furious?"

Her father waved away the question. "This is what's so exciting. We don't know what to expect. Bramford is highly unpredictable in his current adaptation."

"You mean he might become even more animal-like?"

"We can't predict what latent genes might be activated. As I said, we have to wait and see."

"Or not," Eden said pointedly.

"What are you saying?"

She leaned close and whispered. "Why risk our lives for Bramford?"

Her father looked stricken. "But I'm responsible for him, Daught."

"You threatened to kill him today."

"It was a bluff." He pulled the syringe from his shirt pocket. "Only a sedative, you see? I would never hurt him."

"But you said he's unpredictable. He might kill us." She paused to let the idea sink in. "Maybe we could cut a deal: Bramford for our freedom. It's not too late."

"What? With Jamal?"

"Never," Eden said, once more worrying her father would discover her connection to him. "You must know someone in science at the Uni-Gov level who could help us."

"And what makes you think I'd want such a deal?"

She threw up her hands; her voice grew shrill. "Why can't you understand? It's our only option. We have to give up Bramford."

In a flash, the beast leapt beside her with a terrifying roar. Her eyes traveled from his strong thighs, thick as tree trunks, to his brilliant eyes. She felt trapped, as if caught in the path of an avalanche. Only, she wasn't sure she wanted to move out of the way.

Trembling, Eden rose to face him. "My father's health is in jeopardy," she said. "You must send us home."

"So you can go back to your FFP friend?" Bramford said.

She felt as if her stomach fell to her knees. "It wasn't like that."

"Don't tell me you didn't know who Jamal was?"

"I swear I had no idea. If I had known, I never would have..." But what could she say?

Bramford snapped at her. "I want the truth."

His broad, naked chest distracted her so she forced herself to look into his eyes, which didn't help much, either. Instead, she stared at a point just over his shoulder, as he often had done to her in the past.

"You saw those soldiers after me at the dance," Eden said. "I wasn't in on Jamal's plan, I swear."

"Dance?" her father said.

"There was an information leak at REA," Bramford said. "Only your father and I knew the extent of the operation. I think we can safely assume that neither he nor I betrayed us to the FFP."

"Don't listen to him, Father."

But Bramford kept up the attack. "Why did you disobey my order to stay in your unit? Jamal convinced you to go, didn't he?"

Eden hung her head on her chest. "I thought—"

"You thought Jamal would option you. And whenever you enjoyed romantic visits with him you just happened to let vital data slip. Isn't that true?"

"What, what?" her father said.

"You don't understand."

Bramford shook his head. "How naïve could you be, Eden?"

"To believe a Coal might want me? Is that what you mean?"

Embarrassment flickered across his face. That was exactly what he meant.

Eden looked him dead in the eye. "Someday, when you're locked up in a cage, Bramford, maybe you'll understand what it feels like to be an outcast."

He flinched. His startling green eyes narrowed as he growled menacingly. Eden braced herself for the unexpected, when his face flooded again with human intelligence.

"We always have a choice in life," Bramford said, matter-of-factly. "If you weren't so self-involved you'd understand that. But since you've proven to be untrustworthy—" His hand snaked forward and tore out her Life-Band earring.

Eden screamed as her hand flew to the spot. How dare he? She felt more violated than if she'd been raped.

She raised her arm to strike him, but he caught it midair, pinning her beneath him. They stood locked together like a pair of impassioned tango dancers. A muscle twitched in his jaw. The hair on the back of her neck prickled.

Something else besides fear gripped her; something Eden couldn't name. A sharp awareness of his powerful body, the warmth of his skin on hers, and the nearness of his lips overpowered her. Or maybe it was the lack of noise in her head that disoriented her. She felt off balance without her Life-Band, frighteningly alone with her thoughts.

"Be careful, Daught," her father said, his voice cutting through the tension.

Bramford released her and she fell back into her seat, breathless.

"I'll need your Life-Band, too," he said, turning to her father.

"Of course." He handed Bramford the wristband, then offered the syringe. "What about a sedative? I doubt it will kill you."

"Father," Eden said in a warning voice.

"Just a little scientific humor."

Like an obedient child, Bramford knelt down, though he still loomed over her father. He arched his back at the jab of the needle, growling through his teeth. Eden had the feeling that he used all of his strength to resist striking out.

"Thanks," he said, sheepishly.

His chilling, measured gaze passed over Eden as he stalked back to his seat.

"I'm really sorry, Father," Eden said meekly.

He shook his head. "Inconceivable, Daught."

Her father was all she had left in the world. Now, she had lost him, too. For Earth's sake, she just couldn't think about it. So she stuffed her despair onto a crowded shelf in her heart and slammed the door shut.

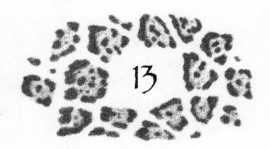

13

TIME? EDEN REPEATED, puzzled by the lack of response in her head. She rubbed her earlobe and felt the empty spot. Like an amputee who still feels the presence of a missing limb, she had forgotten her Life-Band was gone. Bramford had taken more than her earring; he'd stolen her identity. She just didn't know who she was anymore. The random thoughts that skittered through her head like frightened mice were as alien to her as the high-flying scramjet.

In the alcove ahead, Eden saw Bramford's dark head rolled to one side and figured the sedative had taken affect. Her father dozed nearby, his face tight with pain. This might be her only chance.

She quietly slipped into the aisle, heading for the attendant's area. Unable to resist the opportunity to study the sleeping beast, she stopped beside him. A company T-shirt strained over his shoulders like a child's garment, exposing his muscular torso. Long, dark eyelashes swooned over the sharp slash of cheekbones. Fine, dark hair framed his rugged face.

Time seemed to flicker around Bramford, imposing his former self over his animal-like incarnation, as if his old Holo-Image clung to him. Eden suspected that the dual identities waged a mysterious battle. But which did she want to win? The powerful titan that might save them or the savage beast that excited her?

Eden had despised the attractive, top-rated man Bramford had been. And yet, this wild creature stirred something deeply primal in her.

With Jamal, she'd never felt such dizzying emotions. Even while kissing him she'd been outside of it, as if peering in through a window. Only now, she realized she'd never shown him the Real Eden. Was it even possible for two people to truly see each other in a calculated world where its inhabitants mated to improve their offspring's genetics or to control a lesser mate?

She thought about how her mother might have quoted Aunt Emily. *"That Love is all there is, / Is all we know of Love."*

But no, Eden reminded herself, love was dead. Bramford's condition simply piqued her curiosity, as it would any researcher. Possibly, that explained her desire to touch him. Even now, her hand reached towards him. At the sudden twitch of his mouth, she froze.

If he awoke and found her hovering over him, he might attack. She imagined him leaping on her, pinning her underneath him, his strong body pressing her down no matter how she writhed and protested. His jaw would clamp onto her neck and she'd scream.

Sweat beaded on her forehead. Her limbs felt rubbery, as his earthy scent exploded in her brain. In a daze, she stepped away from him. Clearly, the monumental losses of home, Austin, and her Life-Band, had driven her crazy.

She wobbled up the aisle and entered the attendant's area, greeted by Daisy's weary sigh. She'd expected her, Eden realized. The girl shooed Eden inside and angled herself by the entrance, eyeing the cabin through the opening in the curtains.

"I can't help you," she said.

Eden held up a hand. "Wait until you know what's at stake."

"Look, Ms. Newman. I'm just trying to survive."

"Call me, Eden. We've all suffered, haven't we, Daisy? My mom got The Heat when I was ten."

Daisy's shoulders relaxed slightly. "I understand."

She reminded Eden of one of the girls shown on the old Beauty Map—an English Rose. How ironic that long ago the two of them might have been called "hot."

Daisy nodded towards the cabin. "What on Sweet Earth happened to him?"

"Interspecies structural adaptation." Eden sketched out the basics. "Something went wrong. There was an accident." Her fault, but she kept that to herself. "The point is my father's technology greatly reduces the odds of contracting The Heat."

"Really?"

Now, she had Daisy's full attention. Any Pearl would want to know.

"Imagine if we could adapt, too," Eden continued. "Not to the degree Bramford has changed, but enough to increase our pigmentation and resist solar radiation. Imagine how different the world would be."

Daisy's eyes searched Eden's. "It sounds like a pretty big if."

"It's more than we've had; more than we'll ever have again." The truth of it hit Eden, as she said it. "Please, tell me where we're going."

Daisy shook her head and stared off to the side. Her voice softened as she began. "Noah and I knew it was risky to mate, two Pink Pearls. But we wanted to be together, no matter what. Noah was one of Bramford's pilots, the best one. He had rare 20/10 vision. But a violent storm..." She paused as emotion swept through her. "When he died, Bramford gave me this job. I owe him."

Eden figured Bramford found it cheaper to employ the widow than pay costly benefits. He was no tender heart.

"Look," she said. "The best way to help yourself is to help us. My father is the only one who understands this technology. We could trade Bramford for..."

She started to explain her plan when a much better idea popped into her head: loyal Shen had the keys to Bramford's empire. Considering his past behavior, she bet he would come to their aid.

"I need a Life-Band," Eden added. "Everything depends on it."

"You don't understand. I have a young son."

"Then help us, for his sake. Don't you see? If my father's work gets into the wrong hands things will be even worse."

"Sector Six," Daisy said, abruptly. "That's your destination."

Holy Earth, Eden gulped. They might as well be sucked into a black hole. Sector Six was a lawless, barren land. If the drug lords didn't kill them, The Heat or predators would.

The tension swept back into Daisy, like a turning tide, as the scramjet banked into its descent.

"Go, now," she said, holding open the curtain. "Before he wakes up."

"I'm begging you. Please, Daisy."

The girl stood resolute. Eden thought her mother might have made the same choice.

"Well, good luck to you and your son," she said and quickly left.

She ducked into the bathroom, shocked by her reflection in the mirror. Her streaked coating no longer had a Midnight Luster—more Daylight Scary.

Just wipe it off, Eden. That was her idea and not her World-Band voice, right? Yet how could she even think such a thing?

She wet a guest towel with a fancy embossed letter "B" and held it to her face. Still, she hesitated, terrified of showing her natural coloring. But why worry when two of the other passengers were Pearls, and the only Coal didn't look his usual self? Even some Coal was better than none, she decided, throwing down the towel.

Eden reached her seat before the men awoke. She stared with dread out the window, as the broiling sun pushed over the edge of the horizon. Soon, it would hang in the leaden sky like an angry, bloodshot eye of a Cyclops. She found it hard to believe that her prehistoric ancestors had welcomed the burning light each morning and feared the cool darkness.

In the dim amber light, she was stunned to see the Amazon River, once the healthy lungs of the planet, limping through parched land. She'd seen it many times glistening and vibrant in World-Band experiences. Had she forgotten that those images were fake?

They'd started her early. At the age of five, she'd had her first experience. Her parents had stood on either side of her as a pristine redwood forest appeared in their common room. Eden would never forget that first awe-inspiring vision.

—*They're like people. Tree people.*

—*The giant Sequoia,* Sequoiadendron giganteum. *Remember that, Daught.*

—*I can hear them. They're crying.*

Her father had stiffened at her comment but her mother had agreed.

—*Yes, they're crying, Eden. They were once among the oldest living things on the planet. Now they're all gone.*

Eden had started to cry, though she hadn't known why. Was that when she first heard her father's disappointment?

—*She's too sensitive, Lily. Don't indulge her.*

—*But it is sad, John.*

—*It's evolution. Man is programmed to survive. Granted, he got stuck in a conquer and destroy mode and overran his habitat. But history tells us he'll find another way to survive.*

Eden had dried her tears—the last she'd ever shed—and looked from her father to her mother, wishing she didn't have to choose between them.

Now, her bird's-eye view of the devastated earth convinced her that man would never find another way. Even more, she knew she wouldn't survive the coming day. She almost laughed as she recalled one of Aunt Emily's cruel poems.

Will there really be a morning?
Is there such a thing as day?
Could I see it from the mountains
If I were as tall as they?

Has it feet like water-lilies?
Has it feathers like a bird?
Is it brought from famous countries
Of which I have never heard?

Obviously, Eden thought, her aunt hadn't experienced this bottomless terror whenever the golden light had stretched its arms towards her.

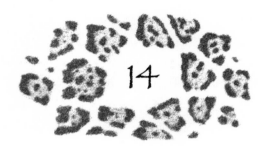

14

EDEN'S NERVES felt as high-pitched as the whine of the scramjet as it touched ground. Outside, the day waited for her, a bright, suffocating prison. There would be no muted grays in which to hide and become invisible.

She didn't think things could get any worse, when the welcoming committee came into view. A half-dozen, short, muscular Indians wearing a rag-tag assortment of clothes stood by a line of ancient, all-terrain vehicles. Machetes hung from several of the men's belts, glinting in the sunlight. Some had long, wooden poles slung over their shoulders. Despite fanciful feathers tucked into simple bowl-cut hairstyles, the warriors appeared fierce.

"The Huaorani," Eden's father said, excitedly.

"Who?" Eden said.

"The world's last independent indigenous tribe. No one knows how or where they've survived."

"What are the poles for?'

"Those are blowguns—quite deadly, as a matter of fact. Most likely, their quivers hold poison darts."

Eden squinted into the sharp glare, spotting the narrow basket that hung down several of the men's backs.

"There, see the palm nut dangling at the end of the pole?"

her father continued. "It probably holds cotton from the ka-pok tree, which forms a gasket around the dart as it blows through the pole. They're expert hunters."

"What do they hunt?"

"*Cowode*, for example, which are non-humans or any-one different from them. Even the name Huaorani means human."

"Wait. They think they're human and we're *cowode*, non-human?"

"Precisely."

"Maybe they'll kill Bramford," she mused. "He's not hu-man."

Her father's owlish eyes flared. "What?"

Daisy approached them. "For your trip," she said, hand-ing Eden a bright red backpack that bore the Bramford Industries logo.

Eden inspected the contents: toiletries, a company T-shirt, and a small bottle of water. But no Life-Band.

"Thanks," she said, dryly. "Just what I need."

Daisy gave her a stony look. "You never know, it might come in handy."

Eden searched the girl's face, hoping for a secret signal, but Daisy abruptly turned to Eden's father. "I added extra bandages, doctor." Then she held out another pack for Bram-ford. "Would you like one, sir?"

He shoved the pack aside with a snarl.

Perhaps it was an ordinary parting gift, Eden thought. But what if Daisy intended to distract Bramford by offering him one, too? That might mean she'd hidden something in Eden's pack. In any case, Eden would have to wait until she was away from prying eyes to inspect it further.

A quivering feather floated inside of her, as Bramford stretched to a standing position. Her eyes betrayed her, traveling the length of his body. She felt embarrassed and, as he shot her a quizzical glance, realized that her flushed, red skin showed zebra-like through her worn, dark coating. Humiliated, her hands flew to her face.

"Let's go, Eden," Bramford said.

"Can't," she said.

"Now!"

"Can't. Daylight."

"Daught, we must leave," her father said, struggling to stand.

Eden shook her head vehemently. Bramford's warning growl sent a shiver up her spine. Still, she didn't budge.

Suddenly, he lifted her into his arms.

"No, I'm not going!" Eden cried. "Put me down, you monster!"

He carried her up the aisle, her screams bouncing off of the cabin walls. Even his blasting roar couldn't quiet her. She pummeled his rock-hard shoulders and yanked his hair, but felt like a fly buzzing around a horse.

Over her shoulder, Eden saw her father leaning on Daisy's arm as they followed. She no longer cared about his disappointment or how pitiful she looked.

"Father, please!"

Only a few feet remained to the exit. Already, she felt the heat blasting through the open door.

"Bramford?" her father said. "Perhaps you could send her back?"

"And let her lead them to us? Sorry, doctor."

With that, Bramford thudded onto the staircase. Eden

shrieked as hot-white light hit her head. Broiling sunrays knifed into her skin, and she gasped for air. Even without her sensors she knew she was in deep trouble.

Below, she saw the Huaorani raise their nut-brown faces. Time seemed to hang in the air as each side, the human tribesmen and the *cowode* visitors, hesitated. For Earth's sake, why didn't they attack the beast?

Eden took matters into her own hands and pointed to Bramford. *"Cowode!"*

"Quiet!" he said, pushing her face into his chest.

The incredibly wonderful feel of his warm body—not a Holo-Image, but a real, live body—stunned her. She registered the sensation of his arms around her bare thighs and shoulders. Pressing her cheek against his hard chest, she heard his heart beat against her ear—*alive.*

Eden's world stopped. Her joints loosened, her heart felt expansive, even her mind stretched to find Bramford remarkably appealing. At the same time, she became aware of a dangerous, inescapable abyss opening up inside of her. If she gave into her feelings, she might be lost forever.

She croaked out a plea. "I beg you, Bramford, put me down."

Then a loud cry rose up from the Huaorani. Unbelievably, they fell to their knees and began to chant in ecstatic voices.

"El Tigre! El Tigre!"

Eden couldn't understand them without her Life-Band. However, their body language reminded her of reverent penitents in bygone churches. Was it possible the warriors worshipped Bramford? Only one thing was clear: they weren't going to kill him.

He didn't seem surprised by the praise, either. He puffed out his chest and grinned, as arrogant as ever.

Her father peered out the cabin door, quickly assessing the situation. "They think you're *El Tigre,* the Jaguar Man. Imagine, the long-awaited Aztec God."

Ronson Bramford a god? Eden laughed out loud.

Now, the tribesmen looked at her with equal reverence.

"See, Daught?" her father added. "You're divine by association with *El Tigre.*"

For once, her father seemed proud of her—for being the beast's sidekick.

The way Bramford sucked up the glory revolted Eden. He made a stately descent, bestowing his new subjects with a regal look. Then he dumped her into the backseat of the lead vehicle. She scooted under a tattered tarp and watched him rip off his puny T-shirt. Probably unfit for a god.

In spite of her disgust, Eden's eyes riveted on his broad, dark chest that gleamed in the sunlight. Even the molecules of air seemed to fall away from his powerful physique. Maybe he did deserve to be worshiped, she admitted. Then, as he waved imperiously to his adoring public, she wanted to slap him.

For once Aunt Emily had gotten it right.

I'm Nobody! Who are you?
Are you nobody, too?
Then there's a pair of us—don't tell!
They'd banish us, you know.

How dreary to be somebody!
How public, like a frog

To tell your name the the livelong day
To an admiring bog!

Two tribesmen set Eden's father on the seat beside her. The tarp didn't cast enough shade for both of them. Already, she felt the prickly heat in her body, the sweat dripping down her back. She inched towards the border of hot light, begrudging her father each centimeter of shade, and hating herself for it. *Promise you will take care of your father.*

As usual, he seemed oblivious to any physical threat. He took out a small notebook from his shirt pocket and began to scribble.

"Incredible," he said. "The Huaorani have waited since 3,000 B.C. for the Jaguar Man to save them."

"And just what is he supposed to do?" Eden asked.

"Appease the spirit world."

"Naturally. Because Bramford is so appeasing."

"What?" Her father laughed but she knew he didn't get it. "The idea of spirits may seen counterintuitive to our way of thinking," he continued. "And yet, thousands of years ago a prophecy was told that one day the greatest of shamans, a real Jaguar Man, would come to save the people from the destruction of their lands."

Eden looked out at the sad, hardscrabble earth and sighed. "Well, he's too late."

"Perhaps not," her father said with a thoughtful air.

"Don't tell me you believe in this fairy tale?"

"Often, sometimes centuries later, science validates folk wisdom. The Indians believe the great shaman will fly into the spirit world by embodying the jaguar in form and spirit."

She watched the newly anointed Jaguar Man command the men to load supplies into the vehicles. "So he intended to dominate the world, after all," she said. "Jamal was right. Bramford never had any intention of helping people. He was always a beast at heart."

"Don't be so quick to judge, Daught." Her father looked up from his notes, adding, "This is the happiest day of my life."

How then did her birth rank? Or did Eden count at all?

She gasped as Bramford leapt into the passenger seat from several yards away. *Show off.* The rusty vehicle creaked, listing to one side with his weight. Her father beamed, while Eden wished she'd never been born.

Behind them, the Huaorani climbed into the packed cars. Bramford turned to face the company and raised a triumphant arm. He announced their destination in a booming voice.

"*Vamos a la Zona Intangible.*"

"Where is that?" Eden said.

He gave her a nasty grin. "No Man's Land."

Exactly what she most feared: now, she'd never find anyone to mate.

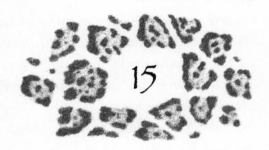

EDEN SHIFTED her aching back on the wooden seat, as the vehicle jounced along a rutted road. If only she could relax. But she held her body rigid, as if she could ward off the boundless, sunlit world. For hours they'd driven past miles of mud-baked shanties and desolate fields with an occasional tree or small rodent scurrying past. Not a living soul appeared.

She felt dirty and grimy from the layers of dust that coated her skin. She'd tied the company T-shirt around her nose and mouth to filter the dust and the nauseating smell of plant petrol. The shirt stuck to her skin, wet with sweat. Even if she'd been brave enough to jump out of the car, she lacked the energy. Gummy humidity chained her listless body to the seat. She lifted a hand with the odd feeling that it didn't belong to her, and waved away dive-bombing mosquitoes.

Burning rays edged under the tarp onto her legs, as the relentless sun marched across a baked sky. Eden considered a sunburned patch on her thigh with numb desperation. Had her white blood cells shouted an alarm? *Hurry to the defense.* Still, it would be a losing battle. She might last a week or two before she got The Heat.

She stared daggers at the back of Bramford's head. The

beast seemed to enjoy the ride. His broad back and alert posture reminded her of a big cat attuned to subtle signs. Signs
Eden couldn't read without her Life-Band, thanks to him.

For the umpteenth time, her fingers crawled like spiders
over the red backpack that lay on her lap, hoping to feel
the outline of a hidden Life-Band. Once more she thought
of Shen, whose Chinese name meant strong spirit. It was an
odd choice in a soulless world. If only Eden could connect
with him, she just hoped he'd live up to his name. And what
if Shen came? Would she be able to convince Bramford to
send her and her father back home? Maybe by then her father
would have served his purpose. If he lived that long.

Wait and see. That's what Father would say.

The memory of a sterile laboratory flashed in Eden's mind
in sharp contrast to the bleak landscape around her. How
eager she'd been at the age of six to please her father. But
she'd botched her first DNA analysis by adding a twenty-
fourth pair of chromosomes. It was the first time he voiced
his simple philosophy.

—*Wait and see, Daught.*

—*For what?*

—*Progress.*

—*But I failed.*

The edges of his mouth had curled into a half-smile, the
best he could offer.

—*Some of the biggest discoveries have come from plans
gone awry. Think of Albert Einstein unable to obtain a uni-
versity job. For two years he suffered odd jobs and even questioned his goal of becoming a physicist. Imagine that.*

Forced to take a lowly position as a clerk at the patent

*office, Einstein found 'a kind of salvation,' as he put it. The
regular salary and stimulating work of evaluating patent
claims freed him to think, even to dream. He began to publish
important physics papers and change the world.*

*You see, Daught, we must be patient. One door closes
and another opens. Wait and see.*

Eden believed her father knew everything. And so she
had waited for someone to see past her skin color and recognize the Real Eden. After all, didn't everyone share the same
DNA? In the end, there had been nothing to wait for but a
treacherous Coal. All over again, Eden felt the sting of Jamal's betrayal.

Lost in the bouncing rhythm of the car ride and the mer-
ciless heat, she began to obsess on his evasive remarks, the
double-sided meanings and clever prodding. His deception
had been plain to see if only she'd looked. How Eden wished
she'd listened to Austin's warnings, or been smarter, prettier,
darker, better.

By the time the convoy arrived at a small encampment
along a river, Eden was desperate to burrow into a shady
spot. At least the sun hid like a gauzy pearl in the hazy sky.
Sad, gray clouds nestled in the treetops, as if abandoned there.

She shook off the T-shirt and stretched her limbs. Waves
of blackness passed behind her eyes, as she stood. When had
her last meal been?

Leaning against the vehicle, she eyed the surroundings
with little hope. Patches of wild jungle encircled a string of
ramshackle huts. Native women and children in tattered rags
stood by, staring blankly at the new arrivals. They looked ill
with patchy hair, and red, scaly rashes on their brown skin.
The children's stomachs were swollen, their eyes lifeless. Two

drunken men sprawled in a heap of garbage. One of them raised his head, eyed the commotion, then spit and turned over.

An antique boom box filled the air with pounding music, each beat twisting the knot in Eden's head tighter. The fast, driving, spoken lyrics told a gruesome tale of violence and revenge. A typical example of man's headlong race to destruction in the late twentieth century. If only they had understood, she thought, staring at the blighted environment.

Bramford's gaze raked over her as he passed her by. She watched him head into a palm grove, mesmerized by the rippling of his muscled back and hips. He moved with the simple grace and powerful confidence of a predator. No wasted energy, no self-consciousness. What must that be like?

Eden hefted the backpack, following the men towards the river that appeared in layers of green and black at the edge of the camp. Suddenly, the ground seemed to shift underneath her. But no, she realized, dozens of columns of leaves moved around her. *Atta colombica*, known as leaf-cutter ants, carried the leaves on their backs.

She screamed as the ants scrambled over her feet. She tried to slap them away but they kept coming, hundreds of them. She started to run when her high heels caught in the dirt. Headlong, she tumbled into a mud puddle, to the delight of the children who laughed at her.

At least that pompous action hero hadn't witnessed her fall.

Eden wiped herself off with the T-shirt and, in the process, shed even more of her dark coating. The Indians found that especially funny, but she was too tired to care.

She collapsed onto a boulder by the moribund river. A

thick, black film coated its surface. Gobs of debris—diapers, clothes and animal carcasses—cluttered the shore. Nearby, several canoes with small outboard motors bobbed beside a rickety dock.

One of the Huaorani with a surprisingly gentle face carried Eden's father towards her. A heavy-set warrior pulled a huge leaf, at least nine feet long, from a giant banana tree and laid it next to her on the ground. To Eden's surprise the men set her father down on the huge leaf. He looked like a fragile baby cradled in a green boat. That was the extent of comfort here—a leaf for a bed.

"Residue from oil mining," her father said, indicating the murky water. "My hypothesis is the tribe sold their oil rights long ago, probably for worthless cash. I suspect no one ever explained the consequences."

Eden could see what the trip had cost him. His eyes were pinched and red, the bandaged leg, bloody, once more.

"How are you, Father?"

"What? Fine." He stared off at the nearby trees. "Just look at the amazing variety of flora. I imagine we could find a new species or two here."

The gentle warrior returned with two coconut bowls full of white mushy liquid.

"*Chicha,*" he said with smiling eyes.

"*Gracias,*" her father thanked him and then tasted it. "Hmmm. Yucca plant. The women chew it up, mix it with water and then spit it out. It's a complete and nourishing meal."

Eden declined with a polite wave of her hand. Even if she could stomach the repulsive, sour smell, she doubted she could digest real food.

Her father frowned. "When you're starving you'll eat anything, Daught."

Always the failed daughter. She pressed her fingertips against her throbbing temples.

The Indian pointed to himself. "Lorenzo."

He couldn't have been much older than her. She liked his soft brown eyes, she decided.

"Eden," she said, tapping her chest.

"El soroche." Lorenzo touched his temples and grimaced, as she must have. Then he reached into his pocket and offered them each a handful of small, oval, dark green leaves.

Eden noted the distinctive small circle they bore. "Coca leaves," she said.

"Precisely, Daught. *Erythroxylum coca.* A traditional remedy for altitude sickness." Her father's short-lived approval disappeared, as she tucked the leaves in her backpack. "You're supposed to chew them," he said.

"But they're dirty," she whispered.

"What? That's illogical. Your skin provides housing for millions of microbes. Without them you wouldn't be able to fight any number of diseases."

Lorenzo nodded, whether or not he understood, and told her how good the leaves were. *"Muy bueno."*

Eden responded with a pained shrug. Lorenzo simply smiled and left to join his tribesmen, who transferred supplies onto the canoes. A sinking realization hit her.

"We're not going over water, are we?" she said.

"It appears so," her father said.

"But I can't swim! Neither can you."

He chuckled. "Then don't rock the boat, Daught."

Her insides twisted, like a strand of DNA. Like any Pearl,

Eden was terrified of water, which had the power to expose. She never even had experienced swimming or any other by-gone water sport on the World-Band. She'd rather die than ride in a canoe.

She clutched the backpack, hoping for a miracle. Now was her chance.

"I'll just be over there," Eden said, pointing towards a large trumpet tree. At her father's quizzical look she added, "For privacy."

"Hurry," he said. "We must leave at once or wait until the next day."

"Why?"

"Elementary. There are no lights here."

Unable to absorb the concept of living by day, she gave him a blank look and then walked away. She struggled to form a little prayer as she stepped into the dark thicket.

Mother Earth, please, let me find salvation in this back-pack.

It was pointless, Eden knew. There was no omniscient power to substitute the objects that already lay inside the pack. Back home, she would have ridiculed any idea that violated the laws of physics.

But then, Eden never imagined she would have to survive by her wits alone, either.

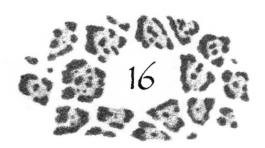

16

EDEN SQUINTED as she stepped into a shadowy grove, clutching the backpack to her chest. Sunrays strafed through a high canopy of trees, piercing dark pockets of vegetation below. The high contrast between dark and light made it difficult to see. Her eyes darted towards silvery specks that glinted, here and there, as if dozens of eyes watched her.

A monkey pant-hoot startled her and she looked up to find a troop of capuchin monkeys, *Cebus capucinus*, gathered in the branches. Somehow they didn't look or sound like their World-Band Holo-Images. And how reverential they seemed with their caps of brown fur around solemn, light-colored muzzles. Now she understood why they were named for the ancient Capuchin Friars.

Eden knelt down, spilling the contents of the backpack onto the ground. Just as she thought, there was nothing special inside. A rain of empty seedpods fell on her, followed by the capuchin's hysterical jeering. *So much for reverence.*

Eden waved her arms and hissed. "Go away."

Instead, the bothersome pests renewed their assault.

She turned her back on them, hurrying now. She flipped the bag inside out and ran her hands over it. There, along the bottom, she found a bulge. New thread was stitched over the seam. Her hopes soared as she ripped it open with her teeth. Something fell to the ground with a small *plink*.

Sweet Mother of Earth. A Life-Band. It was a standard flexible bracelet. *Thank you, Daisy.*

"Daught?" her father called out.

Any minute someone might come looking for her. Even Bramford.

Eden repacked the Life-Band and other items. As she stood up, pinpoint of lights danced in front of her eyes. She took a deep breath and, as her surroundings came back into focus, reached for the backpack. But it moved away. Confused, she tripped after it.

Then the bag flew into the air—in a monkey's grasp. The nimble thief carried it onto a limb from which he and his conniving friends heckled her.

"Hey!" Eden shook her fist. "That's mine."

To her surprise, the thief drew back. The monkeys shrieked.

In the distance Bramford's deep voice boomed like thunder. "Eden?"

The troop scampered away with the backpack—her salvation.

"No!" she cried.

She kicked off her heels and plunged into the forest after them without a second thought. She struggled to keep an eye on the red backpack, but unlike running at home on the World-Band, she actually moved forward. When she smacked into a tree limb, she fell down, more surprised than hurt.

In a panic, she heard Bramford's pounding feet.

Don't lose the bag, Eden. Stuck here if you do.

She scrambled to her feet and ran ahead. Her head screamed with pain. Her legs felt like wet noodles.

"Stop, Eden!" Bramford said.

Only the monkey thief obeyed him and came to an abrupt halt. It swung the stolen bag into the air and sent it sailing. Eden had a sick feeling, as it spiraled over a steep cliff. She skidded to a stop and looked over the edge.

The backpack hung on a bush several yards down slope. Frothy white river rapids carved a serpentine path through a steep, narrow canyon below. If Eden fell she'd drown, or be pummeled to death on the rocks, or both. But she couldn't think about that now.

She sidestepped her way down the incline, using large rocks as footholds. Don't look down, she told herself, as she inched closer. Nerves on fire, she reached a spot above the bag. She hung onto a branch behind her and stretched forward, working the strap free. A little more and she would have it.

Pebbles skittered down the slope behind her, and she heard Bramford's throttled roar, half curious, half menacing.

"What are you doing, Eden?" he said.

Why risk her life for a silly bag? Best to ignore him, she decided.

Determined, she yanked the pack free. She glanced uphill, terrified to find Bramford coming towards her. Like a fly trapped in a glass bottle, she batted back and forth, looking below for an escape route. Her hand slipped from the branch, as she twisted around. She dropped the backpack to find purchase but only grabbed thin air. With nothing to stop her, she plummeted through the air towards the raging river.

"Eden!" Bramford cried.

Her mind drew a blank. There was no time to wish for anything. Not even death.

To her relief, Eden hit the water feet first. At least, she thought that was lucky. As if luck might save her now.

The churning rapids pummeled her underwater until she lost all sense of direction. Her heart hammered like an anvil. Just when she thought her lungs would burst, something grabbed her from behind. Images of the lethal anaconda flashed through her mind. The giant monster propelled her to the surface, holding on tight, as Eden thrashed about, gasping for air.

"Relax, I've got you," Bramford said.

Too shocked and too grateful to speak, she simply grabbed onto his arm around her chest. He kept her head above water, as the rapids carried them downstream. Ahead, Eden spied a series of large boulders. She screamed as they hurtled towards the first one.

Just in time, Bramford twisted her out of harm's way by wedging himself between her and the rock. He vaulted them past the danger with his powerful legs. Over and over, he navigated the tortuous obstacle course. Twice, his legs slipped and he bashed against a huge rock.

And yet, he never let Eden slip from his grasp. She coughed and sputtered as she took in water. Numb with pain, her flailing legs struck the rocks underwater. But she was safe with him.

The current slowed as the canyon walls widened, carrying them into a calm lake. Panting hard, Bramford swam with one arm towards the shore, burdened by her dead weight.

When her foot scraped bottom, Eden tried to stand but her legs gave way.

Bramford dragged her onto land, coming to rest in the shade of a palm grove. Even half-dead, he had remembered to protect her from the sun. With a start Eden saw how necessary it was. Not a shed of her dark coating remained. The water had washed it all away. Finally, she didn't care. She was just glad to be alive.

She collapsed onto the sand beside Bramford, her limbs intertwined with his. Her head rested on his chest, rising and falling with each labored breath. His warm chin brushed the top of her head. The rapid drumming of his heartbeat in her ear reminded her of the risks he'd taken.

Why on Blessed Earth had *El Tigre* saved her?

Eden shivered from the wet, clinging dress, or maybe the fear lodged in her spine. She snuggled closer to Bramford. For warmth, she told herself. He didn't protest, as if it were the most natural thing in the world to be wrapped in each other's arms on a sunny day in the wilderness.

Of course, Eden knew it wasn't natural, though she had a hard time convincing herself at that moment. She couldn't deny how good it felt to lie beside his strong body, which grounded her like a ship's anchor. Exactly, she thought, delighted to grasp the outmoded concept. For the first time since she'd left home, she didn't feel adrift in a rocky storm.

Eden brushed her cheek against Bramford's chest and he made a soft, vibrating sound. Was he purring? He tightened his arms around her, rolling her against him. Her long golden hair fanned over his dark torso, the contrast startling her. She never had felt more exposed in her life.

At the same time, a curious, buoyant feeling welled up inside of her. Eden had experienced some pleasure with Jamal, although her sensors had manufactured it. She always had been in control, never losing sight of her goal to be mated.

Now, she felt captive to the strange, pleasurable sensations that stampeded like wild horses up and down her body. She never wanted to leave Bramford's side. Amazingly, her abysmal circumstances and even the loss of her Life-Band suddenly seemed trivial.

Unpredictable, her father had called this beastly man. But he hadn't warned her how unpredictable *she* would be.

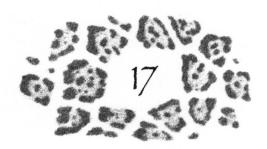

17

AN ETHEREAL birdsong floated on the torpid air, bewitching Eden. She immediately identified it as that of a black-faced solitaire, *Myadestes melanops*. But there was something new and mysterious in its call, unlike any she'd heard on the World-Band. The actual bird, long thought extinct, sounded unreal. But then, cuddled with Bramford beside a placid, sparkling lake, nothing seemed real.

He began to stir, his hand falling down the length of her back, leaving a trail of electric sparks. She gasped, as they exploded in her brain. She shut her eyes tight, drawing in deep breaths. Bramford didn't seem to notice her response. In fact, he knocked her to the side as he rose from the ground. Standing over her, he gave a curious grunt. Had he forgotten she was there?

Breathless, Eden stared up at him. Mottled light played against his muscular body. His pants hung in tatters, his strong legs bursting through the seams. She didn't know where to look. Her entire existence had narrowed to the small patch of earth they shared. Then, for no good reason, Bramford growled at her and walked away.

The beast.

Eden only had imagined a tender connection between

them. Her oxy-deprived brain and the infernal noonday heat that pressed like an iron on her throbbing head had induced the ridiculous fantasy.

She shaded her eyes against the glare, watching him fish for something in the trees that ringed the edge of the jungle. A minute later, he loped towards the lake, carrying a gourd. He smashed the top of it against a rock, then filled it with water. Diamond-like pinpoints of light danced on the lake and silhouetted his incredible body. Eden quivered, as Bramford arched his back and took a long drink.

She forced herself to look at a brace of fulvous whistling ducks among the water reeds. The clear, high-pitched calls of the *Dendrocygna bicolor* somehow lightened her mood. In the distance, a majestic mountain range shimmered through a bank of white clouds. All that open space and blinding light—it was beautiful, wasn't it?

From far away, the rumbling sound of the rapids reminded Eden how far she was from her poor father. She caught herself as she tried to connect to his Life-Band. No wonder things seemed so unreal. She couldn't be certain of anything when there was no one to mirror her life.

"Drink this," Bramford said.

Eden jumped, startled by his presence. How on Good Earth could she stay on guard when he moved like the wind?

Her hand brushed against his, as she took the gourd from him. Once more she felt a crazy, magnetic pull towards him. She could feel his eyes burning into her as she gulped thirstily. She had never tasted water so fresh, and murmured with delight. After estimating her proper quota, she gave the gourd back to Bramford.

"Is that all you want?" he said.

It took a second for Eden to grasp the reality. Plentiful water, whenever she wanted!

She looked at him, wide-eyed, and laughed out loud. His expression darkened, and she saw the usual disgust flood into his eyes. Why didn't he just say it? More than ever, she looked like a freak.

"At least I'm alive. Thanks to you." It sounded like an accusation, which Eden immediately regretted.

Bramford stiffened. "You could have gotten us both killed."

"No one asked you to come in after me."

"What was I supposed to do? Let you drown?"

"What do you care?"

A muscle in his jaw twitched. His fists clenched, as if he wanted to grab her. Eden half hoped he would. Instead, Bramford reached in his pocket and offered her a handful of small, purple berries.

"Açaí berries," he said. "They'll relieve the oxy-deprivation."

Eden knew about the all-purpose food used by jungle dwellers for everything from a sleep aid to beauty treatments. But she wasn't a jungle dweller, and she didn't want his help anymore. She looked away, ignoring him.

"Eat," he ordered her.

"You eat," she said, nastily.

She tried to rise but her head spun. She plopped down and rolled on the ground. The bemused look on his face only added to her humiliation.

"Suit yourself." He popped the berries in his mouth.

"How will we get back?" she said, anxious to be away from him.

"We're not going back."

"But what about my father?"

Bramford's eyes narrowed with a faraway look. Eden had the eerie feeling he could see into the future, maybe like *El Tigre*, after all. But that was impossible.

"The Huaorani will track us to the water," he said, looking towards the rapids. "They'll see where you fell, figure out the rest and meet us at camp."

And the backpack, would they see that, too?

"And where is camp?" Eden said, desperate to get her hands on the Life-Band again.

Bramford continued to study the scenery. He wasn't going to say, she realized.

"What? Do you think I'll tell someone?" she said, with a pang of guilt. That was exactly what she hoped to do.

He cocked an eyebrow. "Given the chance, you'd betray me in a heartbeat."

"Betray you? I didn't ask to come here. I just want to go home."

"We don't always get what we want, Eden."

We? What did Bramford know about disappointment? But as she took in the feline eyes and his hybrid form, Eden figured he finally knew what it felt like to be different.

"I guess you're sorry you volunteered," she said.

Bramford looked weary. "I'm done with regrets."

"But look what it did to you."

He flinched and Eden wasn't sorry her words had stung.

"Maybe I should have let you sink," he said, turning on her.

"Well, why didn't you? How am I supposed to survive by day? And what's going to happen to my father in this sinkhole? Did you think of that when you kidnapped us and brought us here"—she jerked her arm in an arc—"to this deserted, sunny place? No, as usual, you only thought of yourself—"

Bramford jumped on her, pinning her beneath him. His brutally handsome face hovered over hers. Eden stared, transfixed, into fiery eyes as an unfamiliar fluttering darted in her chest, like a small bird released from its cage. She kicked her feet and squirmed, but she was powerless against him. So she used her words, the only weapon she possessed.

"Are you going to rip me to pieces?" He flinched as if she'd slapped him. Eden went on, heedless of the danger. "You're a predator, aren't you? You'd enjoy it. You planned this power trip all along—you can't fool me."

He roared angrily and she shrank back. "You don't know what you're talking about," he said, his face a mass of contradictions. Then he gave her a look that could kill. "You know, you're a pain in the ass, Eden."

"So I've been told."

"Now eat," he said, and forced a berry to her lips.

The tart juice burst into her mouth. An immediate feeling of well-being surged through her. *Almost as good as oxy.*

Bramford stood up and dropped more of the berries at his feet. Eden grabbed for them, gnawing the pulp off the large seeds. She didn't care if she looked like an animal. When she finished, she sighed with relief.

"Thanks," she said.

He grunted softly. *You're welcome,* perhaps? In any case, Eden believed it was the most civil exchange they'd ever had.

She watched him tie one end of a vine round the neck of

the gourd and knot the ends together. He slung it diagonally across his chest. Then without warning, he grabbed her by the waist and lifted her onto his shoulders.

"Hey," Eden cried, wobbling on her perch.

Bramford gripped her thighs to steady her. His warm hands burned against her bare flesh, giving her goose bumps.

He barked out a command. "Hold on."

"I can walk," she said, unconvincingly.

"Not where we're going."

Eden tentatively wrapped her legs around his broad back, barely able to encircle his girth. In spots, Bramford's downy fur rubbed against her skin, surprisingly pleasant. A faint shudder ran through her.

She began to slip backwards, as he sped towards the forest. To stop herself from falling, she squeezed her legs tight around him. Once again, she thought she heard him purr. He placed her hands on top of his head.

"Hold on," he repeated, though his voice was gentler.

She sunk her fingers into his long silky hair, like reins on a horse. As if she controlled the beast. Eden knew it wasn't true, but she enjoyed the illusion just the same.

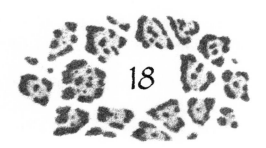

18

THE MYSTERIOUS maze of the jungle swallowed Eden into its dark, forbidding folds. Like craggy monsters, an army of trees reached for her. She glanced over her shoulder, desperate to see the lake, but not even a sliver of it showed through the dense brush. In a minute, she was disoriented.

Only Bramford's easy, confident step reassured her. What did she have to fear when she rode on the shoulders of a mighty predator? His instincts and power would protect her.

"How far is it?" Eden asked nervously. "If the men go by canoe, will they arrive before us? I wish there was a way to signal—"

"Be quiet," Bramford said.

"I just wanted—"

"How am I supposed to find the way when you make so much noise?"

Eden shrieked. "You mean you don't know how to get there?"

"Shhh!" He pinched her thigh.

"Ouch!" she cried.

"Quiet!"

Eden stared at the large hand that gripped her legs and fumed. *Some predator.*

With little cries she fanned away cobwebs that caught in her hair. Something soft fluttered in her face, and she screamed. Each time she made a noise, Bramford squeezed her again. In return, she groaned. From despair or pleasure, she couldn't say.

Gradually, Eden's eyes adjusted to the flickering shadows and she began to decipher the dark chaos around her. High up in the overhead canopy, she saw sunbeams float like golden streamers through narrow gaps in the trees. At least, she realized, the thick foliage provided her with shade.

At eye-level from her perch on Bramford's shoulders, Eden saw another layer of trees that spread laterally through the forest. Not unlike the Combs at home, it created a network of pathways, only for animals and birds. The forest floor, cast in shadows, appeared to be made of huge roots, bogs and piles of vines, which Bramford negotiated with ease, thanks to the superior eyesight that the harpy eagle had donated.

A profusion of smells and sounds grew more distinct, assaulting Eden from every corner. Masses of sensuous orchids wrapped their spindly roots around tree trunks. Their passionate colors and exotic smells amazed her.

A tribe of small, bald uakari monkeys, *Cacajao melanocephalus*, swung from branch to branch alongside of them. Their red faces puckered as they jabbered with loud shrieks. What did the uakaris make of the strange creature beneath her? Or, she wondered with a start, did the eerie white thing with long yellow hair cause a stir?

She was the alien here, not Bramford.

Unlike the dry heat in the tunnels, the jungle was a steamy cauldron. Soon, sweat ran down Eden's back. Bramford handed her the gourd at the exact second she felt thirsty. Just a coincidence, she decided.

"Thanks," she said, and took a long swig.

He didn't respond, he just kept moving. He never flinched at the unseen movements nearby, as she did. If he was nervous, Eden couldn't tell. Now and then, he changed direction for reasons she couldn't fathom. In fact, her mind felt dull and spongy, entirely incapable of reasoning. Her sanity fell behind like a trail of crumbs.

At each mysterious croak from the dark recesses, Eden pressed her knees tight against Bramford's neck. Her fears drove her to cling to him. To her delight, a soft, low murmur rumbled through him. It washed over her, calming her anxiety and yet, arousing her desire.

If he'd confused her before his transformation, she now found him as mysterious as this jungle. How could she even begin to understand someone as complicated as Bramford? Or trust her instincts after suffering Jamal's betrayal?

A rat-a-tat-tat of loud squawks burst in the air with a colorful display of yellows and blues. Probably the last macaws, *Ara ararauna*, on Earth, Eden realized with awe. Something must have startled them. Then she heard a sharp sound from where they had taken flight.

"Did you hear that?" she said, yanking Bramford's hair. "Something's there."

He cocked his head to one side. "Nothing," he said, though she sensed his apprehension. He sniffed the air. "Storm coming."

"What? How can you tell?"

"A lull in the sounds, the slight drop in temperature. Don't you feel it?"

"I'm not receiving any data, remember?" *Thanks to you.*

"Before you would have noticed the signs."

The sound of his voice soothed her so she tried to encourage him to talk.

"Really?" she said. "When was that?"

"About a million years ago, when you looked something like me."

"Like you?"

Even uglier than now? And yet, Bramford wasn't ugly, was he? He was raw and sexy. Maybe she wouldn't have looked so bad.

"I bet you would have been one hell of a she-cat," he said, and she was glad he couldn't see the pleasure creeping into her face.

Thunder rolled overhead, trailing a whip of lightning through the trees. Eden shrieked as it cracked nearby. The lack of weather alerts from her sensors unnerved her.

Bramford laughed. "Okay, maybe just a she-kitten. But you'll learn."

"Not without a Life-Band," she said.

"Just watch and listen," Bramford replied, with surprising patience.

"To what?"

"It's all right in front of you, Eden, if you're willing to open your mind." Bramford held out his hand to catch the falling rain. "Trust me, your basic instincts are more reliable than any Life-Band."

Well, maybe if she had Bramford's new mix of DNA she also might understand nature. Then she thought of Aunt Emily, living shuttered for decades inside The Homestead, her family home. How had she opened her mind to a world beyond her doors?

> *To make a prairie it takes a clover*
> *and one bee,—*
> *One clover, and a bee,*
> *And revery.*
> *The revery alone will do*
> *If bees are few.*

But Eden wasn't prone to imagining. Nearly two decades of oxy drips had drowned out the impulse.

And yet, an idea slowly formed in her mind, as she began to relax to the rocking motion of his shoulders that kneaded her tired legs. It was as if no actual separation existed between her and Bramford, like one mixed-up creature, half-natural-Pearl, half-beastly-Coal. Like a centaur from Greek mythology, she thought, unable to suppress a giggle.

"What is it?" he asked.

"You wouldn't understand." *If only you could.*

Bramford grunted. He didn't even pry. The selfish beast simply dropped the subject and ignored her.

They were nothing at all like two halves of a centaur. More like creatures from different planets.

Rain cascaded down through the levels of trees, falling intermittently on Eden. Cool and refreshing, it washed away the broiling heat. She leaned back her head, catching the droplets in her mouth. Like tears from heaven, she thought.

Soon, her perch grew wet. Bramford caught her waist as soon as she began to slip. He gave her a gentle squeeze before he released his grip. It was a small gesture, maybe even timid. He seemed to communicate something. *Don't worry. You're safe with me.*

Eden began to analyze other unspoken signals that had passed between them. Could he tune into her, as if she were connected to and an important part of the world around them?

Only one way to find out.

Just then, thunder clapped, and even as a scream rose up in her throat, she felt the brush of his hands along her sides. Maybe she wasn't alone. She smiled as an expansive feeling floated through her. Like a burst of fire, but soft as melting wax.

Even more, his response gave evidence to support her theory. If she gave off subtle signs, why wasn't the reverse also true? Why couldn't she tap into her unknown senses and read such subtle signs? Maybe even Bramford's. *Open your mind, Eden.*

Bramford leaned into the steepening angle, as the path rose. A stiff wind rattled the leaves and filled Eden's head with his wild, tangy scent. An irresistible urge to run her hands along his face seized her. She clung to him, pressing her hips against the back of his neck. His breathing grew labored, and for the first time, he stumbled.

"I can walk if you're tired," she said.

He snapped. "I'm fine."

"For Earth's sake. I was just trying to help."

"By running away?"

"You kidnapped me!"

A deep growl thundered through Bramford. He grabbed her waist—too tightly this time. Furious, she raised her arm to smack him, but he caught it without looking.

"I'm watching every move you make, Eden."

She struggled against his tight grasp. "You don't know a thing about me. You never will."

He tossed her hand free and laughed bitterly. "This is my world. Nothing escapes me here."

Really? Could he also see her absurd attraction to his beastly self?

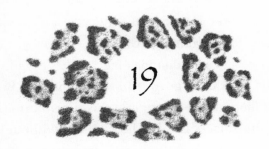

19

BONE-TIRED, Eden slumped on Bramford's shoulders, wondering when her nightmare would end. The uplifting effect of the açaí berries had worn off many hours ago. Bramford already had given her the last of the water. Her mind and body screamed for relief with every step he took.

Through the gathering darkness, she heard the quavering, mournful sound of the great tinamou, *Tinamus major*. It was a nocturnal bird, which meant twenty-four hours had passed since she had left home. It felt more like a lifetime, and even the tinamou's song seemed to echo her despair.

At last, Bramford carried her along a foot-worn path that led into a small clearing. Eden lifted her head, dazed by a sublime sunset that trailed a fiery train of peach and red across the clear sky. She forgot her discomfort and the threat of radiation, if only for a moment. She simply stared, humbled by its perfection, though not in a submissive way. She felt small and human, but sort of good. Because if something so beautiful existed in the world, then maybe some part of her also held such beauty.

To her surprise, a young Indian woman stepped out of the shadows. Eden wondered at the lucky coincidence, and hoped she would lead them to food and water.

She greeted them with a simple hello. *"Hola."*

"Hola, Maria," Bramford replied.

He knew her, Eden realized, her hopes rising.

Maria wore the distinctive bowl-shaped haircut of the Huaorani. A strip of bark-like cloth hung around her wide hips. Her headdress of bright feathers and yellow *Oncidium* orchids seemed to contrast with her plain voice and mild demeanor.

She stared at Bramford with quiet reverence, warmly welcoming him home. *"El Tigre es bienvenido a esta casa."*

"Gracias."

Unlike her tribesmen, however, Maria cringed when she looked up at Eden. Fear lurked behind her startled eyes.

Was it because Eden now lacked a shed of dark coating? She didn't mind not being the Jaguar Man's sidekick, but she hated feeling like dirt.

Maria turned without another word and led them through a well-camouflaged gate. They entered an orderly compound that looked nothing like the decaying river settlement. In fact, Eden wondered if she was the first white visitor. Or hopefully, her father already had arrived.

The forest was cleared to form a large circle. In the middle a huge fire burned, casting a glow over a half-dozen neat, palm-thatched huts. Bramford seemed familiar with the place and headed towards the largest dwelling. Set apart from the rest, it was built on stilts with a wooden front porch. Eden wondered if it was his hut, although he hadn't branded it as usual. But why this remote jungle hideaway?

Past the other huts, and directly across from Bramford's, sat a smaller hut behind a vine-covered fence. Unlike the rest, it had no visible entryway, and Eden guessed that it faced away from the camp onto the thicket of trees.

At the far edge of the camp she spied yet another hut. Overgrown with weeds, it had a bar across a wooden door. *Like a prison?* Eden shuddered at the thought of being locked up there at the end of the world.

Two little girls, naked but for the flowers in their hair, sprang from one of the nearby huts and ran towards them. Their shrill cries and happy, even exuberant, faces shocked Eden. She watched in disbelief as a scarlet macaw trailed after them like a multi-colored banner fluttering in the rosy light. It landed on the older girl's shoulder, its long, graduated tail feathers reaching to her feet. Could an *Ara macao* possibly be a pet?

The children, maybe ages seven and eight, stopped and stared in amazement at Bramford. The macaw fixed one beady eye in his direction.

Bramford sounded hesitant as he greeted the girls. *"Hola, chicas."*

"El Tigre," Maria told them.

Wide grins split their small, round faces. But the excitement dancing in their soft brown eyes flamed out as they took in Eden. They began to tremble.

"Rebecca," the older one said, the color draining from her face.

Eden felt Bramford's shoulders stiffen. She glanced around to see if anyone was there but saw no one.

"Rebecca," the girls called in unison, as Eden turned back.

Did they mean her? Was it the native name for some white-skinned animal? Whatever the reason, Eden understood that she terrified them. Not beastly Bramford. Just the ugly Pearl.

"Rebecca! Rebecca!" the children cried.

Bramford's body began to shake with a thunderous roar and he dropped Eden into a vegetable patch. Maria seemed to scold the girls in a dialect Eden didn't recognize. They grew hysterical, repeating the mysterious name. The pet macaw imitated them with loud, throaty squawks. The louder the noise grew, the more intensely Bramford roared.

Eden dusted herself off, more puzzled than angry. "Who's Rebecca?" she said.

Bramford sunk his weight into a crouch and directed his rage at her. Eden's knees wobbled. The name had struck a nerve in him. If she said it again, he might make her pay. He might grab her with those big, rough hands and pin her down.

Eden couldn't help herself. "For Earth's sake, Bramford. What did you do to this Rebecca to make the children so afraid?"

Just as she feared, he pounced on her. She screamed louder than the children. In a blink, he threw her over his shoulder and bounded across the camp.

My Earth, towards the prison hut!

"No!" Eden cried, struggling against him. "You can't do this to me."

"I can and I will," he said.

Sure enough, he stopped beside the dreadful hut and pulled her down. She pounded her fists on his chest.

"Is this where you lock up your victims? You're an animal, Bramford."

To her surprise, he let her blows rain down on him.

"You've caused enough trouble," he finally said, his voice ragged.

He pushed Eden inside and, before he closed the door, threw a handful of nuts and berries on the floor. Then he shut her in. With a thud, she heard the bar fall into place.

"Let me out!" Eden cried, banging on the door.

Only the wailing voices of the little girls, still calling Rebecca's name, reached her.

She shook her head, dazed. *What just happened?*

Just like at the lab, Bramford had confined her to quarters. She examined the small hut. Air flowed through a high window but there was no way to reach it. She was trapped, like one of her father's lab rats. Like that beast should have been.

Eden slumped to the ground, humiliated. The unfamiliar sting of tears surprised her. She let them spill down her cheeks, tasting their salty wetness with the tip of her tongue. She hadn't even cried when her mother died. Emotional relief always had been an oxy-drip away.

But not for her mother, Eden recalled. Near the end she had refused to take it.

—*I want to feel something, even pain.*

Naturally, she had cried all the time, which had embarrassed Eden. Her father hadn't hid his displeasure. Grim-faced, he had left for the lab because random chaos ruled the world. If he could identify and catalog the chaos, he might establish order. That was all that mattered to him.

Alone, Eden had attended to her mother. For weeks she had puzzled over why her mother smiled, even as she cried. One day she'd found the courage to ask.

—*Why are you smiling, Mother?*

—*Because I have hope.*

—*For what?*

—*For love. For even more after this life.*

Years earlier, Eden had undergone the mandatory death experience and knew to expect only a calm black void. To appease her mother, she'd nodded vaguely.

—*Eden, don't you remember what Aunt Emily said?* '*Hope is the thing with feathers / That perches in the soul, / And sings the tune without the words, / And never stops at all.*'

Nonsense, Eden now thought, brushing away her tears. For example, to which species of bird did Aunt Emily refer? Eden's father was right. She needed to organize her chaotic feeling with logical thought.

And yet, she found herself longing for the warmth of Bramford's body and the tingling excitement of his touch. She strained to listen outside, hoping to catch the sensual purring sound that drove her crazy.

Could a little bird called hope possibly sing for her?

Eden gathered the food Bramford had left; surprised that even in his fury he'd thought of it. It suggested that his mind was still more powerful than his raw emotions. Therefore, from now on, she would use pure objective reason to tame the primitive creature. No matter how wild he became, she would remain cool and objective. She wouldn't give in to the base emotions that threatened to swamp her logic.

Mind over body would save her.

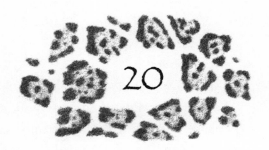

20

EDEN TURNED in her sleep, enjoying what she thought was a fantasy on the World-Band. *I'm running across a beautiful, shaded, grassy field that slopes down towards an endless sky.* Then she heard a knocking sound and woke with a start. She took in the dirt floor and the thatched roof, her new reality coming back to her.

Then what was that? Eden wondered. She closed her eyes, trying to recall the sweet images. Slowly, they began to flicker in her mind.

Why, Bramford is chasing me. I laugh as he tumbles with me onto the grass. We roll like playful kittens. He's smiling at me, really smiling. I'm so happy, I feel as light as a feather.

Eden's eyes flew open as she grinned. It was a dream, wasn't it? She had been dreaming in her sleep—and at night-time, too.

She recalled that long ago, before the aid of oxy, people were prone to such mental distortions. And yet, this dream delighted her. Her happiness in it felt almost real. Certainly, her romantic experiences with Jamal paled in comparison. The grassy knoll appeared more vivid than any heathery cliff she'd seen in Old England. In fact, the dreamy sensations of Bramford's touch still lingered in her body.

Again, she heard a knock.

"Eden?" a man's voice called.

She jerked to her knees and the blood rushed from her head. Woozy, she braced her palms against the ground. She heard the bar being lifted. The door opened and she blinked as daylight flooded into the tiny hut.

"Lorenzo?"

"*Hola.*"

Eden tensed, recalling the girls' violent reactions to her white skin. The gentle warrior only smiled. Touched by his kindness, she smiled back.

Then she saw that he was naked except for a thin rope around his groin. She stumbled to her feet and leaned against the wall, her cheeks flush. Her brain sent out a jumble of distress signals—food, oxy, sleep.

Luckily, she recalled a few Spanish words she had learned whenever her sensors had translated.

"*¿Mi padre?*" Eden said, concerned for her father.

"Okay," Lorenzo said.

He handed her a coconut bowl filled with lumpy *chicha*. Once again, the sour smell repulsed her, though her stomach rumbled with hunger. Already, the torn, dirty dress was slipping off her frame.

Eden dipped a finger into the unappetizing mess, hoping she wouldn't pull out a bug. She tasted it, tentatively. Like vomit, she decided, spitting it out.

Embarrassed, she stared at the floor until she heard a shuffling sound. She looked up to find Lorenzo gone and the door open. Had he meant to free her or simply forgotten to shut it? Eden dropped the bowl and dashed outside.

Lorenzo waited beside a stately royal palm, smiling as she came up beside him. No judgment or anger. Just acceptance. She thought she might cry again if he showed her one more ounce of kindness.

He led her through the compound, taking care to skirt the sunlit center. Eden walked gingerly, wishing she hadn't lost her shoes. The dirt clung to her bare feet, filling in between her toes. And yet, the shaded earth felt cool against the soles of her feet, and somehow gave her a weighty feeling, like she mattered. She even found the temperature outside almost pleasant, and breathed in the sweet-smelling fragrances that laced the air.

Another day, and it hadn't killed her. Not yet, anyway.

Eden heard a small child's cry and turned to see a naked toddler standing in the vegetable garden. The boy tunneled under the arm of an Indian woman who looked up in surprise from her work.

Real food—maize, sweet potatoes, chili peppers and peanuts. What Eden wouldn't give for her daily meal pills.

"Lucy y Carlito," Lorenzo said, nodding towards mother and child.

She smiled at them, but they simply stared. Were they also thinking of the dreaded Rebecca? Eden turned away with a deep sigh.

She followed Lorenzo round a bend onto a narrow path lined with giant bird of paradise plants. Huge flowers with dark blue beaks and spiked white helmets peered down at her like haughty women. Several yards ahead, Eden saw another clearing in the jungle around a wooden, dome-shaped structure. Thick, antiquated solar panels covered the roof over which a cloudless blue sky soared.

At her questioning glance, Lorenzo explained. *"Padre."*

Eden's step quickened. She peeked inside the door to find a rudimentary laboratory large enough for three or four workers. Light streamed in through the tinted panels, bathing the room in soft, amber hues. A few crude wooden desks, gathered in the center of the room, housed old-fashioned boxy computers and hand-held microscopes.

A big step down from the sophisticated laboratory of REA, Eden thought. And yet, her father already seemed at home. He sat at the main desk, against which a crude crutch leaned, deep in conversation with Bramford.

The beast's naked back was to the door. Eden's stomach somersaulted as she traced the line of his muscles. Just hungry, she told herself.

A slight twitch of his head told her he had registered her presence. But her jailer ignored her. Probably too ashamed to face her.

"Daught!" her father said, turning to her.

"Hello, Father."

In just one day he'd grown feeble. Pain clouded his eyes. His face had a waxy cast. He looked sharply away. Probably to spare her from his weakness.

"What's that?" Eden said, pointing to a patch of yellow-stained goo that covered his wounded leg.

"An herbal poultice," he said. "Maria prepared it. I expect it will draw out the toxins."

"You'll assist your father here, Eden," Bramford said over his shoulder.

If she had hoped for an apology, she realized he wasn't going to offer one.

"Does that mean I'm freed from prison?" she said.

Her father began to blink rapidly, though he continued to avoid her eye. "Prison, Daught?"

"Didn't you know? Either our host thinks I can escape this hellhole or he's a sadistic beast."

Bramford jerked around, trapping her in the crosshairs of his gaze. "I've seen what you're capable of, Eden. Just don't forget, I'm watching you. Do you understand?"

"I understand that your power has driven you berserk."

He growled menacingly. His eyes blazed with hot light. A secret smiled tugged at Eden. She might be powerless, but she sure could get under his skin. She strolled past him, inches away, and flicked her hair against his chest.

Go ahead, do something.

Instead, his anger softened to a frustrated moan. Her heart skipped a beat and she wobbled onto a stool. *So much for mind over body.*

"She understands," her father said, his gaze unnaturally fixed straight ahead. "Don't you, Daught?"

She could have been killed in the jungle for all he knew. But let's not upset the prized prototype. And why wouldn't he look at her? With a sick jolt, she realized that her white skin embarrassed him. She stared at the ground, wishing just once he'd accept her for who she was.

"I understand very well, Father."

He wiped his glasses on his shirt and resumed his conversation with Bramford. "You see, you present the full capabilities of *Homo sapiens* as well as the leading animal's characteristics, namely the jaguar—"

"But can you reverse the process, doctor?"

Her father hesitated, checking his notes. Eden's urgent, heartfelt response surprised her. *Say no, Father.*

"An interesting question," he finally replied. "Even at stage one the projection for reversal was slim. In your advanced adaptation the mostly likely outcome will be the demise of the subject."

"What you're saying is a reversal might kill me?"

"Correct."

"Otherwise, I'll remain like this..." Bramford grimaced. "This animal?"

"Exactly. An amazing interspecies adaptation."

Eden resented the feverish glow in her father's eyes. Far from ruining their lives, the accident had provided him with the opportunity for scientific investigation and possible glory.

"This isn't what I bargained for," Bramford said.

"Can't you appreciate the advantages?" Her father looked disappointed as the question hung in the air. "Well, the choice remains with you."

Bramford walked to the doorway and stared out. A trio of chestnut-mandibled toucans, *Ramphastos swainsonii*, sat perched upon a long branch that slashed in front of a tangle of trees, like a restraining cordon. The birds turned their huge bills to one side and stared at him. Their croaking sounds seemed to echo Eden's anxiousness.

Bramford began to present his argument to the feathered jury. "If even a slim possibility of reversion existed, then I assume the possibility of accelerating a transformation may also exist. Since I don't wish to remain in this half-state, which reminds me..." His voice faltered and the toucans swung their bills to the other side. "But if I could fully adapt, perhaps I wouldn't know the difference. Can you do it?"

"What? Speed up the adaptation?" Her father almost

spilled off his stool. "Yes, of course, it is possible to optimize the procedure. However…"

Bramford pivoted to face him. "What?"

"I cannot guarantee that the subject will retain his analytical faculties. However, if we postulate acceleration, factoring in your current state of adaptation and, of course, your particular genome…"

Eden leaned forward as he hesitated. "What is it, Father?"

Bramford summed up the situation. "Either I risk death to regain my humanity or I lose it altogether and become a full-fledged animal. Is that it?"

"Very well put," her father said proudly.

She winced at his lack of sensitivity. But if Bramford felt the sting of it, he didn't react.

"Allow me to show you," he added.

His fingers danced over the keyboard, trying to keep pace with his thoughts. Once more Bramford turned to study the landscape. The slump in his shoulders caused Eden a twinge of pity.

"There," her father said, with a satisfied nod at the screen.

She edged beside him and gasped at the image of a super jaguar. Dark fur covered the large, muscular body that now walked on four legs. Mother Earth, it even had a tail. The only remnant of humanity showed in the creature's discerning eyes.

The toucans' piercing tumult increased. After all, she recalled, the jaguar was their most dangerous enemy.

Like a man to the gallows, Bramford took his time crossing the room. He viewed the formidable image without a word. Still, Eden saw his jaw clench. If he continued to adapt, he might not even know her. With a pang she realized how much she would miss him.

"What will it take?" Bramford said.

Her father's voice climbed to an excited pitch. "Additional stem cells from our donor species, particularly the jaguar. I'll also require samples from an anaconda and a harpy eagle, if we are to follow the exact pattern."

Fear flashed across Bramford's face. He might be superhuman, but she doubted he would survive a battle with born predators.

"I'll get what you need," he said, once more composed.

"Are you insane?" Eden said, jumping to her feet.

"What?"

Speechless, she watched Bramford glide up to her. Lovely, golden light fell on his muscled chest. Like a sleight of hand, the arrogant man she detested disappeared, leaving behind his primal self. Here was the one who had saved her from drowning. His touch thrilled her. His confidence inspired her.

He looked deep into her eyes. In that instant, Eden felt truly seen. The sultry sound of his breathing washed over her. Her chest grew soft and velvety. She felt herself sinking into the green, fathomless pools of his eyes.

His coarse voice filled the small room. "Did you want to say something, Eden?"

She struggled to form a sentence, to be logical. "It's just that my father needs medical help. That should be the priority, not this ridiculous experiment. Or don't you care?"

A lifetime seemed to pass before Bramford answered. "It must be nice to look at life so simply. But it's more complicated than you realize." His gaze never strayed from her, as he added, "Start making preparations, doctor."

"You understand," her father said. "Once the adaptation has accelerated beyond critical mass, the change will become permanent."

"It doesn't matter. I'm never going back."

Eden's heart sank. *Never?*

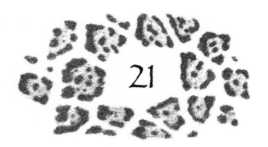

21

AN EAR-SPLITTING din rose up around the laboratory like a hundred sirens. Eden froze. Had the FFP found them? She watched in amazement as Bramford's body began to pulse. His eyes flared and the predator in him sprang to life. In a blur, he leapt outside.

She flew after him but stopped in the doorway. A fierce, feline growl cut through the noise. She caught a flash of him bounding through the trees, the powerful body extended, muscles rippling. The Jaguar Man, she thought, weak in the knees.

Her father hobbled near on his crutch.

"Howler monkeys, *Alouatta nigerrima*," he shouted in her ear. "The loudest land animals in the world."

Eden pressed her throbbing temples. "It's giving me a headache."

"Excellent bush meat. I assume Bramford will catch dinner."

Again, a big cat's growl pierced the air, followed by a painful squeal. Eden quivered as she pictured Bramford, lusty for the kill, ripping into the howler.

"That's my boy," her father said.

The monkey riot stopped as suddenly as it had begun. In

its wake, Eden felt a strained silence fall between her and her father.

When he spoke, he sounded irritated. "Why did you remove your coating, Daught? You know better."

"I didn't do it on purpose," she said. "It washed off when I fell into the river."

"You should have stayed with the group. Lucky for you, Bramford was there to save you." He started to shuffle back to his desk.

Yeah, lucky me.

Eden stared blankly at the jungle while, unbidden, her five-year-old self handed over a forgotten memory. Snappy music had awoken her one afternoon. Something jazzy. She had tripped into the main room, stunned to find her parents dancing. The forbidden lyrics about a beautiful, blue-eyed woman still shocked Eden.

Her father had swung her mother in a circle and laughed.

—*Look, Daught, your mother's eyes are the color of bluebells.*

—*Oh, John.*

—*But Lily. The color is exact.*

Something about the incident puzzled Eden. Then the clear recollection of her mother's cheeks, flushed with pleasure, hit her. *Mother wasn't coated! And Father, too.* It was the only time she had seen them natural.

—*You mustn't tell anyone about this, Daught.*

—*Secrets can be fun, Eden.*

For once, her parents had agreed. Was that when Eden's deep shame began?

She spun around and marched to her father's desk. "Why did you do it?" she demanded.

"Hmmm?" he mumbled, once more absorbed in his calculations.

"Mother was right. Fooling with nature is dangerous. You're not some infallible god. It was wrong to twist Bramford into this savage creature." *Who's so exciting and yet, so infuriating.*

His head jerked up. "Impossible. Lily believed in my work."

"Mother believed in a ridiculous thing called love and some stupid gentle wind that supposedly brought it into your heart. She had her head in the clouds just like you. Dreamers ruining people's lives, her with her crazy ideas and you with your crazy experiments."

"I don't understand, Daught."

"Is that all you can say?" *Not even my name!*

At his blank look, Eden banged out the door. She careened down the pathway, past the towering birds of paradise that seemed to mock her with their regal beauty. Veering behind the main hut, she came upon a watering hole. She collapsed in the cool, wet sand, as tears threatened to spill.

How pathetic, she thought, fighting them back. For once she'd been truly seen—by a beast. No doubt, she had imagined it, just as she'd imagined a connection between them at the lake. Bramford wasn't capable of such feelings. Then, as the memory of lying beside his hard body filled her, Eden groaned.

She just couldn't think about him anymore.

She quickly retreated to her catalog of labels for the natural world. *Dipterids*—a ghost of giddy gnats spun round the glossy surface of the water like dancers whirling on a polished floor. And there, among the reeds, a cattle egret,

Bubulcus ibis, stood on one spindly leg, dotting the air with its beak.

A plain wren, *Thryothorus modestus*, fluttered past and lit on a branch. The small brown bird's effervescent song seemed to sneak up and hit her with a punch. How could so much beauty come in such a drab wrapping?

Nor could Een resist an intoxicating whiff of jasmine that brought a smile to her lips. So different from her leaden response to Mood Scents. Slowly, she began to relax. She cupped the inviting water in her hands. Cool and silky, it dripped between her fingers and ran down her arms. She splashed her face with a little laugh.

In the distance, the children's high-pitched squeals mingled with deeper voices. A nauseating, burning smell floated on the air. Curious, Eden walked to the edge of the hut, hiding behind a guava tree. Several yards away, the women gathered vegetables while the children tumbled around two rows of logs that circled the fire. She spied Lorenzo adding wood to it and beside him, Bramford turning the dead howler on a spit. Her father pegged his way up the path from the lab. He was right. Bramford had caught dinner.

Eden studied him, intrigued by the startling changes. The lab pants, ripped short and split at the seams, were nothing more than a loincloth. Red scratches marked his naked torso, probably from the howler. His long hair was a knotted, wild mess. More than Bramford's increasingly savage appearance, she detected a new, smug confidence. The big kill had increased his arrogance. As if he needed it.

Before Eden knew it, her feet propelled her towards him. She wanted to hurt him. And yet, her heart demanded something else. *Look at me. See me like before.*

Bramford ignored her, as she drew near. For Earth's sake, why didn't the beast look at her? Shaking, Eden raised a hand to slap him. He turned towards her with a lazy look. She was like a pesky gnat, buzzing around his head—nothing more. Her arm fell limp.

"It's not ready," he said, cocking his head towards the dead monkey.

Eden wrinkled her nose. "I won't eat that," she said, aiming to hurt him with her words. "I'm not an animal."

Bramford shrugged. "Too bad. If you were, you wouldn't be so much trouble."

She swept past him with a frustrated huff. Pins and needles stabbed her chest. She could barely see through her anger. She slipped on a pile of Brazil nuts and fell onto a log. From the corner of her eye she caught Bramford smirking. What was wrong with her, anyway? She didn't care about him.

Her father eased beside her and gave her an impatient look. Eden didn't want to talk to him, either, and turned her back on both of them.

She saw Maria heading towards the fire, carrying a basket of vegetables. From the way she brushed against Lorenzo, Eden understood they were mates, although neither wore a white mark on their foreheads. Of course, with no pressure to mate, why bother marking one's status?

Eden also noticed a peculiar glow that the couple shared. Could it possibly be evidence of love? Perhaps, she thought with growing excitement, remnants of it still existed in this untainted corner of the world.

The little girls flitted nearby but kept a wary distance from Eden. Maria called the older one Carmen. *Bossy little thing.* She pointed at the nuts Eden had scattered and the

younger girl, named Etelvina, immediately fetched them. Her
pretty, upturned mouth and soft eyes made her seem sweeter
than her sister.

The girls appeared to anticipate each other's intentions as
they ran towards the pet macaw. It looked up from its perch
in an avocado tree and squawked. They threw the nuts up in
the air for the bird to catch. A game, Eden realized.

Lorenzo sat across from her and pointed at them.

"Mis hijas." he said, explaining they were his daughters.

Eden nodded, surprised. The possibility of sisters hadn't
occurred to her. Of course, why limit the number of children
when resources were plentiful? She saw the girls' subtle com-
munications with each other in a new light. Not unlike the
way Austin had understood her, she recalled with a pang.

Soon, the portly tribe member joined the group. He
smiled shyly at Eden.

Lorenzo introduced him as his brother. *"Mi hermano
Charlie."*

"Hola," Eden said.

Like Lorenzo, he was naked except for the thin string
around his hips. But no, Charlie also had red straps over his
shoulders—her backpack! And the Life-Band, she hoped.

He sat down beside her, unaware he controlled Eden's
future. The little boy toddled over and draped himself on his
father's knee. Lucy scooped up her son and began to nurse
him from her breast. *The poor woman.*

Eden couldn't stand the swirl of emotions any longer. The
soft looks between the couples, the nakedness, and the girls'
relentless laughter—it was all too much. Dizzy, she lurched
towards the girls.

They began to shriek once again. "Rebecca! Rebecca!"

Maria immediately scolded them. They rattled back, something about Rebecca.

Bramford aimed his burning gaze at them. The distraught mother appealed to her brother-in-law Charlie, who shrugged off the backpack, waving it towards the children.

Her bag as bait. To distract them from the forbidden name, Eden realized.

The girls seemed to agree with a quick glance at each other. And yet, they scampered off and climbed over the fence that separated the lone hut. They disappeared around the back, confirming Eden's suspicion that the entrance must face the jungle. But where were they going?

Bramford's worried gaze fixed upon the hut. For once, he looked threatened.

The bag sat unguarded. Now was her chance. *Get it, Eden!*

She lunged, her heart firing. Just as she reached down, however, Carmen ran past and snatched it. Her sister offered Charlie a wooden carving, maybe a small bird.

He took it and thanked his nieces. *"Gracias, sobrinas."*

The girls skipped off and threw the bag to the macaw. Playing catch with salvation, Eden thought. After several tries, the bird nipped it in his beak and tossed it onto a branch where it lodged.

Now what?

"A Huaorani custom," her father explained. "A gift is always returned with a gift."

"But who gave them the carving?" Eden said, looking towards the gated hut. "Is someone there? Is it Rebecca?"

"Forget it," Bramford said, the threat clear.

Now Eden was sure someone or something hid there. If she discovered the truth, she might gain leverage over him. Her legs worked like pistons as she hurried towards it.

"Stop!" Bramford said.

She began to run, calling out. "Hello! Rebecca?"

Behind her, she heard Bramford's pounding feet. His furious growl ripped into her. She screamed as he grabbed hold of her. The blood seemed to drain out of her, and she fell limp.

"Eden!"

But why did Bramford sound anguished? He didn't care.

Then a dark curtain dropped over her world.

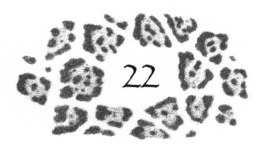

22

EDEN'S EYES flickered open. She wondered why Bramford cradled her in his arms. A wave of relief seemed to pass through him. She must have fainted, she realized. She drew her arms round his neck and cuddled close. His tender purr lit a flame in her. How could such an ornery animal sound so tame?

Maria approached, insisting he bring Eden inside the main hut. There, she pointed. *"Ahí."*

"No," Bramford said, carrying Eden towards the jungle.

Maria blocked his path and said that Eden was sick. *"Ella está enferma."*

His confused gaze fell on Eden, then cut over to the hut. To her surprise, she glimpsed something in his expression that she knew all too well—suffering. What ghosts lay hidden in that place, she wondered.

She thought Maria said, "It's time."

A hard edge returned to Bramford's face.

"You've done everything in your power to destroy our mission," he told Eden. "If it weren't for your father, I would have farmed you out long ago. You're a blind and selfish girl who cannot see the greater good."

"And you do?" she said, jerking her arms away. "With your power-hungry plans for domination?"

"I'm warning you."

He began to shake with a deep, angry rumbling. His chest heaved against her. Eden felt torn by rage and desire. What strange phenomenon held her in its grip and obliterated all reason?

"Please, stop," her father called, hobbling near.

Bramford put her on the ground. "This is your last chance. I've got better things to do than look after you."

"Then let me go," Eden said.

"No one's stopping you. Leave if you want."

His offer cut her deep. She silently watched him slip like a shadow through the trees. *Moody bastard.*

She laid her hand on her chest, aware of an awful ache. Had she caught The Heat? Did that explain this madness?

Maria took Eden's arm and helped her across the clearing to the main hut. Behind her, Eden heard the slow thump of her father's crutch on the porch steps. Inside, the one-room hut had the lonely air of a long vacancy. Thick dusk layered the wooden floor, though there were recent tracks. Cobwebs hung from the rafters like lace curtains. A protective mesh of woven reeds, unlike any in the other huts, covered a window in the back wall. Overgrown brush nearly blocked a view of the watering hole.

Eden took in a family-like grouping of hammocks—two adult sizes, one much smaller. There were even three small stools around a low table that had fallen on its side. Clearly, this once had belonged to a family. So it couldn't be Bramford's residence.

Her father came up beside her and pointed the tip of his crutch at a hammock. "They're made from hemp," he said. "Quite comfortable, I discovered last night."

Even in the grip of pain his inquisitive nature couldn't be dampened. If only he were as curious about her as he was about everything else.

Eden started towards one of the hammocks, but Maria directed them to the far end of the room. Come, this way. *"Vengan por aquí."*

Eden gasped, as they rounded the narrow corner. A frightening figure appeared out of the shadows. It was a large wooden carving, she realized, part jaguar and part man. Even the fierce expression resembled Bramford's.

"El Tigre," Maria said proudly.

"Just as I thought," Eden said, her worst fears confirmed. "Bramford planned it all along."

"Point of fact," her father said. "Using the jaguar as a donor was my idea. Of course, I told him about the legend. But how could we have predicted things would turn out so well?"

"Yeah, just great."

Maria held up a hand, as her eyes cut nervously to the doorway. Then she slipped past the carved figure and pushed aside a wooden screen. Behind it, Eden spied a small room.

"Vengan," Maria repeated, ushering them inside.

A cold shadow fell over Eden's heart, as if she'd seen a ghost. Even the wavering light that streamed through a mesh-covered window seemed anxious not to disturb the room's unseen occupant.

Against one wall stood a simple but modern bed. In fact, everything in the room reminded Eden of home, from a bedside stand to standard pillows. There was even a silver hand mirror on the stand. Not your usual jungle décor. It might have satisfied someone who felt as alien here as Eden did.

"Whose room is this?" she whispered.

Maria told her not to be afraid. *"No tengas miedo."*

Eden looked round, surprised to see two paintings tacked to the thatched wall. The larger one depicted a sleek, black jaguar prowling through a lush landscape. The silhouette of a girl hovered in the brush. Eden couldn't tell if the jaguar stalked the girl or if they were companions. In the corner of the painted board the artist had signed two initials.

"R.B.?" her father said, stepping beside her. "Ronson Bramford?"

"Don't be ridiculous," Eden said, admiring the sensuous images. "Bramford is no artist."

She took in the second painting, stunned by what she saw. It was a portrait of a young woman, her white skin visible. Eden couldn't deny the thrill of seeing a Pearl so well represented, a girl just like her. More like her than she could have imagined. The girl's youthful skin shone with the luster of a sea pearl. Soulful, blue eyes stared back at Eden with familiar longing.

The slender figure and graceful neck also resembled Eden's, though it shocked her to think of herself in such flattering terms. A rare, velvety red *Cattleya* orchid adorned the girl's long, blond hair. She wore an old-fashioned white dress. In fact, except for the flower and clothing, the resemblance to Eden was uncanny.

Eden's father echoed her thoughts with astonishment. "She could be your clone."

A shiver traveled up her spine, as she recalled the children's reactions to her. She pointed at the painting, turning to Maria.

"Rebecca?" she said.

"*Sí*, Rebecca." A weary sigh escaped the woman, and Eden considered how their arrival must have upended her peaceful existence.

Eden's father cleaned his glasses, then peered closer. "If I didn't know it wasn't my own daughter, I might be convinced."

"It must be a self-portrait," Eden said, noting the same artist's signature. Again, she looked to Maria for confirmation. "R.B. for Rebecca Bramford?"

This time Maria met her question with a blank stare.

Eden pushed harder, pointing outside for added emphasis. "But where is she?"

Stone-faced, Maria turned to leave.

Eden's father sank down on the bed, sending a puff of dust into the air. "I assume Bramford doesn't want us to know," he said.

"I wonder what he's hiding?" Eden mused.

"I'm not suggesting he's hiding anything."

"Then tell me, Father, why is there a prison here?"

"It's none of our business."

"What if Rebecca is in trouble?"

"Now who is being ridiculous, Daught?"

"He locked me up."

"You were excitable."

Deserved it, that's what he meant. Well, Eden was sick of his and Bramford's grandiose schemes and lack of feeling for anyone's aching heart. She crossed to the window, staring at the gated hut on the other side of the compound.

"I bet he's holding her prisoner over there," she said. "That's why it's off limits."

Her father sputtered. "What? He's not a kidnapper."

"He brought us here against our will, didn't he?"

"That is not my recollection of events."

Eden spun around. "Against *my* will, then."

"This is pure conjecture, not facts. How can you be prone to such illogic?"

He started to rise but Eden pressed a hand on the crutch.

"Okay, here are the facts, Father: There's a portrait of a girl named Rebecca. It's signed by R.B. Rebecca is a Pearl, so obviously, she's not Bramford's sister. It's also clear she wasn't his mate because arch Coals don't option Pearls."

"A false absolute. Such mating has been known to happen."

"Maybe." Still, Eden doubted that anyone as status-conscious as Bramford could see past a woman's color. "But you can't deny that he's never been mated—it clearly says so on his profile."

"Also not a fail-proof test. Those with the means may bribe the authorities. For now, I concede the point, however, as I see no reason for Bramford to have lied about it."

"So who's Rebecca? Since her portrait is here, let's assume this was her room. And yet, it was sealed off. We don't know where she is. Clearly, Maria is afraid to tell us."

Eden let her questions settle in the air. She picked up the hand mirror, noting the antique patina and engraved letter "B." The thought of looking in the mirror tugged at her, but she couldn't confront her white face. Instead, she showed her father the engraving.

"See this? It's how Bramford marks his territory. Maybe he mated Rebecca and then regretted it. He had to eliminate his mistake so he killed her."

The rapid blinking began. "What? Impossible."

"Perhaps she's buried in that hut."

"I insist you stop this line of reasoning, Daught!"

"No, Father. For once, you're not being objective. We have to get away from Bramford. Why can't you see that he's a monster?"

Her father drew in a deep breath, regaining his cool detachment. "Bramford is a predator. Precisely for that reason, your attempts to excite him are dangerous."

"I don't know what you're talking about," Eden said, turning abruptly.

"It's evident that you have a talent for aggravating him. A common female tactic to attract the male's attention."

"Are you insane?"

"Perhaps. However, that does not assume a diminished capacity to observe your growing attraction to him."

"Bramford and I aren't even the same species." *Thanks to you.*

"Quite true. As a matter of fact, his affection might kill you. Therefore, since you are willing to risk life and limb, I can only assume you are desperate to win his favor."

"In this case, you're dead wrong, Dr. Newman. I loathe Ronson Bramford."

"Hmmm." He pushed to his feet. "Wait and see."

"There's nothing to see. You're investigating a dead end."

"I'm afraid I'm not the one who lacks objectivity here, Daught." He took one last look at the mysterious portrait, muttering as he left. "Extraordinary."

Eden heard him sink into the squeaky hammock in the next room. Weary, she fell onto the feathery mattress and stared up at Rebecca's image. Sweet Earth, they could have been sisters.

If only she could grasp the mystery of Rebecca, she might also understand the strange yearnings that tugged at her heart. She wondered what her imagined twin would think of Bramford's transformation. Would she also experience a whirl of sensations at his touch?

Go ahead, Eden told herself as she picked up the mirror. She took a deep breath and, picturing Rebecca gazing into it, studied her own reflection. Her hand trembled with the initial shock. She brushed a strand of hair from her check, startled by her pearly whiteness. And her eyes—the water had washed away the brown caps—were the color of bluebells, just like her mother's.

Like a punch in the gut, the FFP's offensive logo flashed into Eden's mind. She glanced at Rebecca's portrait, drawing courage from it, then looked in the mirror again. She couldn't deny the amazing resemblance.

And Rebecca is beautiful, isn't she, Eden?

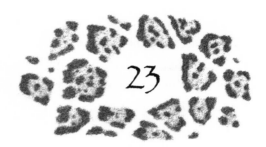

23

AT FIRST Eden thought the odd, rustling sounds belonged in her dream. As they grew louder, scratching at her awareness, she realized someone or something was inside the room. She opened her eyes. *Mother Earth.*

The palm-thatched wall creaked as Eden shied back in the bed. Immediately, the noise stopped. Breathless, she squinted into the shadows. The peachy light of dawn folded through the window mesh. Beside it, she sensed the intruder staring back at her.

Eden fumbled for the small mirror and threw it across the room. "Go away!"

The mirror bounced off the mesh and fell to the floor with a loud crack. She heard an animal shriek. She screamed as the creature scurried past her towards the main room.

"Father!"

The animal's footsteps were light on the wooden floor. It must be small and harmless, Eden decided. So she ran after it, pounding her feet to sound threatening.

"Watch out, Father!"

Wheeling around the carved jaguar statue, she glimpsed the creature, as it cut through the doorway. She noted its small, upright frame and dark body. Possibly, a black spider monkey. They often walked upright on the ground with their tails stiff against their backs.

She rushed after it onto the front steps, but it had fled. Arms akimbo, she caught her breath. She'd scared off an *Ateles paniscus* all by herself. Maybe she wasn't as helpless as she thought.

Eden doubted the monkey would return to find itself trapped indoors again. Why did she find comfort in stark boundaries when they confused a creature of simple intelligence? The Huaorani also lived in a seamless way. Was that why they seemed so happy?

Her eyes darted across the compound, searching the avocado tree for a sign of her backpack. It was gone. Anything might have dragged it off, even the adventurous spider monkey. Hope was so close, and yet, so far away, once again. Would she ever be able to count on anything or anyone?

The woods cranked to life with a sputtering of mysterious sounds. A dark sky groaned with its heavy load of storm clouds. Even the lighthearted, chatty warble of an *Aramides cajanea*, or wood-rail, couldn't dispel the gloom that pressed in on Eden.

She scanned the forest just in case the backpack lay nearby. But she knew she really hoped to see Bramford. If only she could talk him out of his foolhardy decision to accelerate his adaptation. *For his sake, really.*

"Daught?" her father called.

"Here I am, Father," she said, hurrying to his side.

The hammock threatened to tip over as he sat up. Eden rushed forward to steady it. He glanced up at her with dull, lifeless eyes. His coating, which had worn off in large patches, revealed a sallow, greasy complexion. Each day, his condition worsened.

How devastated her mother would have been to see him nearly as ill as she'd been. The guilt of Eden's betrayal weighed heavily on her. There were so many things she wanted to tell him, to explain how she felt and, possibly, make him understand.

But all she said was, "Why not wash the coating off your face, Father?"

"Impossible," he said, with a withering look.

"Do I look that bad?"

"Bad?" He looked puzzled. "That would require a subjective opinion."

"Forget it." He would never understand.

Maria appeared in the entryway without a sound. Eden marveled at how little her solid frame disturbed the world around her. Like water, she seemed to move along with the earth rather than against it. A warm smile lit her face.

She set down her supplies beside the hammock, including a bowl of pungent, yellowish paste. Her daughters trailed behind her. To Eden's surprise, Carmen approached her with tentative steps, offering *chicha,* sprinkled with açaí berries. Etelvina handed another bowl to Eden's father, then smirked at her sister, as if to say, *Loser.*

Eden wondered if Carmen had lost a contest in which the loser had to serve her. She smiled at the girls, hoping to dispel their fright, but her smile felt tight and fake.

"Gracias," she said, as she accepted the food.

The sisters froze. *Ah, the monster speaks.*

Their mother signaled them to leave and they couldn't

run away fast enough. Eden shrank within herself, trying to disappear. She hardly realized she had begun to sip the *chicha,* more from nervousness than anything else.

"Not bad, eh?" her father said.

Eden shrugged. Actually, it wasn't as revolting as she had thought. At least her father was right about one thing. When you're hungry enough, you'll eat almost anything.

Squatting on the floor, Maria began to clean his wound. A sickening odor filled the air as she removed the old poultice. Eden tried not to gag. And yet, Maria never reacted. She delicately layered on a fresh coat of paste with a handmade brush of soft bristles and fur. Eden knew the woman meant well. But then, the road to Earth's destruction also had been paved with good intentions.

She pointed out the obvious. "Father, do you really think this jungle medicine is working?"

"Precisely." His tired face brightened. "The poultice contains bark from the slippery elm, you see. Its antibacterial properties are known to be an excellent treatment for gangrenous sores."

For Earth's sake, his life was at stake, not some hypothetical subject's.

"Yes, but is it working?" she repeated.

Maria pointed towards the mountains. *"Más fuerte."*

"I believe she's telling us that something stronger exists in the mountains," Eden's father said.

Maria nodded. *"La Puerta del Cielo."*

"Heaven's Gate."

"We'll never make it there," Eden said.

"El Tigre go."

"But isn't he busy chasing predators?" *The selfish beast.*

"A pity so little remains of the rainforest," her father mused. "Miracle cures, valuable information—all destroyed."

Maybe it was better if he didn't face the facts. Denial had its advantages, after all.

"You can imagine the pressure on Bramford to sell this land," he continued. "Instead, he's invested a great deal of money here in research on plant life, with no guarantee of return, I might add. And another thing—he believes in the Huaorani. If he sells the land, their way of life will end. I suppose you could say he's a purist."

Eden scoffed. "Trust me, Father, you don't understand his greedy motives."

"You misjudge him. I can think of no one finer to be the Jaguar Man."

Maria referred to *El Tigre* as a shaman, adding, *"El habla con los espíritus."* She waved a hand in the air, probably to indicate that he talked to the spirit world.

"Spirits?" Eden said. "That's impossible."

Maria mimicked drinking something. *"El bejuco de oro."*

"Oro that's gold, isn't it? What's *bejuco?"*

"Gold, indeed," her father said. *"Bejuco* refers to filaments or vines. In this case, a woody vine, *Banisteriopsis caapi*, is used along with a companion plant to prepare the shaman's drink. Therefore, *bejuco de oro* is an herbal medicine as precious as gold.

"It lifts the shaman to another level of reality, what we call the Fourth Dimension. You may recall that Albert Einstein said, 'Time and space are modes by which we think and not conditions in which we live.'

"Of course, long before him, the shamans understood this. How else to explain their encyclopedic knowledge of plants—healing properties, poisonous traits? They even foretold the white man's destruction of their world."

"I'd like some *bejuco de oro*," Eden said. "Maybe then I could figure out how to get us out of here."

Maria gave her a warning look. *"Bejuco de oro muy fuerte."*

"Yes, it's more powerful than any modern medicine, in fact," Eden's father said.

"If it's so strong, why don't you take it, Father?"

"I expect it would kill me."

Eden considered what it would be like to be as fearless as *El Tigre*. Her reactions to the harmless black spider monkey seemed silly in comparison.

"What's *El Tigre* afraid of?" she asked Maria.

"Coatlicue."

At their puzzled looks, Maria searched the thatched ceiling, as if the translation hung there. Then she set aside her work and lay on the ground, playing dead.

"Charades," Eden said.

Maria's eyes blinked open with a dreamy look. She stood up and pretended to climb up several steps. Then she came to an abrupt halt, stricken with fear and awe. Something or someone seemed to block her path. She opened her arms wide, three times, to indicate the size of the obstacle. She gave them an encouraging look as she twisted her arms and body in a serpentine fashion.

"A snake," Eden guessed.

"Or a snake god, more likely," her father said.

"*Coatlicue,*" Maria repeated.

When she tried to step over the imaginary snake it bit her. She fell down and crouched into a little ball. Then, with a sweet chirping sound, she spread her arms like wings.

"Hmmm," Eden's father murmured. "I don't recognize that particular birdcall."

"I get it," Eden said, perking up. "If the Big Snake in the Sky bites you, then you return to earth as a bird."

"Or anything at all," her father said. "For example, a *Tapirus terrestris*, a common jungle animal also called a tapir. You might appear as the pig-like creature with a short snout and splayed, hoofed toes."

"That's disgusting." *Sort of like how Bramford must feel.* Suddenly, his temper didn't seem so outrageous.

Maria returned to the starting point. This time she vaulted over the imaginary snake to the other side. She smiled happily as she greeted dead relatives and friends.

"A nice fairy tale," Eden said, pleased at how well she had understood without a Life-Band. "Make it past the snake god and you live happily ever after. Fail, and you come back to earth as an animal. I guess killing animals is like killing your friends."

"It certainly explains why it was so difficult to obtain the DNA of an anaconda," her father said. "Killing an animal like *Coatlicue* must be the worst sin of all."

Satisfied with their understanding, Maria bent down to finish her tasks. Eden's father moaned as she began to lay thin strips of bark over the paste. His bloodshot eyes seemed to beg Eden to do something. If she failed him again, she feared he soon would meet *Coatlicue.*

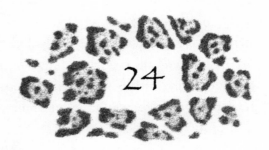

24

EDEN SAT on the steps of the main hut in the shade of a palm tree. She waved a fan she'd made of its fronds, stirring the hot, humid air. The unforgiving noonday sun bleached the compound with stark light. Her hair stuck to the nape of her clammy neck, the dirty dress, to her sweaty skin.

The minutes slowly ticked by, cycling into hours, then long passages of the day. She never realized how long an hour was or how much time she had at her disposal. What had she done with all her time? She had frittered it away with fantastical World-Band experiences. That had helped bury her feelings—she could see that now. At least she hadn't felt this stifling boredom.

For the hundredth time her eyes searched the forest, and once more, she sighed. That dumb beast had been gone since yesterday afternoon. Where on Holy Earth was he? What if a real predator had killed him? She just couldn't think of it.

The children's shrill cries caught her attention and she turned to see them scampering around the vegetable garden. They seemed content to play with whatever was at hand, a wooden tool or a cucumber to bat a bean pod into the air. Neither Maria nor Lucy, who tended the plants, grew

irritated by the kids' frequent calls, always ready with a patient answer or tender glance.

In fact, the Huaorani met the most trivial events with a
happiness that puzzled Eden. Maybe they didn't know how
boring their lives were.

Carlito began to toddle towards her, dragging a large cucumber that was nearly as long as his leg. Its dark, glossy skin
glowed in the sunshine, as if it were more than a vegetable.
As if it were strangely alive. Carmen and Etelvina stopped to
watch their cousin's progress, their faces anxious.

The determined boy finally reached the bottom of the
steps with a proud smile. He dropped the vegetable at Eden's
feet, presenting his gift. She felt awkward as she picked it up,
and yet, deeply pleased.

"Gracias," Eden said.

Carlito's wide, innocent eyes were insistent. *Eat it.* Even
a toddler could make his intentions clear without a single
word, apparently.

"Why not?" she said.

She brushed away the dirt as best she could and took a
small bite. At once, the little boy began to retrace his wobbly
steps. Mission accomplished.

Eden ran her tongue over the wet, fleshy piece. Not at all
like cucumber flavoring in meal pills. In fact, she liked the
fresh, clean taste and took another bite. Maybe she'd try the
other vegetables, too.

Lorenzo stepped out of the shadows, startling her. She
wondered how he'd reached the porch without her seeing
him approach.

"Hola, Eden."

"*Hola,*" she responded.

He walked into the hut without asking anyone for permission, just as his mate often did. Perhaps their disregard for boundaries made them feel more connected to the world, allowing them to move through it with so little effort.

Eden followed him inside, just as her father awoke from a nap. She feared these naps would get longer and longer until he wouldn't wake at all.

"Ah, Lorenzo," he said, pulling a piece of paper from his shirt pocket. "I wrote down a few supplies. Anything you need, Daught?"

She gave him a blank look.

"*A la ciudad,*" Lorenzo said, and imitated driving a car. He was going to the city.

Eden's heart skipped a beat. She asked when he would leave. "*¿Cuándo vas?*"

"*Ahora.*"

"Now? Right now?"

"It could be a year from now," her father said.

"How is that possible?"

"The Huaorani never use the future tense, you see. For them, only the present exists."

"Then how do you know when something will happen?"

"I suppose it doesn't matter."

But it did matter. Bramford's words came back to taunt her. *Leave if you want.*

That was exactly what she planned to do.

"A comb would be nice," Eden said, and mimicked combing her long hair, which had become a tangled mess.

Lorenzo left as quietly as he'd arrived. Her father settled

back into the hammock and closed his eyes. Eden returned to the porch, surprised by the startling change in the weather. In the short time she'd been inside, the sky had flipped over and now hid the sun behind a sheet of gray. As changeable as Bramford's moods.

Dark silhouettes of trees wove together like old-fashioned lace. Lightning cracked so near that she jumped. The sky burst open, pelting the ground with thick raindrops.

Despite herself, Eden wondered where Bramford would find shelter. She pictured him lying across a tree branch, his powerful body balanced with effortless grace, licking his lips from some tasty treat. Her body turned to jelly.

She started to go inside when a sharp movement near the gated hut caught her eye. She peered through the rain, uncertain of what she saw. It was Bramford, wasn't it?

He pounced towards the hut, and out of view. Eden watched, breathless, as he sprinted back. He lashed out but his punches only struck air. Was this some sort of primal dance or demonstration? Or was he trying to intimidate his prisoner, Rebecca?

Lightning crashed down, illuminating him. Eden saw his wet face, mashed with hair, and forgot all about her missing twin. His strong legs kicked and jumped, making her feel small and delicate, and at the same time, aggressive and full of daring. An earthy moan escaped her lips.

Bramford immediately zeroed in on her. She swore she could feel the heat coming off of him. Her yearning grew unbearable. Was it for her sake or Rebecca's that she flew towards him? She no longer cared why. She simply knew she had to be with him, whatever that meant.

She clattered down the steps into the rain. She didn't heed her father's call or Bramford's warning growl. Neither one understood. For Earth's sake, neither did she.

Bramford leapt over the gate, running to meet her. Something wild and crazy came over her and she yelled his name. Did she hear a frightened cry answer from inside the hut?

Bramford caught her in his arms. Through the crashing thunder she heard him say, "Go away, Eden."

And yet, he held her tight. His magnetic eyes burned into her. This time she knew without a doubt that he saw her. *The Real Eden.* It was all she had ever wanted.

Why then did she struggle to see past him to the hut? She couldn't understand why she said it, either; the words didn't match her desire for him, but they came anyway.

"Hello, Rebecca?" Eden called into the wind. "Are you there?"

Her knees buckled as Bramford's mouth found her neck. Sharp teeth grated against her skin.

Maria appeared beside them, tugging at her arm, telling her to come. *"Ven."*

Bramford pushed Eden away. She slid down his legs and crumbled to the muddy ground, desperate to understand. She needed to talk to him, but he disappeared among the stormy shadows.

Dazed, Eden followed Maria back inside, met by her father's worried gaze.

"What did you do to Bramford?" he said.

"Rebecca's there," Eden said, numbly.

"Please, leave it alone, Daught."

"That's the way it always is. Just ignore it?"

"Yes. I mean to say, no." He blinked hard. "I don't understand you."

"No, you don't."

Eden hurried past him and curled up on poor Rebecca's bed. Wrenching sobs hit her one after the other. The wind threatened to split the thin walls into pieces. Rain leaked through the thatched roof, pooling onto the floor.

She shut out the storm and the whole crazy world. In her mind's eye, she only saw Bramford's piercing gaze. She ran her hands over her arms, recalling his indelible touch.

Good Earth, she simply had to get away from him or she would die.

Eden started at a sound and looked up to find Maria standing there. She averted her eyes, embarrassed by her uncontrollable display of emotions. Something soft fell on the bed beside her.

"Para ti," Maria said.

For me?

"Gracias," Eden murmured to the woman's retreating back.

She slid her hand over a bundle of white fabric. A row of buttons. It was a dress. *Rebecca's dress!*

Eden held it across her hips, judging the size. The width fit her fine, but the dress reached almost to her calves. Was Rebecca taller, she wondered with a pang of disappointment. Silly, but she imagined that they were identical in every way. Then she recalled that the old-fashioned style was worn long.

She happily slipped off her ruined dress and threw it in a corner. *Let it rot.* She wiped her skin clean with a blanket. A whiff of jasmine floated in the air as she slid Rebecca's dress over her head. *See?* They both liked the intoxicating scent.

Eden smoothed out the long skirt, surprised by its wide sweep. The fitted top scooped under her shoulder blades, exposing bare shoulders. A bright blue string threaded through the edge of the bodice—the perfect accent to her eye color, *their* color.

She never considered how color or shape might affect her mood. Or how empowering such a personal choice could be. She thought of Aunt Emily, who had worn only white for many years, and in a similar style, too. Had such pretty clothes made her and Rebecca feel beautiful?

The delicate dress swished, as Eden moved. So unlike the stiff, techno fabric she'd worn. Delighted, she began to sway. The skirt captured the soft air underneath it, brushing it against her bare legs. Once again, the jasmine perfume filled her head, and made her think that anything was possible. Even for her.

Eden examined herself in the silver hand mirror, which was cracked thanks to the intrusive monkey. She smiled, pleased by what she saw. More than ever, she resembled the lovely Rebecca.

Eden twirled around and laughed lightly. What would that callous beast think of her now?

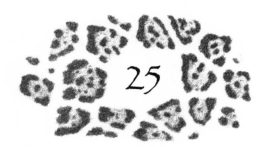

25

ONCE AGAIN, soft rustling sounds woke Eden. *Probably that damn monkey, again.* She noticed that it had pushed open the window mesh. Thin wands of early light poked through.

There, by the window, she saw the dark creature moving. She heard something fall and roll across the floor. The animal turned towards it with a soft pleading sound. Spider monkeys were highly intelligent, but could they beg?

"Shoo—go away," she said with false bravado.

Its frustrated begging increased. What could be so important to a monkey?

Eden screamed as it darted towards the mysterious object. The animal screamed, too, and shot through the window.

Curious, she scooted to the edge of the bed to see what it had dropped. She tapped her foot around the boards, which were still wet from the rain. Her toe met something thin and round. But as Eden leaned forward, her weight sent it rolling under the bed. Possibly, a well-worn stick, something a monkey would use to extract bugs from the ground. Or the pest might have stolen one of Maria's tools. Not worth reaching for into the dusty hollow.

If only Austin were there to protect her. If only she had

paid attention to his warnings. Never again would she be blinded by pride. For Earth's sake, she had bought into the hatred against her own kind. She had longed for a color-blind mate when she was more prejudiced than the worst of the FFP.

She glanced at Rebecca's portrait. Sorry, Eden's eyes pleaded. *Thanks to you, I'll do better.*

She stepped to the window, surprised to see the compound transformed. Strewn with leaves and small branches from the storm, it appeared startlingly new in the soft blush of dawn. In the same way, Eden decided to shake loose old habits and thoughts. If she wanted to survive, she would need a personal evolution.

Open your mind, Bramford had said. It seemed like strange advice from such a stubborn man. And yet, look at how brave he was in the face of unfathomable change. How did he do it?

Of course, she had managed to retain her inner sense of normal, despite a lifetime of oppression, hadn't she? Possibly, if she gave the Real Eden a chance to live and breathe, she might accept herself just as she was. If Bramford could open his mind, why couldn't she?

She looked towards the gated hut. Did poor Rebecca languish there, filled with similar regrets? How Eden longed to sit and talk with her, like sisters in an Old World novel. They'd laugh and cry over how foolish they'd been to fall for a couple of jerks like Jamal and Bramford.

Eden spied a beautiful pair of snowy white umbrella cockatoos perched on a nearby branch. The male paraded back and forth with slow, deliberate steps to woo his female friend. He cocked his head to one side and gave her the eye-blaze, constricting his pupil to reveal the edge of the iris. If he succeeded, the two *Cacatua alba* would bond for life.

If only Eden had another chance to find her true mate, she promised herself she would be wiser next time.

Soft voices floated in the air, and she turned to see Lorenzo and Charlie leaving their huts. They wore ragtag clothes— their city clothes. They were leaving, she realized with a jolt. Here was her chance to escape.

They stopped beside the fire pit as their faces registered surprise. Then Eden saw it too. The carcass of a massive bird, nearly three-and-a-half feet long, lay on the ground. It was a harpy eagle, the world's most powerful raptor and one of Bramford's genetic donor species. The bird's showy, feminine crest of head feathers contrasted with its stern vulture-like features, bringing to mind a harpy, the half-woman, half-vulture creature of Greek mythology. Dark wings splayed open like huge, angry hands. Blood dripped from vicious bite marks on its neck.

Bramford's bites, Eden realized with dread. He had begun to gather the DNA her father needed to continue the adaptation. *One down, two to go.* If he also captured a jaguar and an anaconda, the balance in him would tip forever from man to beast. If he failed, he'd be lunch. Either way, he was doomed to a cruel fate.

Eden heard Lorenzo murmur, *"El Tigre."*

She followed their gaze, as they scanned the area. But Bramford was nowhere in sight. Probably gathering his energy after what must have been an incredible fight. Harpy eagles nested in trees over a hundred feet high. It was no small feat to capture one.

Eden imagined Bramford stalking the raptor, as it tracked

its own prey, possibly a sloth or monkey. He must have am-
bushed the surprised eagle with lightning speed and impec-
cable timing. She shuddered to think of the actual attack—
Bramford's springing action, the desperate harpy flailing its
long talons in defense, the bloodthirsty roar as Bramford
lunged at the huge bird. Hot and dizzy, Eden leaned against
the window to catch her breath.

The brothers hefted the heavy carcass, carrying it
over their shoulders towards the laboratory. Soon, her father would discover the prized specimen as well as Eden's
absence.

When the warriors returned, she would follow them into
the jungle where hungry predators and poisonous animals
waited. The idea paralyzed her. Why couldn't she just stay
there at camp and wait for a better option? She was just a
Pearl, after all.

And yet, she could almost hear Rebecca nudging her. *Remember your promises, Eden.*

True, not all Pearls were cowards. Some, like her mother,
were brave. The image of her diseased body, soft and useless against the hard utilitarian furniture, came to Eden. Her
curled posture had formed a question mark that punctuated
Eden's terrified thoughts. How would she go on after Mother
was gone?

—*Please, brush my hair, Eden.*

—*Won't it hurt?*

—*Not if you're gentle.*

She had lain still, smiling, always smiling, while Eden
brushed the dry strands, easing over the scorched scalp.

—*Tell me. Are you afraid, Eden?*

—*Sometimes.*

—There's nothing to fear. I won't be far away. You'll see.

How happy she'd seemed, despite the sorrowful words she had quoted from Aunt Emily's poem.

—'Because I could not stop for Death, / He kindly stopped for me; / The carriage held but just ourselves / And Immortality.'

Of course, the notion of a soul living past the grave was as illogical as love. Still, Eden admired the fearless grace with which her mother had made her exit. The least she could do was be brave.

Just as she expected, Lorenzo and Charlie reappeared, heading towards the main gate. Time to go, she told herself.

She took one last look at the painting of Rebecca gliding through the forest beside the protective jaguar. *See how easy it is?*

Eden quietly entered the main part of the hut, greeted by her father's gentle snore. The wounded leg jutted out over the edge of the hammock. His ravaged face broke her heart.

Especially to save Father, she must be strong.

Hurrying outside, she glimpsed the men passing through the main gate. From one of the huts the little girls' singsong prattle floated into the air. Any minute they might spring outside. Eden could just imagine their horrified reactions to seeing her in Rebecca's dress.

She sprinted down the steps and hit the ground running. Mud splattered on the white dress. But she couldn't think about that now. She wove through the shadows until she reached the gate. Ahead, she saw Lorenzo and Charlie turn down the mountain path.

As she stepped outside the compound, she heard a high-pitched cry. She glanced over her shoulder, expecting to see the two sisters' troubled faces. Instead, a sharp movement near the gated hut caught her eye.

Rebecca?

Eden hesitated, fighting a strong pull. It might be her only chance to discover the truth. And yet, what hope could she possibly offer?

The seconds ticked by. Soon, the men would disappear in an impenetrable maze of jungle and she would lose her chance.

Eden waved to her twin. *I'll be back with help.*

Then she latched the gate behind her and hurried after her unsuspecting guides.

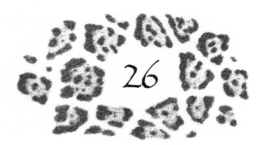

26

EDEN MAINTAINED a safe distance from Lorenzo and Charlie, as they wound their way down the mountainside. If they discovered her, she feared they'd return her to camp. She tried to keep an eye on the palm nut that bobbed from the end of Charlie's blowgun. *Like a game, Eden.* But she wasn't having any fun.

Her bare feet tripped over piles of vines and sank into the muddy ground. The long dress hampered her movements. She slapped away swarms of insects, stifling the impulse to scream.

The brothers wove in and out of the shadows, disappearing at heart-stopping intervals. Each time she lost sight of them, she panicked. The jungle closed in around her. Anything might happen.

When she stepped on a dry twig, it snapped in half. To her ears, it sounded like an avalanche. Her guides came to an abrupt halt. Eden ducked behind a cluster of huge, sappy leaves. Through a small gap, she saw the men fan apart, their eyes searching. Lorenzo held his machete ready, while Charlie reached into his quiver.

What if they mistook her for prey? For Earth's sake, with her blond hair and pale skin, Eden presented a bull's-eye target in the dark forest. She felt faint as she imagined a poison dart sailing straight to her heart.

She inched back against the tree trunk. She could almost hear the warriors' steady breathing, wafting through the moist air to reach her feverish cheek. Somehow, she knew they had located her position. Deep inside, she had a heightened feeling, as if she also had sprung a finely tuned antenna like Bramford. *Eden, a she-cat?*

A scratchy sound from above her head distracted her. Heavenly Earth, a swarm of stout ants marched down the tree trunk. Why hadn't her newfangled instincts warned her that it was a cecropia tree? Bullet ants, *Paraponera clavata*, took shelter in its hollow trunk in exchange for warding off intruders—like her.

Eden recalled the dreaded nickname: twenty-four-hour ants. That's how long the pain from a sting could last. In fact, in order to become a warrior, a young Indian boy had to survive the sting of dozens of them at once. Not everyone passed the cruel initiation. And neither would she.

Wasn't she full of useful tidbits?

The black mass of ants advanced in lockstep towards her neck and shoulders. She could either die from waves of burning pain or a quick, lethal dart. Sweat trickled down her face, as she considered her dismal options. *Decide, Eden.*

She waved her hand, hoping for a truce.

Nothing happened.

Just in time, Eden jumped away from the tree trunk. But she had escaped one deadly fate, only to be met by another. Lorenzo and Charlie were nowhere in sight. They probably had decided that the odd, hidden creature was no threat and moved on.

She looked around, anxiously debating which route to take, when an azure-hooded jay swooped in front of her. The blaring cry of the *Cyanolyca cucullata* sounded an alarm that sent Eden running.

Long tendrils reached out to grab her like the bony fingers of a giant, green monster. They knotted into her long, oak-colored hair. Trembling, Eden tore at the shoots and pressed forward, only to feel the clawing tentacles quickly smother her again. She was a small offering walking into the forest's hungry mouth. *Feed me, little Pearl.*

The idea of Rebecca strolling through the dangerous terrain accompanied by her animal protector now seemed laughable. For Earth's sake, Eden should have stayed where she belonged—safe inside the tunnels or even in a flimsy hut. Aunt Emily had been a recluse for good reason.

Eden glanced over her shoulder, wondering if she should turn back. But there was no clear path, and she pictured herself wandering in circles. Sick with fear, she pushed deeper into the forest, searching for the men.

Tears of relief sprang to her eyes, as she caught sight of Lorenzo and Charlie crossing a boggy marsh. Eden crouched low, studying their graceful steps across a log that spanned the brackish water. They quickly reached the other side and, once more, slipped into the flickering shadows.

Easy, right? But then, the Huaorani weren't terrified of water. Eden just couldn't think about that now. She had no choice but to try.

She took a deep breath and stepped to the edge of the pond. A little blue heron on a craggy rock seemed to egg her on with its snapping sound. *You can do it, Eden.* Unlike the generous *Egretta caerulea*, a colony of ugly, gold-striped frogs croaked ominously. Probably about the disastrous spill she would take.

Better crawl, Eden decided, tucking the hem of her impractical dress into the waistband. She knelt onto the log and inched forward with a tight grip. Her knees hurt from the rough surface; splinters lodged in her skin.

The frogs' throats bulged with incandescent lights as they bellowed. The gruff sounds of *Lithodytes lineatus* played like a competitive roundelay. Probably laying bets on how long it would take before the white creature fell into the mucky mess they called home.

Never mind.

Eden focused on the next step and then the next, aware of each passing minute. Halfway across, she raised her head, straining for a sign of the brothers. In that instant she lost her balance, one leg sliding into the slimy bog. The water gobbled up her skirt, which grew heavy around her leg. She kicked against the water, desperate to hoist herself back on top of the log. But her hold slipped, and she fell off with a loud shriek. A riot of victorious croaks filled the air.

At least the shallow water only reached her waistline. Eden grabbed for the log but it bobbed out of reach. She'd never make it across, anyway. She had no choice but to wade to the other side of the marsh, a few yards away.

She slowly moved through the warm, sticky water, trying not to think of a crocodile or a snake lurking below, eager to strike her bright white legs. But huge, untamable fear welled up in her. She couldn't even pretend this was a bad experience on the World-Band. Too late, she understood that hope and courage weakened denial.

At last, Eden crawled onto dry ground, her chest heaving.

She stumbled to her feet, a lump in her throat. Her guides were gone again.

Pell-mell, she plunged into the forest. Sunlight glinted through the upper canopy at a more oblique angle. A half hour had passed, she guessed. How much ground could they have covered in that time? Perhaps enough that she would never find them.

"Lorenzo, Charlie!" Eden cried out, only hoping they would drag her back to camp.

She passed a broken branch still oozing sap, and hesitated. *This way.* She told herself she would see the palm nut dangling from Lorenzo's blowgun any minute now.

Again, she shouted her friends' names, desperate for a response. Instead, the thunderous cries of howler monkeys beat the air.

"Help!" Eden screamed, her voice lost in the din.

Blind with tears, she tripped ahead. Through a thicket of teak trees, she spied an opening of stark light. She veered towards it, wild with hope. She could hardly believe her good luck when she burst onto a riverbank. The small tributary might lead her to the mighty Amazon River and an Indian camp.

A breeze lifted off the dark green river, offering Eden a cool respite from the scorching heat. Dazzling sunshine lit the narrow embankment and danced upon the lazy water. She walked downstream, hugging the shaded rim of trees.

To avoid the blinding contrast with the sun-baked ground, she lowered her gaze. Blue eyes refracted more light against the back of the cornea than dark eyes, she recalled. One more reason why she didn't belong there.

Nearby, the sound of the howlers intensified. Eden

pressed her temples, which throbbed from the terrific noise. Were they following her? Was it possible they were trying to warn her of something? That would explain the strange, niggling feeling in her gut.

Don't be ridiculous, Eden. It was only a cartload of howling monkeys.

Just then she tripped headlong to the ground.

But why didn't she feel the sandy shore beneath her?

Instead, something cold and rubbery slithered around her.

A giant monster had broken her fall.

Oh, Holy Mother Earth.

Eden was caught in the grip of an anaconda.

Immediately, the howlers' cries stopped. And her curdling scream rose up into the sudden, sharp silence.

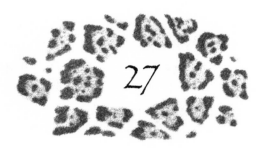

EDEN QUICKLY ticked off the cold, horrible facts about *Eunectes murinus*. The anaconda was at least eight feet long and weighed around two hundred pounds—probably a male. A female would have been twice as long and heavier. Not that it mattered. The male would kill her just as well.

Inch by inch, the water snake, as the name anaconda translated, would constrict its muscular body round her, rolling her into the loop of its tail like a present tied with a bow. The painful process would last about three or four minutes. *An easy day's work.*

When Eden was nice and dead, the hungry snake would swallow her whole. Its teeth angled backwards, the better to ratchet her into its gullet. She often had marveled at its efficient killing design during her research. Of course she never imagined she would experience it firsthand.

Funny, how life could surprise you. She didn't know half as much as she thought she did.

Eden lay on her back, one leg caught in the anaconda's tail. Snatches of forest, then a patch of sky whirled overhead, as the snake flipped her over. Just as she feared, it began to roll its long body around her. Desperate, she clawed at the ground, trying to squirm away. She used her free leg to kick sand at the giant reptile. It seemed to sneer at her useless efforts and twisted her closer, trapping all of her limbs.

Already, she could feel the rhythmic pulsing of its muscles around her torso, as it tightened its hold on her. Her death certificate would read, *suffocation by anaconda*. But then, no one would ever know what happened to Eden Newman. Her death would be as invisible as her life had been. *How appropriate.*

The seconds slid in seeming slow motion towards a final count like bright colored balls on an ancient abacus banging together with a loud *click!* Soon, she expected to hear the brittle cracking of bones.

Wouldn't Father be fascinated to see a live anaconda? But no, what was she thinking? He cared deeply for her and would be horrified. Her unexpected insight upset her almost as much as her grisly predicament. She'd gotten it all wrong.

What if she had misjudged Bramford, too?

Eden didn't know which hurt worse, the searing pain that spread through her body or the deep feelings of regret. The memory of Bramford's open gaze flashed in her mind. Why had she ruined their connection by calling for Rebecca? Now she would never have the chance to show him what was in her heart.

At least she would leave this earth knowing she had experienced one true thing in her life.

The monster jerked Eden sideways, draging her towards the river. The short journey would stall the constriction process—a reprieve of maybe a minute. Hopefully, she would drown as soon as she hit the water. *Small mercies.*

Black inkiness dripped behind her eyes. She couldn't fight the paralyzing slide into darkness any longer.

Sleep, Eden.

Then, for some reason, the anaconda stopped moving. In a daze, Eden forced her eyes open. The snake's head pointed towards the jungle. What was it waiting for?

Eden heard feverish birdcalls in the distance. They bounced closer and closer, as if the birds passed a baton of terror down the jungle route. Dozens of small animals scampered in the undergrowth. The ground began to shake. Dear Earth, something was coming.

Eden didn't know what to wish for.

A flock of green parrots ringed the trees, crying out like spectators in a coliseum. Just then a furious roar ripped through the air. Eden's heart leapt as an awesome gladiator burst into view: the Jaguar Man.

He had come for her. *I'm watching you, Eden.*

Bramford sprang forward, snarling. His feral eyes flared. His brow pressed in fierce concentration. His muscles rippled, as he attacked the anaconda faster than her dulled senses could follow.

Oh, he was magnificent.

The anaconda whipped its long tail into an upright S shape, flinging Eden free. She landed in the water and slapped at the surface, fighting to stay afloat. Her rubbery limbs tingled pins and needles as oxygen flowed back into them. She could barely breathe from the pain in her lungs. Her feet paddled fast, but once again, the dress weighed her down.

Through slashes of water and swirling sand, Eden caught scenes of a gruesome battle. Intertwined, the Giant Reptile and Jaguar Man fought to the death. The anaconda's tail beat the water like a drummer keeping time as it writhed and twisted. Green and brown scales glistened in spots of sunlight. Bramford held it by its throat with one hand while he pummeled the top of its head with the other. The snake's snapping jaw lunged for his heart.

"No!" Eden screamed.

Bramford shot her a look and, in that second, lost his advantage. The enraged anaconda caught his free hand in its teeth. Bramford doubled over with a sick roar. She felt his pain as if it were her own.

Your fault—do something, Eden!

She locked her limbs round the snake's long tail when it came down beside her. The snake dunked her underwater then swung her high into the air. Her heart was in her throat, but she dug her nails into the leathery skin and held tight.

Too briefly, she locked eyes with Bramford and felt the thrill of a powerful connection. She wasn't imagining it. They were allies, if only in their fight to survive.

Bramford also seemed to gain strength from their new-found bond. The brilliant fury of his roar electrified the air. Eden watched in amazement as he thrust his captured arm deeper into his foe's jaws. Only man wielded such counterintuitive intelligence, she thought proudly.

And it worked.

The anaconda flung open its jaws with a gagging sound. Bramford was free. In a blur, he butted his head between the snake's eyes and it fell into a heap. Its thrashing tail grew still. The reptilian giant fell into the river, pulling Eden down with it.

Her chin jutted above the water, as she took one last look at her savior. Crumbled on the shore, he bent over his wounded arm, oblivious to her distress. She sputtered a small squeal, water seeping into her mouth. The river closed around her, shutting off the world with a deafening sound.

Eden struggled to reach the surface but it kept moving farther away. With a sickening feeling, she realized she was caught under the dead snake, sinking towards a watery grave.

Her heart pleaded. *Bramford, help.* Was it her growing intuition or the certainty of their connection that told Eden he had heard her?

And yet, quiet darkness closed around her. She couldn't breathe. Her mind grew numb. This is it, she thought, as the world disappeared in a soft, quiet rush.

From far away, Eden registered something grabbing hold of her. Then a bewildering rush of air hit her face. She wondered at the sound of her name.

Bramford was calling her, she realized.

"Eden! Wake up, Eden!"

She felt a hard slap against her cheek. Solid ground beneath her. Her body, alive. Her eyes blinked open. Bramford pressed his hands onto her stomach, over and over, until she coughed up water.

Her Jaguar Man had saved her once again. Contentment filled her as she pillowed her head against his heaving chest. She breathed in his musky scent and felt a lovely lift, as if a bird were trilling inside the top of her head.

What else did she need in life besides the warmth of his body next to hers? She was done with regrets. From now on, she would follow her heart. In fact, she would forgive the past and start fresh with Ronson Bramford.

Eden licked tiny beads of water that clung to the hairs on his chest with the tip of her tongue. His full-throated rumbling sounded full of yearning. She threw her arms around his neck with a little cry. Pulling her tight against his body, he groaned heavily.

"I'm sorry, Bramford," Eden whispered in his ear. "For everything."

His weary eyes lit up. "I understand."

She smiled at him, and for a long, blissful moment, his warm, open gaze was all for her. Once more, the Real Eden felt truly seen.

Why had she ever wanted to leave this wonderful creature in the first place?

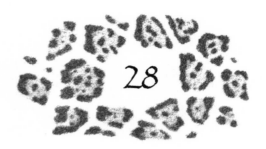

28

EDEN CUDDLED closer to Bramford as a sharp pain knifed into her right side. Woozy, she reeled in his arms.

His burlap voice softened with concern. "Are you all right?"

She shook her head yes, then no. There beside him, she never had felt happier. Still, her body ached all over.

Bramford wasn't in much better shape, Eden realized. His eyes were shot with pain. His left hand, torn and bleeding from the snakebite, hung limp.

For her, he'd risked his life. It made no sense, but it thrilled her all the same.

Her savior crouched over her, examining her ribcage with his good hand. At his touch warmth pooled in her belly.

"Here?" Bramford said, trailing her side.

Eden grimaced. "Uh huh."

"You broke a few ribs. But you'll live."

His gaze traveled down her wet dress. Plastered against her skin, it hid nothing. She felt shy as his eyes devoured her, inch by inch. He licked his lips and reached for the blue bow tied at her breast. Eden held still, though a storm rocked inside of her. His thick fingers brushed against her skin as he fumbled with the ribbon. She titled towards him with a little shiver. Inexplicably, Bramford jerked away, as if burned by a hot flame; his seductive expression turned hostile.

"Where did you get that dress?" he demanded.

Eden shrank back, perplexed. "Don't you recognize it? It's Rebecca's."

He shot to his feet. She had a worm's-eye view of his towering figure. The wet loincloth molded to his hips. Tousled hair fell down his shoulders. Fits of sand clung to the dark skin. Bramford was a wild, angry beast.

"Take it off," he said.

"What?" she said, struggling to sit up.

Eden wondered what triggered the door between them to open, then slam shut. And why had she thought the dress would please such an insensitive brute? Or didn't she look as pretty as Rebecca, after all?

"Take if off," Bramford repeated. "It doesn't belong to you."

She stammered. "But. But I have nothing else to wear."

"There's no one here to see."

Meaning he wouldn't even look?

Eden's temper flared. "When I find Rebecca I'll give it back. Where is she?"

His jaw muscles pulsated. Flinty hardness armored the eyes. Somehow Rebecca seemed to get deeper under his skin even in her absence than Eden did in the here and now. After all that they had shared, why wouldn't he tell Eden the truth? If only she could get him to open up to her.

Bramford growled half-heartedly—more of a grunt, really. She saw that the ferocious battle had weakened him. He turned away, loping towards the river. The tessellated ground, whipped into small dunes, reeked of violence. He picked up something and stood with his back to her for some time, perhaps watching the river meander on its course.

Eden longed for him to look at her like he had before. But no, that wasn't true. She ached for more, only that wasn't possible. Sadly, she recalled her father's warning. *His affection might kill you.*

Bramford returned to her side, though he avoided her searching gaze. He held out a razor-sharp tooth of the anaconda. Was this his attempt at sharing?

"It's horrible," Eden said, stating the obvious.

Naturally, Bramford took a contrary position. "If you choose to look at it that way. I see one of nature's greatest creations. I'm sorry I killed it."

"But it would have killed you. And me."

"Is that so terrible?"

Eden's mouth gaped. Didn't he care for her at all? Then she recalled Maria's fairy tale and decided to give him the benefit of the doubt. *"Coatlicue?* Is that what you mean?"

"That, too," Bramford said, and she caught his disdainful glance at his body, or more likely, at hers.

"You don't believe it's guarding an afterlife, do you? It's no worse killing an anaconda than any other predator." *Like him?* "I mean, it's just a silly myth," she quickly added.

"Is it?"

Again, felt she'd said the wrong thing. But if he wouldn't tell her what was on his mind, how on Great Earth could they ever really communicate?

Bramford abruptly turned and walked to the edge of the forest. His torso rippled as he gathered long, stringy vines with his good arm. His wide shadow tipped behind him like a buttress to a tree. Eden's gaze never left him, as if she feared the warm feeling in her chest might vanish, and maybe the whole world with it.

"We're all connected," he said over his shoulder. "If I'd lost the fight I would have provided fuel for the anaconda. Instead, its tooth becomes my tool. Does it matter?" He snapped the vines with the tooth, as if to prove his point.

"Of course it matters," Eden said. "We have to survive."

He cast a withering glance over his shoulder. "You only think so because you're human."

There, he admitted it. They were different. But the truth burned a hole in her heart.

"You're wrong," she said in a small voice. "You have no idea what I think." *Or how I feel.*

Bramford fixed her with a questioning look. He seemed about to say something, and she waited anxiously. Then he shook his head and turned away.

"Man thinks he's above nature when in fact he's its slave," he said, pulling down two huge leaves from a giant banana tree. "Look at you, Eden. Without walls to enclose you you're afraid of everything. Don't you see? Your fear invited the anaconda to attack. Try to think of yourself on the same plane as the animals in the forest. No better. No worse."

How wrong Bramford was! Only one thing frightened her now. What if he never touched her again?

He dragged the gigantic leaves towards her and, aware of her injuries, set them by her good side. Then he sat down and handed her one end of the vines.

"Hold this tight," he said.

Eden took it, and he began to braid the ropes together with one hand. The warmth from his body reached her like an embrace. She looked away, fighting the pull.

Pinpoints of light flickered like fireflies on the opposite shore. Their fickleness reminded her of Bramford's changing moods. Was there some clue in nature that would help her decipher his strange meanings? Maybe then she could calm this impossible, hammering need for him.

For Earth's sake, he was a beast who could offer her nothing. And yet, her body seemed to have a will of its own. Logic failed in the face of uncontrollable, ridiculous emotions and lusty desires. However, Bramford's only concerns were for the dying earth and fairy tales and animals. She wanted to scream as he calmly worked the braid. Some antenna he had.

"The more man ruins the planet, the sicker he becomes," he went on. "He doesn't even know why he's heartbroken. It's solastalgia—homesickness for the loss of one's habitat. Like the Huaorani." He looked up at her with a soulful expression. "You suffer from solastalgia, Eden, whether you know it or not."

No, something much worse than that broke her heart. But she couldn't tell him. She simply stared at him, wondering if this was the same man who once had wasted precious resources and belittled the loss of her dog. Maybe Bramford really had become a shaman.

Eden flinched as he leaned over her with the finished rope. When she realized he intended to bandage it around her ribs, she regretted her reaction. Why hadn't he just said so?

Bramford looked wounded. "Do you think I'd hurt you?"

"Sorry," she mumbled.

The observation that only recently he'd imprisoned her caught in her throat. She swallowed it because she couldn't bear his sad expression.

She let him tie the rope around her, thrilling to the touch of his hands. A thin cough sputtered from her like a dying flame as he knotted it at her side.

Bramford gave her a searching look. Once more, it seemed he wanted to say something.

"What is it?" Eden asked.

Again, for no clear reason, a door seemed to close shut.

"Hold on," he said, lifting her gently.

She put her arms around his neck and pulled close. He stood still, his sizzling green eyes on her. A deep, primal groan came out of him that made her heart spin.

"Lay still," Bramford said, setting her on top of one of the giant leaves.

Eden heard her voice through a gauzy filter. "But for how long?"

"A day, maybe two."

"Here?"

"Yes."

"And what, sleep in the jungle? That's impossible."

"Nothing is impossible, Eden."

If only that were true.

At least, Bramford would be there to protect her while she recuperated.

"What about your arm?" she said. "It'll get infected."

"Just rest," he said, and walked away.

Eden watched him head downriver, hypnotized by the powerful movements of his hips and shoulders. Long, tubular orange canna lilies brushed against his torso, like vibrant women luring him into the forest. It hurt just to look at him.

An explosion of bird cries popped in the direction he'd taken. Eden marveled at the jungle's built-in warning system—*the Jaguar Man is coming.*

Soon the only trace of Bramford was the coarse scent that clung to her skin and filled her with deep longing.

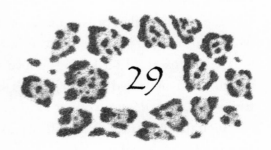

29

EDEN LAY rigid on the huge leaf, alert to every sound and movement in the jungle. The dappled light had thinned and angled west. From the passage of the shadows, she guessed Bramford had been gone at least two hours.

Panic clawed at her, as she wondered if she'd misunderstood him. *A day, maybe two.* She only had assumed he would stay with her. But what if he planned on leaving her alone? Why couldn't the beast ever say what he meant?

Eden jerked her head at a loud splash in the river. A pretty, little rainbow fish leapt into the air, its tail flailing in vain against gravity. The frenzied attack of piranha fish cut short its escape. They diced the luckless prey, their scales flashing. Her stomach turned as blood fanned across the water.

It was evolution, her father would say. *Pygocentrus piraya* represented the water police that killed off the weak, making room for the strong. She nervously scanned the ring of forest, hoping she wouldn't be nature's next victim.

Now, a whistling sound behind a gumbo limbo tree startled her. She twisted towards it, a terrible ache in her side, and squinted at the waxy trunk. Cold fear iced her spine as the sound moved closer. Pure instinct told her there was another human there.

"Bramford?" she said in a thin, wavering voice.

No one answered.

Everywhere Eden looked she felt hungry eyes staring at her, closing in on her. The hysterical crescendo of a laughing falcon rippled in the air. She couldn't fight the feeling, however illogical, that the evil *Herpetotheres cachinnans* mocked her plight.

Please, protect me, Mother Earth.

Eden promised to be good. She'd heed good advice, even Bramford's. Wait and see—always, she swore.

Something upstream caught her eye, and she did a double take. Bramford seemed to materialize from out of the shadows, in the opposite direction from where he'd left. Relief, and then anger washed over her. He hadn't even bothered to call out to her.

Her shrill voice lit into him, as he approached. "For Earth's sake, Bramford. Why didn't you tell me you'd be back? Or did you enjoy scaring me?"

He stood his ground in front of Eden and grunted. In his good hand, he cupped a bunch of leaves and nuts and berries. A thick, woody vine trailed over his shoulder. Bruising eyes bore into her.

One minute he was a pussycat, then, for no reason at all, he slayed her with just a look. She let loose a torrent of emotions, too agitated even to feel the pain of her heaving chest.

"I don't know why you bothered to save me in the first place, if you were going to leave me here to die. There are *things* everywhere; things that want to kill me. Just now, I heard someone." She wagged a finger. "Right there—"

Without warning Bramford pounced on her, scattering

his pickings into the air. Eden flattened her back against the leaf and screamed. He knelt over her, his weight supported on one arm. His loincloth brushed against the top of her thighs. His irresistible scent shot like a hot arrow through her galloping heart.

Eden yearned to caress his savage face but feared he might hit her. From a lifetime of habit she knew what to do.

"I'm sorry, sir," she began, speaking in the flat, unthreatening tones of a Pearl. But she had to reach for the right note, as if it was packed away on a shelf. She hung her head on her chest as she continued. "I didn't mean to upset you. I only wanted—"

"No!" Bramford said.

"I said, I'm sorry."

"Why? I left you here without explanation. You have a right to complain. Go ahead. Attack, don't whimper."

"You mean you wanted to teach me a lesson? Is that it?"

He cocked his head, as if a good idea had struck him. "It's certainly one you could learn."

The bastard hadn't changed one bit.

"How could you leave me defenseless here?" she said.

Bramford sat back on his haunches and heaved a weary sigh. "Did anything bother you, Eden? Even come close? Anything at all?"

She had to admit nothing had. Not even a rodent had scurried near. In fact, now that she thought about it, a protective bubble seemed to exist around her.

He arched an eyebrow. "Well?"

"No," she said, evenly. "But that doesn't mean something couldn't have attacked."

Bramford took a frustrated swipe at the sand, spraying the edge of her leafy pad.

"Why can't you understand?" he said. "The jungle isn't chaotic. Order exists here. You just don't recognize it. Don't you realize that I marked you with my scent when we laid together so that nothing would attack you?"

The tender closeness—a survival technique. Nothing more? An icy feeling stabbed her heart. She'd never let him see the Real Eden again. Never.

"I see," she said, quietly.

Bramford frowned. "You sound different."

"Do I?'

"If you trusted me you would understand."

Eden laughed bitterly.

"What's so funny?"

"Nothing." *Just that I'd never trust someone so cruel.*

She watched the scribbled line of shade slide over the opposite embankment, for once, dreading the coming night. She wished she were anywhere else in the world other than stuck here with him. Bramford grumbled, and she guessed he felt the same.

He waded into the river and plucked out a giant Amazon water lily. Eden noticed that the enormous, foot-long white flowers, which during the day lay huddled like baby Pearls, began opening to the night. She winced as Bramford tore off the flower and tossed it over his shoulder. He probably wished he could be just as easily rid of her.

He gathered the nuts and berries he'd dropped, placing them onto the large, flat lily pad.

"Eat," he said, setting it down in front of her.

Eden kicked away the pad. "Don't tell me what to do."

His hand snaked out and caught her ankle. Hot, burning signals traveled up her legs, exploding in her brain. Furious, she threw sand at him. A satisfied smile spread across his arrogant face.

She simply hated him.

"Good, you're angry," Bramford said. "You can't survive in the jungle without anger."

"I don't want to be in the jungle," Eden hissed.

"You want to survive, don't you?"

"That's a stupid question."

"Is it? As far as I can tell you invite danger. You don't eat, you walk alone in the jungle." He narrowed his gaze at her and spoke pointedly. "And you take up with dangerous men."

Eden's hand shot out, and she slapped him before she could stop herself. His emerald eyes grew cold and, beneath the blank façade, she detected simmering rage. He drew the back of his hand across his cheek.

"Don't push me, Eden."

"It was one man," she protested. "And I told you I didn't know about Jamal's plans."

"Didn't you?"

Eden hesitated, recalling her ex-boyfriend's wicked grin. His treachery was plain to see, if only she'd dared to look.

"I thought so," Bramford said.

"You thought wrong," she said. "You don't understand anything."

"When you get to where I am you'll understand a lot more than you could ever imagine."

"Why on Holy Earth would I want to be like you?"

Bramford's face went blank. Eden saw that she had hurt him. Well, he deserved it. Still, she felt a lump in her chest.

Cold as stone, he moved away. She pretended great interest in a Brazil nut while stealing glances at him. He piled branches and twigs a few feet in front of the leafy pads. Then he started to rub a stick against a small rock with blinding speed. To her surprise, a small flame sparked. Building a fire, she realized with delight.

Bramford looked at her, beaming. Eden smiled back. Then, as if he remembered who she was, his enthusiasm quickly waned.

Why was he so difficult?

She wondered if the scene had looked similar eons ago when the first clever creature had discovered fire. Perhaps he also had showed off for his mate. *Look what I've done.* And had that girl fluttered with amazement? Maybe she, too, had regretted a thoughtless remark.

Of course that trailblazing pair had been two of a kind. While she and Bramford could never mate.

He hunkered over the woodpile, fanning the growing fire. The flickering light played over his feline cheekbones and rugged chin. Eden told herself to look away. Unable to resist, she traced the lines of his glowing body. And felt her heart do a little flip.

"You'll have to tend the fire when I'm gone," Bramford said, rigging a trestle over the fire.

"Where are you going now," she said worriedly.

"The *bejuco de oro* will carry me far away. Don't worry. I'll be right here—at least, my body will be. But my spirit will depart. It's the only way to tolerate the pain. The herbs have to be strong to clean out the poison."

He hung a gourd on the trestle. Piece by piece, he added bits of the woody vine as well as the leaves he'd foraged.

Eden recalled Maria's prophetic words as he continued speaking. "Only the shaman drank the *bejuco de oro* in special ceremonies long ago. It allowed him to see far ahead so he could protect the people. They called him *El Tigre* because his spirit flew with the speed of a jaguar." Already, Bramford sounded far away as he added, "It's the next step for me."

He stared into the gourd, his expression growing anxious. Had he seen something ominous in the future? Of course, that was impossible.

Again, his mood abruptly changed. He looked at her, almost grinning.

"You'll have to hold the fort, partner," he said with a cowboy drawl.

Partner? Like a mate. Even if it wasn't possible, Eden liked the sound of it.

"But what can I do?" she said.

"A lot more than you think."

"When will you—your spirit—return?"

A ribbon of moonlight fell across Bramford's face, as he searched the starry sky. He looked devilish, she thought, and achingly handsome.

"By dawn, I'll be back," he said, though he sounded hesitant. "No matter what happens to me, don't be afraid."

Dear Earth. Eden realized she'd be left alone all night with his lifeless body. How would she ever hold the fort against snapping, hungry creatures? Even if he had marked

her with his scent, predators certainly would sense his help-
lessness—and hers.

"You can't do this, Bramford."

"If I don't, I'll die. Is that what you want?"

Her heart protested, *never.* Why couldn't she just say it?

Instead, she stammered. "But, don't you see? What if it's
dangerous?"

Bramford looked her dead in the eye. "Oh, it'll be dangerous, Eden. You can count on that."

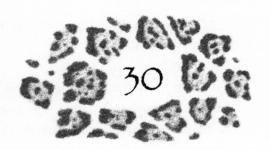

30

WITH DREAMY eyes Eden watched Bramford stir his herbal concoction over the fire. She breathed in the pleasing smell of wood smoke that mingled in the night air with the heady perfume of the water lilies. Moonlight trickled down from an ebony sky, casting a mellow glow upon their little camp. Twinkling stars, aligned in ancient patterns, reminded her of the cool indifference of time.

Her old life in the tunnels with the ever-present voice in her head and the dark coating that fit like a second skin seemed nothing more than a bad dream. Had it really happened? Only the present felt real, and comforting. Somehow, Eden believed she and Bramford always had been together in the jungle—how had he put it—as partners.

Attuned to him, she sensed the anxiety hunkering behind his impassive face. Soon he would head into battle again. *No matter what happens to me, don't be afraid.* Was he kidding?

Bramford leaned the stirring stick against the trestle and walked over to her. Angry red streaks zigzagged down his swollen arm, like just accusations of her stupidity. Eden held still, her nerves on fire, as he kneeled beside her.

His touch electrified her, as he slid one arm around her. Perhaps it was simply easier to hold her since he only had one good hand to retie the knot at her side. In any case, she was happy for an excuse to lean against his warm, bare chest.

"How's the pain?" he said.

She put on a brave face. "It only hurts when I breathe."

"Take shallow breaths."

"I am." *Except when you look right through me.*

He'd finished with the bindings and yet, he lingered. A soft but powerful sound like a babbling brook rolled out of him. It both excited her and swept her into a place of deep contentment. Why couldn't it always be like this?

She was on the verge of asking Bramford that very question when he pulled away.

There was a hitch in his voice as he said, "The *bejuco de oro* is calling me. Are you ready, Eden?"

"Do I look like I'm ready?"

"Yes, you are. Even if you don't know it."

She shrugged. "It's up to you, anyway."

"Only if you choose to give away your power. If you know your place here then your strength will equal mine."

"You can't be serious."

"Listen carefully to what I tell you," Bramford said, his tone emphatic. "Even now, the herbs may speak through me. The *bejuco de oro* will say things to test me. And you."

"But I'm not part of this."

"You're here for a reason. Try to understand."

"I'm only here because you kidnapped me." It was a fact, though for once Eden presented it without malice.

"But you came along, didn't you?" he said, with equal matter-of-factness.

"I had no choice," she said softly.

He looked off into the distance as he spoke. "In everything we do there's always a choice. We can choose to see ourselves as victims of circumstance. But when we act beyond our personal needs we become part of something greater. The choice is ours."

Eden gave him a blank stare. Riddles, she thought. As mystifying as love.

Bramford shook his head, as if to say, *I tried.*

Her pulse raced, as she watched him lift the gourd from the trestle. *Here we go.*

He returned to her side, his hold on the medicine reverential. When he set the gourd on the ground between them, Eden peered inside at an unappetizing dark brown watery soup, surprisingly odorless.

Bramford settled onto the other giant banana leaf, his wounded arm away from her, so that their injuries were like damaged bookends. He closed his eyes and blew out a slow, deep breath that rattled the air. Without a single word of encouragement or even so much as, "see you in the morning," he took one long swallow.

Immediately, he began to shake. The empty gourd slipped from his grasp. Eden gasped, as he doubled over with an agonizing moan. Then he lurched like a drunkard to the bushes, where she heard him retching.

Good Earth.

She snapped as soon as Bramford wobbled back into view. "What kind of medicine is this?"

Swaying, he collapsed beside her. By the flickering light she saw his glassy eyes, his face, taut and sweaty.

"Bramford?"

He didn't seem to register her voice. He simply stared into space, like a dead man. She called his name again. Only the crackly fire and the bubbly, laughing hoot of a tropical screech owl peppered the night.

Eden nearly shouted. "You're scaring me. Please, say something!"

Still, Bramford didn't respond.

She poked his shoulder, tentatively at first, then with a little shove. At least his body felt warm so she knew he wasn't dead. And yet, he seemed as far away from her as the world was from their lonely encampment. Had the spirit of *El Tigre* really flown away as Bramford had predicted?

Her eyes traveled over his magnificent, inert form. She would have laughed at the irony if she weren't so scared. The helpless Pearl guarded the Jaguar Man.

Till dawn, he'd said. Eden hoped she would last that long.

She settled back, her eyes fixed on her charge. From time to time his face twisted, as if his thoughts fought to escape. An occasional twitch of limb or weird moan startled her.

In a short while, Bramford began making strange, indecipherable sounds. Perhaps it was a shamanistic language. His brow furrowed before he slipped back into his silent world.

The snap of the fire and the buzz of insects grew loud around her. Her fears loomed large in her mind, as the night wore on. What if Bramford's spirit never returned to earth? What if the great *Coatlicue* killed him in revenge for the anaconda's death? And sent him back as one of those ugly piggy tapirs that her father had mentioned?

For Earth's sake, she sounded as superstitious as the Huaorani. *Think logically, Eden.*

She wondered if she called Bramford by his first name, would he respond? She wouldn't have dared before—that implied deep intimacy. But hadn't he called her 'partner'?

Eden hovered close, speaking gently. "Ronson? Ronson, please talk to me."

She thought she saw his eyelids flutter. But no, his spirit stayed away.

Resigned to wait, she lay next to him with a weary sigh. Overhead, the stark beauty of the sky filled her with unbearable longing. Why did true beauty do that?

Slowly, she reached for Bramford's hand and laced her fingers through his. He wouldn't even notice. The warmth of his touch comforted her. And there was something else—her hand belonged in his, even if his was paw-like.

To her surprise, Bramford squeezed her hand, as if he were trying to communicate. He rolled over to face her, the catlike eyes insistent.

"Please, don't go," he said, though Eden hardly recognized the angst-ridden voice.

"What?" she said.

"Promise you won't leave me."

Bewildered, Eden replied. "Of course not."

"Say it."

"Okay. I promise I won't leave."

"But you did," Bramford said, his face lined with pain. "You deceived me."

A heavy knot of guilt tightened around Eden's heart. Could he have confirmed in his altered state that she had betrayed him to Jamal?

"I didn't mean to hurt anyone," she said. "I only wanted to survive."

"But you knew I would protect you."

For a while, perhaps. But once her father had finished his work, Bramford would have cut loose the Newman family.

"We had no guarantees. You can't deny that, Ronson."

"How could you doubt me? Do you think I would ever let anything happen to him? I'd give my life for him."

"Really?" *For a Pearl?*

"You don't understand how important he is to me."

"I guess not."

"Because you're still afraid," Bramford said, gently. "Tell me why."

"Look at me. I'm…" Did she have to say it? "I'm not strong like you."

"But I'm teaching you and you've made good progress."

"You can't understand what it's like for me or him."

"I realize that now," he said, regretfully. "I've suffered, but I'm better for it. I'm sorry I hurt you. Both of you."

Tears sprang to her eyes. "I'm sorry, too."

Bramford caressed her cheek. "I didn't think I could forgive you, but I have. I come to you with an open heart." He paused, his sad eyes begging. "Can you forgive me?"

"Yes. I've already forgiven you, Ronson." And it was true, Eden realized. "But why did you bring us here?"

"I had no choice," he said, becoming agitated. "They would have taken him."

"Maybe, but he'll die here."

"Don't you see?" His face glowed feverishly; his voice grew loud. "I laid out a precise plan. If you had trusted me you would have understood. My only goal was to protect you from The Heat—both of you. But you were susceptible to

the FFP and gave in to your fears." Sadness seemed to flicker
across his face as he added, "If only you'd waited."

Eden grasped for understanding. "You did it all for us?"

"For who else?" Bramford said.

"Not for power?"

"What is power to me without love?"

Love? The word exploded inside of Eden. Was it possible
that Bramford loved her?

"Is that why you risked being the test subject?" she asked.

"Time was running out," he said. "They already knew
my secret."

Eden recalled his well-timed arrival at the Moon Dance.
"You tried to stop them from getting to me?"

"Of course."

It all made perfect sense. The startled look in Bramford's
eye when they first met. He was attracted to her from the
beginning, though her stupid prejudices against her own kind
hadn't allowed for that possibility.

She smiled at him.

"Now do you understand?" Bramford said.

"You...?" Eden could hardly say it. "You love me?"

"I've proven my feelings."

Just like that, the whole cock-eyed world righted itself.
For Earth's sake, this crazy, heart-shaking feeling was a thing
called love. Aunt Emily was right, after all.

Wild Nights! Wild Nights!
Were I with thee,
Wild Nights should be
Our luxury!

Futile the winds
To a heart in port,—
Done with the compass,
Done with the chart.

Rowing in Eden!
Ah! the Sea!
Might I but moor
To-night in thee!

"Oh, Ronson," Eden murmured as she fell into his arms.

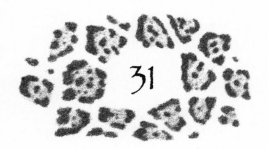

31

EDEN SOFTLY moaned as Bramford nuzzled her neck. His bare chest grew hot to the touch, his breathing heavy. His lips found hers, teasingly at first. Then he pressed harder, kissing her with hungry passion. She wanted this kiss to last forever.

She caught her breath as he whispered. "My mate."

Really?

But she didn't question him, not now. She simply reveled in the hot, sensuous sensations that danced in her body.

Bramford tipped up her chin, gently forcing her to meet his gaze. He smoothed her tangled hair away from her face and smiled at her. Just like in her dream. But this was real, she told herself. Wasn't it?

"I never thought I would see this day," he said.

"I wish I'd understood," Eden said, dumbfounded but delirious. "Couldn't you have given me a hint?"

Bramford looked puzzled. "You were unreachable."

She sadly recalled her blind prejudices and foolish anger. "I guess I was."

"Nothing can separate us now."

Nothing. Not ever. That was what Eden believed. Until his next words knocked the wind right out of her.

"Thank you for coming back, Rebecca."

"What?" She shook her head, hoping she'd heard wrong. "What did you say?"

"I'm glad you changed your mind."

Powerful Planet Earth, what kind of sick joke was this? And yet, Bramford looked so sincere. Eden braced a hand on his chest to steady the world, which had begun to reel.

"And, who am I?" she said.

"My mate, Rebecca," he replied, with just a hint of irritation. "Who else could you be?"

"And you funded the research to save *me* from The Heat? For *me* you became the test subject?" Eden gulped for air. "And you love *me*, Rebecca?"

"Of course."

A birdlike shriek flew out of her. His love wasn't meant for her, but the girl she resembled. She struggled to get away but he clung to her.

"Rebecca, what's wrong?"

Eden flailed against his chest. "Let me go!"

"I thought you understood."

She bit his shoulder, drawing blood. Confusion rushed over Bramford, as he stared at the spot. He slumped to the ground, his head weaving like a drunkard's. Then his warning came back to Eden like a slap in the face. *The bejuco de oro will say things to test me. And you.*

Even without mind-bending herbs it was easy to mistake her for Rebecca. The girl's dress and perfume must have added to the confusion. Drug-addled Bramford believed he was with his mate, either in the past or present.

The joy Eden had experienced only minutes ago disap-

peared as she saw her relationship with Bramford in yet another light. Yes, he had reacted to her uncanny resemblance
to Rebecca right from the start. Only he had resented her
for it because he loved Rebecca; that much was clear. Even
worse, he had never seen the Real Eden, not once. Whenever
he looked in her eyes, he only thought of his real mate.

For Earth's sake, was it Eden's fate to be attracted to men
who wanted a different girl?

Well, if the herbs could test her, she also could test Bramford. She would capitalize on his confusion to discover the
truth about Rebecca. Then, like a scorpion, she would sting
him with it. She would balance out this cruel equation, his
suffering for hers.

She leaned forward and rubbed his arm with long, gentle
strokes. "I'm sorry, Ronson," she said, softly. "I want to understand what happened."

Bramford looked at her expectantly. "Really, Rebecca?"

"Please, tell me."

"I tried to reach you. But I was too late. You'd already
gone to them."

"To who?"

"Don't pretend you don't know." He clenched his fist,
and Eden slowly sat back. "The FFP used you to get to me. I
warned you, but you laughed and said I was paranoid."

"How could they get to you?"

"You must know that you and I made a terrible mistake."

"By mating?" Eden asked.

"No," Bramford replied, then hung his head. "Yes."

"How can I trust you if you won't tell me the truth?"

"We deceived each other, that's the truth." He scrubbed

his face with his good hand, as if he could wash away the
sorrow etched there. "If I had discovered your lies, I never
would have chosen you. But what were the odds?" He gave
her a pleading look. "Tell me, Rebecca, did the FFP hire you
for the job? Did you ever care for me?"

It would have been so easy to crush him. But not yet,
Eden decided. *First, his secrets, then make him suffer.*

"You know I care, Ronson. Our kiss..." Her voice broke.
She had to stuff her feelings down into the pit of her stomach
to continue. "They tricked me. I wish I hadn't listened to
them. I'm sorry, but deep down I couldn't believe you really
wanted me."

His attention seemed to flicker in and out of the present.
From nearby, the quick rattling of a black guan sent a cold
shiver up Eden's spine. The *Chamaepetes unicolor's* ominous
birdcall sounded like a warning. *Be careful, you're playing a
deadly game.*

But what more did she have to lose?

"You're lying," Bramford finally said, the accusation cool
and quiet. "You lied to me from the start. They chose you for
the job. You only pretended to care."

He closed his eyes briefly, and Eden saw a change in his
expression—acceptance, perhaps.

"I guess I always knew I couldn't trust you," he went on.
"Thank Earth, I protected Shen. Only a promise to my wise
father stopped me from answering your persistent questions.
If the FFP knew Shen was my half-brother, they would have
used him against me, too."

Shen Bramford? So that explained his devotion.

Steeliness seeped back into Bramford as he continued,

"When our son was born, the truth was plain to see. But how could I let him pay for our crimes?"

Eden's head spun. "You—I mean—we have a child?"

"You'd like to forget about him, wouldn't you, Rebecca? I'm sorry to say I once felt the same way." He pummeled the ground. "But what were the odds?"

"Odds of what?"

"Having a child with someone like you. Our son, Logan. A terrible mistake." He stared at her with haunted, vacant eyes. "You were very clever, Rebecca. You begged me to go back home, swore you needed to see your dying father. Even then, you had planned your escape. If I had given you our position here, you would have let them destroy us and never shed a tear."

In a flash, Bramford pinned her down. "Admit it!"

"I, uh..."

"No more lies!"

Eden trembled underneath him. He just might kill her, thinking she was his traitorous mate.

"It was for the money, wasn't it?" he said. "You abandoned me and your son—*my son*—for a bunch of worthless uni-credits."

"They tricked me," she repeated, grasping at straws.

Bramford nipped her neck, the sting sharp. He pressed his body hard against her. Eden could hardly breathe. Tortured, groaning sounds came out of him. Her screams only seemed to incite him.

Desperate, she spoke to him as she had when she worked for him, hoping to undo the dangerous spell she'd cast.

"Mr. Bramford, sir!"

There was a brief halt. Then he roared, and she heard her dress rip.

"Stop, sir!" Eden cried louder. "Please, stop!"

He grew still and grunted, as if to say, *What on Earth?* Rising to his feet, he stood over her with a puzzled look. The dark night and the crackling fire and the devastating heartache pressed in on Eden. She knew she should quit. But curiosity won out.

She propped herself up on her elbows. "What happened to our son, Ronson?"

Once again, Bramford seemed eager to talk to Rebecca. In fact, he seemed relieved to discuss the past. It wasn't the kind of sharing Eden had imagined, but it was a start.

He began to pace in front of her, talking fast. "When they offered to return you for a price, I suspected they intended to double-cross you. I was angry but willing to forgive, for Logan's sake. After all, the boy needed a mother."

"I came back to you then?"

His step faltered. "The price. Too high. They demanded our son in exchange for you. When I didn't agree—how could I—they killed you."

Rebecca, dead?

Bramford stumbled to his knees. "Because of my lies, you and Logan suffered."

"What lies?" Eden said.

"The same as yours." He beat his chest, over and over, the wretched sounds echoing in the night. "This is my punishment. Look at me, now. I'm a beast."

He writhed on the ground, his eyes rolled back in his head like a man possessed by evil spirits. Again, he made babbling sounds. Eden guessed that his spirit had fled, just like she wished she could. And yet, she dragged herself beside him, worried he might kill himself in his hallucinatory state.

"Stop it! Please, Bramford, don't do this."

But the frenzied fight with his inner demons raged on. At least he couldn't see her shame and humiliation.

What a pair of lonely, unloved freaks. Neither one of them belonged anywhere on this hopeless planet.

Numb with exhaustion, Eden limped to the dying fire and added several sticks. Its warmth enveloped her, reminding her of their passionate embrace. A hand flew to her lips, where the bruising feel of his kiss still lingered. Tears streamed down her face—pathetic tears, useless feelings for a man who loved someone else. Disgusted, Eden wiped her mouth on the dress. She wanted to rip the ugly thing to pieces.

Damn Bramford for picking the lock on her heart. Damn the hunger his kiss had awoken in her. And damn that conniving, selfish bitch, Rebecca.

Love? If it did exist, it hurt like Bleeding Earth.

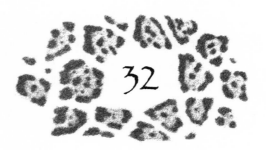

32

THE SLOW, sweet whistle of the quail-like tinamous floated in the air, teasing Eden from a fitful sleep. She peeked at the hazy dawn, surprised to find herself lying on the ground. Then the sight of the smoldering fire brought back memories of her torturous night with Bramford, as well as a bitter, broken heart.

A sharp movement among the trees nearby startled her. She jerked her head towards what sounded like running steps. Her heart beat high in her chest; a scream wedged there. Only the surprise of Bramford, spooned beside her, calmed her.

His chest and hips rounded her like a protective mantle. A heavy arm was slung over her waist. The warmth he generated cushioned the cold, dewy ground. Eden nestled into his embrace—only for the warmth, she told herself. He softly groaned, pulling her closer. His lips tickled the top of her head. But the pleasurable feelings rubbed like salt thrown on a wound.

Probably dreaming of Rebecca.

Eden shut her eyes tight. Couldn't she pretend, just for a moment, that he wanted her? But the fantasy felt hollow, and only deepened her despair. Father was right all along: better to catalog the chaos than to feel it.

Bramford quietly rose and lumbered to the fire. She ate several berries, wondering if he remembered their stolen embrace. He kicked sand over the ashes, then he scanned the area, as if reading the daily news. His gaze passed over Eden just like any other part of the landscape.

Nothing more.

His swollen hand had shrunk overnight to normal size— normal for a beast, anyway. The redness was barely visible. She decided she had underestimated the power of the herbs. Bramford seemed nonplused by the miraculous healing.

Too distracted by thoughts of Rebecca.

Eden blew out a hot breath. At once she began to cough, doubled over from the pain in her ribs. Still, he ignored her. She might be unlovable, but she was tired of being invisible.

"Hey," she called to Bramford. "Remember me? I'm Eden, by the way, not your dead mate, Rebecca."

Hard eyes cut over to her. "What do you know about that?"

She saw that his spirit had returned. At least he wouldn't kill her. Though he probably wouldn't kiss her, either.

"I know you betrayed her and your son. Wait a minute—" Eden realized her mistake. "Your son Logan is hidden in the gated hut, isn't he?"

Bramford's jaw muscle began to twitch. "I'm warning you. It's none of your business."

"That's no way to treat a child."

"You don't understand."

"I understand how cruel you are."

He shook with rage, his weight sunk low. "I didn't know it was all a lie."

Go ahead, Eden thought. *Rip my body apart—my heart is already in pieces.*

Bramford rushed towards her, but then his shoulders sagged. "Let's go home," he said wearily.

"Home?" Even as Eden said it she regretted the sarcastic tone.

"To the compound."

He gently picked her up, and she naturally reached her arms around his neck. After their stolen intimacy, however, she felt uncomfortable and quickly crossed her arms over her chest. He shot her a questioning look, but she dropped a blank mask into place. If only she had never felt the hot press of his lips against hers.

She just couldn't think about that anymore.

She forced herself to concentrate on the sounds and smells of the jungle, as he carried her deep within its shadowy folds. The dank smell of earth and constant chatter of primates and cacophony of birdsong rose up around her like a crushing wall.

And yet, as the miles passed, her natural curiosity began to override her fears. When the air thickened with dampness and her skin turned clammy, she suspected a coming storm.

"Is it going to rain?" Eden asked, not quite trusting her budding instincts.

"Is it?" Bramford replied.

"Yes. I think so."

"Let me know when you're sure."

He added a dismissive grunt and she wondered why she had bothered to mention it. His encouraging words came back to taunt her, words meant for Rebecca. *But I'm teaching you and you've made good progress.* He really didn't care whether or not Eden opened her mind.

A swarm of *Callicore cynosura* butterflies flitted past, their hypnotic black and white markings as fantastical as having imagined that Bramford loved her. She stole a glance at him and caught her breath. A pale ribbon of morning light shone on the rugged, feline face, so at odds with the human intelligence that peered through his captivating eyes. Would she ever know him?

Perhaps if Eden solved the mystery of the FFP's hold over Rebecca, she would understand Bramford. And if they could talk about it, maybe his mate's ghost would no longer torture him. Would he see the Real Eden then?

When the first drops of rain began to fall, Bramford smiled at her. She smiled back, wanting to believe he thought only of her, though she was more confused by him than ever.

He huddled over her, shielding her face from the storm. His heart drummed against her ear. If Eden were a she-cat, would it beat for her?

By the time they reached the gate, the gloomy day had turned bright and steamy. Once again, Maria waited there. She didn't react to either of their wounds—maybe she had expected that, as well—and simply fell in step beside them.

Eden nervously scanned the compound. An eerie quiet hung over it, as if something boiled just under the surface, waiting to erupt. The thump of her father's crutch broke the silence, startling her. She saw him limp onto the porch. Poor Father. He looked like a frail, little bird. A dying bird.

"Daught," he said, his feeble voice just reaching her.

"Father."

He began to blink, as he took in the braided vines around her chest. He gripped the railing for support, his fearful eyes questioning her.

"A few broken ribs, that's all, doctor," Bramford said, as they brushed past him and entered the hut. "She'll mend. If she doesn't do anything foolish, again." He shot Eden a warning glance.

"You're safe, Daught. That's what matters," her father said, following behind.

Eden looked over Bramford's shoulder, wondering if those were tears in her father's eyes. She never had seen him cry; not even at her mother's death. Like father, like daughter. Why did they have to travel to this primitive place to express any emotion?

This time, Bramford didn't hesitate to carry her towards Rebecca's room. Eden studied him, hoping he would react to his dead mate's portrait with indifference. But his eyes never strayed towards it.

"I guess you're glad to be back," he said, settling Eden onto the bed.

She let out an empty laugh. "It beats sleeping on the cold ground."

"It wasn't cold."

"Not for you, maybe." She tamped down the bittersweet memory of spooning together. "You have thick skin."

At first he stiffened, and appeared anxious to say something.

"Eden..." He broke off as her father limped into the room, along with Maria.

"I'm in your debt, Bramford," he said, collapsing at the end of the bed.

Bramford reached behind his back and handed him the anaconda tooth. "Will this work?"

Excitement sparked in her father's waxen face. He adjusted his glasses and examined the tooth with trembling hands.

"It's fresh," he said. "How did you ever get it?"

"There was a battle."

"Oh, Father, it was—"

Bramford cut her off with a sharp glance. "We fought and I won. That's all."

"What?" Her father sounded like a lost child.

"I told you, she's fine."

"Yes, I'm fine," Eden added, surprised that her father's beastly creation understood his needs better than she.

"Ella está bien." Maria murmured her agreement.

She squatted on the floor, using the sharp end of a bamboo stick to cut a bed sheet into strips. For new bindings, Eden guessed. For an uncomfortable moment, only the tearing of the fabric sounded in the room.

Finally, her father addressed Bramford, his voice wavering. "I never dreamed you'd catch an anaconda. But then I've underestimated your power. Tell me, are you still determined to accelerate the procedure?"

"Yes, I am," Bramford said. "More so than before."

"Then we shall need one more thing. *Panthera onca*. A jaguar. Can you manage?"

"I'll have to go deep into the jungle. It might take several days to find *un tigre*."

Maria gasped. "*Un tigre?*"

"It's important, my dear," Eden's father said. "Besides, what is one more jaguar in the face of such progress?"

The Huaorani woman looked at each of them in turn, her eyes sad and disapproving. Then she dropped her handiwork and quietly left.

"But Father," Eden said. "Isn't that the kind of thinking that got us here? One more tree, one more acre, one more jaguar—they matter." She questioned Bramford too. "What about you and your sorrowful solastalgia? How can *El Tigre* even consider killing a jaguar?"

"I'm a hunted man." His hand swept in front of him with a show of disgust. "What can I do for the Huaorani like this?"

"Perhaps if others like you existed," her father said, as his eyes took on a feverish shine. "A new race of highly adapted human. Then we might reset the clock with you, Bramford, as the first New Man. It's the only way."

"I'm just trying to survive, doctor."

Bramford pinned Eden with his penetrating stare. She wished she could read his mysterious expression. Why did he make her work so hard? And why on Holy Earth did he have to go and kiss her?

Then he turned and headed for the door.

"Wait, don't go!" she cried.

He spun around, his expression as expectant as when he'd believed she was Rebecca. Or was Eden foolish enough to think he really wanted to talk to her instead?

She blustered on. "I'm sorry, but it's all wrong. Don't you see? What will happen to us if you get killed? And what about your son?"

His eyes went flat. "What about him?"

"If you're not concerned for our welfare, at least consider your son's before throwing yourself in the path of a deadly animal."

"I'm no good to him or anyone else now."

You're good to me. But the words wouldn't come.

"Exactly," Bramford said.

He gave her one last, cold look and ran out. Eden's heart sank as he sped by the window. *Selfish beast.*

Her father mused. "I'd say the odds are in the jaguar's favor, although if you factor in Bramford's intelligence—"

"Father, you're talking about a real person, not an experiment."

"I suppose you could look at it that way. Certainly, I'll be more disappointed than anyone should he lose the fight."

"You said he had a chance. For Earth's sake, do you think he'll be killed?"

"But Daught, do you care?"

She snapped at him. "Of course not. I'm just thinking of his son, Logan."

"What? What child is this?"

Eden nodded towards the portrait on the wall. "Rebecca was Bramford's mate, though he claims she's dead. I suspect he's hiding their son in the gated hut." She sketched in the story Bramford had told in his dream-state and puzzled once more over the missing details. "What could the FFP possibly use against him?"

"Hmmm," her father said. "As far as I recall no incriminating data on Bramford was available."

Eden wanted to probe deeper but he struggled to his feet, his exhaustion palpable.

"Wait and see," he added as he shuffled off.

Wait for what?

Bramford's affection undoubtedly would be lethal when he reached full adaptation. No, if Eden ever wanted to feel the burning heat of his kiss, or the strong press of his body, or hear his tender purr, only one way remained.

Adapt?

She laughed out loud. Why lose what little physical appeal she had for someone who loved another? Besides, a real jaguar probably would kill him. She simply couldn't think about Bramford another minute.

And yet, as Eden closed her eyes, the wild feelings he aroused ran through her, as inescapable as the blazing light of day. And the kiss—the memory of their long, burning kiss—brought a moan to her lips.

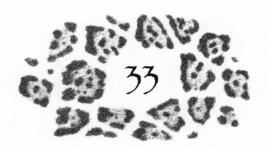

33

EDEN AWOKE the next morning to a startling dream. *I'm speeding through the jungle. Nothing scares me. I'm fearless and free.* It was only a dream. And yet, she had changed, hadn't she?

She no longer flinched from morning's golden light. Even the vast spaces and lack of boundaries intrigued her more than they frightened. And after spending time in the lush jungle, the modern room seemed as garish as makeup on a little girl's face. Or did Rebecca's presence repel her now?

Eden studied the lush painting, which evoked her time with Bramford in the jungle with a bittersweet feeling. Had Rebecca painted it as a ploy to convince him of her sincerity? Despite their strong physical resemblance, Eden now understood that she and Rebecca were as different as night and day. She doubted if her so-called twin ever had wanted to be a brave she-cat.

But I do.

It also struck Eden that if by some crazy circumstances she and Bramford were to mate, their child might look a lot like Rebecca's son. She simply had to meet him. Then, as her eyes fell on the torn window mesh, she thought of the curious spider monkey that had paid her a nocturnal visit or two.

Could it have been a small boy? Logan, perhaps?

He had left a clue, she realized with growing excitement. She gently knelt on the floor, happy to find that the pain in her side had improved. She brushed away the cobwebs under the bed with Maria's bamboo cutter. There, stuck against a bump in the floor, she spied something. She fished it out and examined it by the light of the window.

Why, it was a paintbrush, which must have belonged to Rebecca. That would explain her son's frustration over its loss. Even more, the lost object suggested that, as Eden suspected, Logan had visited her. And he still might be in the gated hut.

How heartless to lock away an innocent child. Had Bramford tried to bully the poor boy when he boxed in the rain? Once more, she puzzled over the fact that the hut opened to the forest. That arrogant bastard probably didn't want anyone to see his son's mixed race.

Eden angled the brush in the window so that it stuck out like a flag, hoping to entice Logan. *Come play, little boy.*

At a soft, gasping sound, she jerked around to find Maria staring. She detected wariness in her eyes, as well as the eerie knowingness she seemed to possess. In fact, she had the weird feeling the Huaorani woman knew what might happen if the boy returned for his toy.

"Logan?" Eden said, fingering the brush.

A sad look came over Maria. She didn't reply but returned to the task of cutting bandages. Her shiny hair closed like silk curtains around her wide face, as she bent forward, and seemed to shut off the possibility of further questioning. Naturally at ease, her bare breasts and stomach pleated against her torso.

Again, Eden's dream of running free flitted through her mind. She tried to imagine herself living like Maria. But the woman's lack of self-consciousness felt out of reach, even dangerous, like swimming or walking in the light.

Eden sat on the edge of the bed, watching the woman's nimble handiwork.

"Maria," she said, pantomiming her question. "How did you know when we would arrive at camp?"

"I talk to you."

Eden shook her head. "But we didn't speak."

Maria swept her hand through the air with a whooshing sound. *"El viento."*

"The wind?"

"Sí."

Love's gentle wind?

"You remind me of my mother, Lily," Eden said, wistfully.

"Lily," Maria repeated, and her face broke into an infectious grin.

They began to giggle, though Eden wondered if they laughed at the same thing. But then again, maybe Maria understood far more than Eden thought. Maybe her mother had, too. And just maybe she could gain some of that same intuitive knowledge.

Maria gently began to wrap a long bandage around Eden's ribs. Eden held up her long tresses, but a lock slipped and caught in the bindings. She couldn't stand the sweaty mess, not for another minute. Once, it had been a small source of pride, but she had hidden behind it. *For long enough.*

"Cut it, please—*por favor,*" Eden said. She touched the ends of Maria's hair then marked the same length on her jaw. "Like yours. Okay?"

The excited gleam in Maria's eye suggested she knew Eden sought more than convenience. She knotted the bandages, then reached for the bamboo cutter. As she held it to Eden's jawline, Carmen and Etelvina burst into the room. At the sight of their mother pointing the sharp instrument at Eden, they stopped short. Etelvina hid behind her sister. Even the delicate *Cymbidium* orchid in Carmen's hair seemed to tremble with fear.

Eden took a deep breath and nodded. "Go ahead."

Maria made the first cut and Eden grabbed her hand as the strands fell to the floor. Long-repressed, painful images of her mother's hair falling out in chunks loomed in her mind. By then, the dark coating only had covered the tips of the red strands, as if her mother's true essence had flooded in before she left.

Breathe, Eden. Stay in the moment. That's what her mother would have said.

Maria made the gentle, calming sound of a breeze, letting her breath rise and fall, over and over. Outside, the ever-changing melodies of the forest reminded Eden that, for the Huaorani, only the present existed. And right now, nothing threatened her but old fears.

If she could stay in this moment and then the next, and the next after that, would she become fearless and free? Perhaps just like in her dream. She had to try. Yes, she admitted, she hoped to be somebody's she-cat. But mostly, she wanted to shed her fear-logged skin.

Calmer now, Eden released Maria's hand. "Go ahead," she repeated. *"Por favor."*

The little girls settled on the floor to watch, their arms wrapped around each other. Snip by snip, the hair cuttings pooled at her feet. She wondered if the children thought it held some potent magic or evil.

Soon, Eden's head grew light; her spirits, frisky. Looking at the growing pile of golden hair, she imagined a bowl of honey, a reverie Aunt Emily might have enjoyed.

> *The pedigree of honey*
> *Does not concern the bee;*
> *A clover, any time, to him*
> *Is aristocracy.*

Maria stepped back to appraise her work when she was done. Eden waited, wondering at the quizzical look on her hairdresser's face. Then Maria offered Carmen the bamboo cutter in exchange for the lavender orchid. The girl seemed happy with the trade. Her mother smiled, as she tucked the *Cymbidium* behind Eden's ear. Its bewitching fragrance drew Eden's lips into a soft smile.

"Tu eres muy bonita," Maria said.

Me, very pretty?

Eden swung her head, delighted by the tickle at her jaw. She felt as naked as when her dark coating first had washed away, but without the fear. More than that, she felt liberated. Maybe there, in that wild place, anything was possible.

Even beauty, Eden.

She studied herself in the hand mirror. Definitely less timid, she decided. If nothing else, she might pass as a tribeswoman.

But not quite.

She held out her long, flowing skirt to Carmen and gestured for her to cut it. The sisters muttered between themselves, deciding. When the older girl stepped forward, Eden had a clear view of Etelvina and caught her breath. The red straps of the backpack were slung over the little girl's shoulders.

That's when Eden remembered the Huaorani principle of exchange. She scooped up the pile of hair and pointed to the bag. Once more, the sisters conferred. Then they nodded, and the exchange was done.

At last, freedom, Eden hoped, shrugging on the pack.

Again, she held out the skirt and Carmen began to cut it. Eden turned around and around until the dress was almost as short as Maria's little flap. Carmen pointed the cutter at the top of her dress, but Eden politely declined her offer. *Not that free.*

The demanding shrieks of the macaw rang out in the air. Its mistresses fled, clutching their golden bounty. Maria quietly left before Eden could thank her.

She laid the backpack beside her on the bed with a heavy sigh. Yes, the Life-Band was there, she confirmed. And yet, it failed to bring her the joyous relief she had expected. From the moment she had been ripped away from home, her only aim had been to return. *Why hesitate now, Eden?*

Thoughts of Bramford produced a dull ache in her chest.

If she left the jungle, she might never see him again. Was that what she really wanted?

Eden gazed out the window at the vibrant forest, imagining him on the hunt. Hungry and dangerous, he would slip through the shadows, his body rippling with energy. Even in deep darkness, he could see and smell his prey. When ready, he would pounce with a bloodthirsty roar. The law of the jungle required that he violently take what he wanted.

She fanned away the heat, wondering if he ever would take her. A lovely blue-vented hummingbird, *Amazilia sophiae*, buzzed up to the paintbrush with a sharp *tsiping* sound. The rapid beat of its sapphire-colored wings seemed to echo the flutter of her heart.

When Bramford returned—he simply had to—he would find a very different girl. Maybe even a wild she-cat.

But what about the Life-Band, Eden?

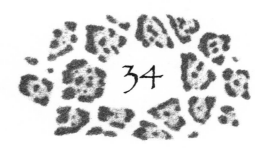

34

"DAUGHT?" EDEN'S father's frail voice floated in from the main room. "Where are you?"

"Coming," Eden answered.

She stashed the backpack under her bed, then thought better of it. What if an animal slipped through the window and took it? She slung it over her shoulders and rushed out.

The sway of her hair against the back of her neck pleased her. The shortened dress moved with ease. How little the world had changed while, there in her room, Eden had shed an old skin. She approached her father with a proud smile that faded at the sight of him.

Had he shrunk in the hammock overnight? A fresh poultice covered the wound on his leg. Useless, Eden thought. She had no choice but to signal Shen as quickly as possible.

"Something is different," her father said, cocking his head to one side.

Her hand fluttered to her hair. "Do I look all right?"

"Aha. Going native. Short hair will cool the body temperature."

Eden sank down on a stool. Why couldn't he see the deeper changes in her? The truth came to her even as she said it.

"I don't want to be a Pearl anymore."

"What?" Always, the nervous blinking. "We can't change what we are."

"Why not? Bramford did."

"An undeniable fact. However, an entirely different scenario."

"Is it?" Again, the words popped into Eden's head. "Suppose I wanted to change like him?"

"I don't understand," her father said, though the flash of fear in his face suggested he did.

Eden didn't quite understand, herself. She stared out the back window at the insects buzzing around the water hole. *Live out there?* That can't be right, she thought, and tried to explain.

"I'm just saying that maybe we don't have to be what other people expect us to be. Maybe I can be who I really am. Although, I'm not sure who that is." She paused, relieved by the admission. "I can tell you one thing, Father. I'll never again be the Old Eden. I'd rather die."

He studied her with the same focus she often had seen him apply to a puzzling phenomenon.

"I see," he said. "Of course if the right variables are in place and conditions permit, then, naturally, change is possible. After all, such is the history of man. Even you and I can change, if only in incremental ways."

A tentative smile creased his face, which Eden took as a sign of pride, however meager. She smiled back, delighted as the invisible wall between them began crumbling. And yet, she soon grew uncomfortable with their unfamiliar closeness.

"How are the sequences progressing?" Eden said, returning to safe ground.

Her father also seemed eager to change the subject. "Quite elegant," he quickly responded. "A very, lucky break that we came here. Too many regulations back home."

Lucky? He was dying. And the only man who ever had touched her heart was about to become a super jaguar—not exactly good mating material.

"It won't be lucky if Bramford is killed." Eden heard the tightness in her voice. "I mean, who will protect us?"

"He'll survive," her father said, matter-of-factly.

"How can you be so sure?"

He chuckled. "Parental knowingness."

"You're not his parent, Father," she said, unable to hide her resentment.

"Only in a metaphoric sense, of course. Creator to creature."

He was the problem, Eden realized. If she couldn't stop Bramford, she had to stop her father and his crazy ideas.

"You can't do it," she said, rising to her feet.

"Do what?"

"Change Bramford again. You've already done enough damage. Why can't you just leave him alone? Think of his son." *Think of me.*

"The son, Logan?" Her father scratched his head. "An unknown variable. Bramford will have to decide his future. It's not up to me."

"But it is. You have real power here." Eden hesitated, struck by how much she sounded like Bramford. "If you change the way you look at yourself, you'll see what I mean," she added.

"But this is an incredible opportunity, Daught."

She drew in a deep breath. "Why don't you ever call me Eden?"

"Daught is your nickname. I always call you that."

"It sounds like a classification."

"Precisely."

"But I'm not one of your experiments," she said in a firm, quiet voice. "I'm your daughter, Eden."

"Yes, I see what you mean. Wait, please," he called out as she turned to leave.

Over her shoulder, she saw his sad, desperate expression. "Rest well, Eden."

"You, too, Father."

It was time, she told herself, as she entered her room—not Rebecca's any longer. It belonged to Eden now. And she would take matters into her own hands.

She dug out the Life-Band and activated it. A slight tingle in her head indicated her sensors had connected to the World-Band. The internal buzz that she had heard all her life flooded into her mind with a bang. She stumbled over to the window, shocked by the crippling noise. Even there in the wilderness, old familiar fears clawed at her once more. *They* were back.

Eden numbly watched a riodinid butterfly land atop the paintbrush, still lodged in the window. Its emerald metallic scales shimmered in the sunlight. The shining *Caria mantinea* rested just long enough for her to sigh before it flew off.

For Earth's sake, do it, Eden.

All she had to do was link to Shen Bramford. She almost hoped there would be no response, but the Life-Band flashed.

Eden sent her plea. *Please, come get us.*

Noting her location along the equator in the last preserve

of rainforest, she imagined the message lifting from the damp, loamy forest floor. It would fly through the dense foliage as it inhaled the exotic scents, or tasted a juicy papaya, and especially took a last gulp of clean air before flying north to the polluted, barren land of Home Sweet Home.

Sadly, she registered Shen's response: *Message received. Will come soon. Hold tight.*

It was done.

Eden quit the connection and buried the Life-Band back inside the pack. She couldn't think about it anymore.

She lay on the bed, drained by her dilemma. She had done the right thing, hadn't she? Why then this nagging feeling?

Outside, birdsong ramped to a fever pitch, announcing the end of another day. And still, Bramford had not returned. Eden closed her eyes, wondering where he was. And did he think of her at all? If only they could glide through the jungle together like the girl and the jaguar in the painting.

Poor Aunt Emily once felt this intense ache.

I envy seas whereon he rides,
I envy spokes of wheels
Of chariots that him convey,
I envy speechless hills

Eden tossed and turned all through the restless night. The relentless hum of the crickets and the cast-iron heat wore on her. In vain she swept her legs across the bed, searching for a cool pocket of air, though it wasn't the thing that would satisfy her.

Too soon, a dusting of pale pink light lay against the

window. She awoke, amazed by the recurrence of her dream. *Bramford and I are on the beautiful, grassy knoll. He's looking at me in that naked way that stirs my blood.*

Eden struggled to catch more of it. *I'm in his arms. Our lips meet.*

Slowly, she became aware of a silent, watchful presence in the room. Father or the little girls could never be so quiet. Maria would have announced herself. And if it were Bramford, Eden would have caught his scent.

Could it be?

She jerked up in bed. "Logan?"

The intruder made a garbled sound. He was halfway through the window when he stopped to grab the paintbrush. In that instant Eden clearly saw the outline of a small boy, six or seven years old. It had to be Bramford's son.

She held still and spoke in a calm, reassuring voice. "I won't hurt you, Logan."

Again, Eden heard a pitiful, choking sound. She rushed forward, as he jumped to the ground.

"Wait!"

Through the soft light, she saw him run towards the gated hut. He skirted around the back, disappearing from view.

Eden didn't want to scare him by giving chase. Besides, if Bramford caught her there, he would be furious. The last thing she wanted was for Logan to see them fight. No, she had to let the child come to her.

She couldn't explain her protective feelings towards the boy or the urgent need to know him. Deep down, she felt certain that if she could win his trust, she might gain something even more valuable. Something a she-cat needed.

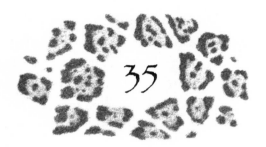

35

EDEN STARED out at Logan's hut, amazed that she had discovered him, when a grass-green tanager landed below her window. She stepped closer and peered over the edge, delighted by the plump little bird's glistening trill. The slash of red across its eyes reminded her of a mask, as if the *Chlorornis riefferii* were a playful bandit.

What was that? Eden's toes met something hard and gooey against the wall. She took a step back, surprised to see a rectangular piece of board. Why, it was a painting, freshly done!

The hair on the back of her neck prickled as she reached for it. At first Eden thought it was another portrait of Rebecca. Then she noted the slightly fuller mouth, the more elfin-shaped face. Could it be? There was no mistake.

Imagine, a portrait of Eden Newman.

The single initial, signed in the corner, equally surprised her: *L for Logan?* Perhaps he had left it in exchange for the paintbrush. However, the time it must have taken to paint it as well as the personal nature of the painting pointed to a gift, made especially for her.

Overwhelmed by the idea, Eden sank down on the edge of the bed. Gifts were rare. Unlike in the Old World, birthdays were a painful reminder of a short life span and marked with sadness. Only a girl's first menstruation—a sign she wasn't toxic and, therefore, might perpetuate the species' survival— caused a minor celebration.

Eden wistfully recalled the gifts she'd received on her special day. From father, a detailed analysis of her genetic predispositions with special emphasis on her advanced intellect. Mother had given her an old, graying book of Aunt Emily's poems. And though she appreciated these things, the obvious message layered into them never escaped her: *you must improve yourself, Eden.*

How astonishing that this young boy who didn't know her had presented a gift without judgment or comment. In fact, unlike the images of Rebecca, which had a serious, almost stern, quality, Eden thought her portrait was light and whimsical. As if Logan alone could see the New Eden emerging, something she barely understood.

She recalled his surreptitious visits along with the soft, rustling sounds, which she decided must have been the stroke of his brush. How many mornings had he stood in the room, studying her? And how had seen her in the dim light? Perhaps, isolated in his hut, he had grown sensitive to subtle shades of light, as well as to the layers of life. Eden longed to hug the sweet boy.

She jumped up, full of glee, and replaced Rebecca's portrait with her own. Much better, she thought, stepping back to examine it. But how could she continue this unusual dialogue of objects with Logan?

Eden never had owned much, but how useless it all seemed now. Finally, she needed so little. The backpack and

the ruined party dress, which lay in a corner of the room covered by spider webs, were all she possessed here. She dusted
off the dress and laid it out on the bed, considering it, when
she heard the chirpy prattle of the two sisters in the main
room. Her father's wheezing cough filled the air, as he seemed
to gasp for air.

Hold tight, Shen's message had said. Eden only hoped her
father could.

Carmen skipped into her room, offering the morning *chicha* and a fresh white orchid. Etelvina trailed behind, a petu-
lant look on her face. They slung harsh words under their
breath at each other. Amazed, Eden understood the tables
had turned. She was no longer a monster but more like an
older sister whose attention they sought.

"*Gracias,* Carmen," Eden said and, hoping to diffuse the
sibling rivalry, also thanked her sister.

Etelvina seized Eden's old dress, her eyes dancing with
curiosity. Carmen took the other end, trying to claim it. Eden
watched the stiff techno fabric fold into odd shapes as the
girls tussled over it.

Maria's entrance immediately calmed her daughters who
settled on the floor. Their mother handed Eden a brittle, ash-
colored leaf with five points. In a pleading voice she spoke of
the powerful healing it would bring Eden's father. "*Es más
fuerte para tu padre.*"

After Bramford's miraculous healing, Eden was anxious
to try anything. "Where is it?"

Maria pointed towards the mountaintop. "*La Puerta del
Cielo.*"

"Heaven's Gate." Eden recalled her earlier suggestion

that Bramford venture there to find the potent healing plant.

She emphasized the danger. "*Es peligroso.* You, *El Tigre* go. Doctor okay."

If only Eden could reassure her that help was on the way. But she couldn't risk word leaking to Bramford. He might steal away Eden's father and Logan, too.

Maria knelt down, pretending to dig in the ground. She pulled out an imaginary object and glanced up at Eden with questioning eyes.

"A plant root?" Eden guessed.

"*Sí.*" Maria pointed at the leaf in Eden's hand, explaining that it wasn't as strong. "*Menos fuerte.*"

"You mean the root has more medicine?"

Maria nodded.

It had never occurred to Eden that various parts of a plant contained different remedies—it was just a plant. At home, she always had dialed in her symptoms to the oxy-drip, never wondering what drugs she received. How cut off from the natural world she had been. No wonder she often had felt like a lab rat, dependent and vulnerable, trapped in the tunnels.

The sisters' squabble over the dress heated up again. Now Eden imagined a comical monkey in the bunched-up fabric, and the perfect idea struck her. She drew her finger along it while making a cutting sound. Carmen's eyes lit with under-standing—Eden needed the bamboo cutter. The young girl sprang from the room with Etelvina in tow.

Once more, their mother appealed to Eden. "You, *El Tigre* go."

"He doesn't need me to go with him, Maria."

She was strangely insistent, as she explained that he didn't understand. *"El Tigre no comprende."*

Dark, silent eyes bore into Eden. She had the feeling her friend was referring to something other than the plant. Well, Bramford didn't understand, did he? Not a thing about Eden, anyway.

"Okay, I'll go with him," she said. "If he comes back, that is." *Unless Shen gets here first.*

Her gaze strayed to the window. Bramford had left on his foolhardy quest two days ago. For all Eden knew he might be dead.

"No te preocupes," Maria said.

"I'm not worried."

She faked a smile but knew Maria wasn't fooled. Eden hardly thought of anything but him.

She welcomed the distraction of the girls' return. They watched as she spread her old dress on the floor and proceeded to cut it. Inspired by the bandit-like tanager, she decided to fashion a mask for each girl.

At last, Eden saw how to catalog the chaos and at the same time, enhance it with reverie.

For Carmen, she made an umbrella cockatoo, *Cacatua alba*, its striking crest extended in surprise. *Saimiri oerstedii*, the cute squirrel monkey with jutting ears suited little Etelvina. She cut tiny holes at the sides of the masks into which Maria braided long strips of palm fronds. She tied them onto her daughters' heads. Wide-eyed, they peeked out from the slits. Carmen squawked and preened like the showy bird while Etelvina scampered on all fours, imitating the chirping, squirrel-sized primate.

Eden beamed, wishing this were just one of many future family projects.

Then it came to her. She also would make a mask for Logan. A nocturnal creature like him: the tube-lipped nectar bat, *Anoura fistulata*, so necessary for pollination in the rainforest, and yet as feared and misunderstood as the poor, isolated boy.

She asked Maria to braid one more strip. *"Uno más por favor."*

"¿Para ti?" For you?

Eden shook her head. "Logan."

A hush fell over the room. Her companions traded knowing glances. To Eden's surprise, they glanced at her portrait, which she thought they hadn't noticed. Now she knew they had been afraid to mention it.

What deep, dark secret could cause the girls' irrepressible spirits to wilt? Even Maria's shoulders sagged. It had to be some superstitious Huaorani belief, perhaps because of his mixed race.

Eden carried on as if nothing had happened. She quietly shaped Logan's mask with oversized pointed ears and wide wings. When she showed it to the girls, they ran away. Maria followed them without another word.

When it came time for Eden to leave the jungle, she would miss them more than she ever imagined. And what would happen to Logan when Shen arrived? She doubted that Bramford would give up his son. But how could Eden leave Logan here to suffer his cruel father?

Wait and see, Eden told herself.

She tied his mask onto the window mesh so that it hung

like an upside-down bat. On impulse she waved towards the gated hut.

Just then, a host of orange-billed sparrows burst through the compound. A barred hawk, *Leucopternis princeps*, chased after them, its white bar flashing like a racing stripe. The hungry predator nipped the tail feathers of the smallest straggler. Eden gasped as the baby bird tumbled downward into the hawk's beak.

Evolution, she mused. Only the fittest survived. Eden would have to be fit, possibly even fitter than Bramford, if she wanted to save Logan.

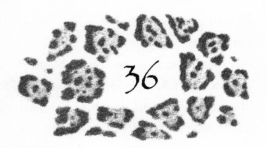

36

ARLY THE next morning Eden heard the telltale rustling sounds in her room and sprang to her feet. This
time, she caught Logan by the arm before he could flee. The
boy made curious yelping sounds as he struggled to get free.

"Logan, please, don't be afraid," Eden said.

He continued to look away from her. She wondered if he
even understood her. Or was he simply shy?

The pearly glow of dawn barely illuminated him. He
wore the bat mask, which had done the trick and wooed him
back. She tentatively touched the tip of one wing.

"Do you like it?" she asked, keeping her voice light. "It's
not nearly as nice as the portrait you painted—which I love.
I'm glad I have the chance to thank you for it. You're very
talented, Logan."

Finally, he made a garbled response, though it sounded
positive. Did he have a speech defect, perhaps the result of
growing up in isolation? Was that the big secret?

"My name is Eden," she said softly. "You have no idea
how happy I am to meet you."

He seemed to relax so she released her hold. She stepped
back to take a better look at him, as a ray of sunlight glanced
through the window. She almost laughed. No wonder she

had imagined a spider monkey—he wore black clothing from head to toe. How hot he must have been in the tropical climate. For Earth's sake, he even had on gloves. Even stranger, Eden saw whitish, kinky hair that puffed over the bat ears. She had expected biracial features, but certainly not Rebecca's recessive coloring.

"You can trust me," she added.

Logan turned and stared at her through the slits in the mask like a frightened animal peering from its hole. Despite the overhang of fabric that shadowed his eyes, Eden detected a pale color. Clearly, he also had inherited it from his mother, despite the low genetic odds. Was that what Bramford had meant? *But what were the odds?*

Anxious to see the boy's face, Eden reached for the mask. "May I take it off?"

Since Logan didn't react, she gently lifted it away. But she wasn't prepared for the sight of him. How could she ever imagine pinkish eyes or the lack of any pigment in his skin?

Eden stared at him, her thoughts slow and searching. Then, as the shock began wearing off, she grasped the truth.

Holy Earth. Logan was a Cotton! *An albino child.*

A small scream escaped her lips. Immediately, Eden regretted it. Logan's sad little face puckered. He snatched the mask from her hand with a pitiful cry. Too stunned to react, she watched him crawl through the window and run back to his hut. Of course, it was gated and opened onto the forest so that no one would see him.

Like a sleepwalker, Eden pushed to the main room. The bewildering image of the young Cotton's face loomed in her mind, along with a noisy zoo of questions. How could

Bramford have produced such a child? The albinism gene had all but been wiped out, at least according to the Uni-Gov's proclamation. True, they found the occasional albino—and murdered the poor thing. Eden shuddered at the ghastly fate Logan had escaped.

She shook the hammock where her father lay sleeping.

"Wake up," she said in a trembling voice. "Logan is a Cotton! I just saw him."

"What?" her father muttered.

He had the humble look of the dying, the eyes soft and accepting. Eden steadied herself against a wooden pole and repeated the news.

"Hmmm. Yes, I see."

Why didn't he seem surprised?

"See what?" she said.

"The mother was a carrier of the albinism gene," her father said with a thoughtful air. "Well, that is news."

"But, Father?" Eden dropped onto a stool, her mind spinning out of control. "It takes two carriers to produce an albino. So how—" She stopped short, stunned by the implication. "Is it possible? Bramford is also a genetic carrier?"

He struggled to reach the crutch. "Yes, it's extraordinary. I must see the child at once."

Eden blocked his path. That explained why he only had remarked on the mother's condition. He already knew about Bramford.

"Tell me the truth, Father."

He released the crutch with a weary sigh. "Bramford swore me to secrecy. But now, with the evidence in plain view, anyone can guess the truth. You said it yourself."

Eden felt the earth tilt, and everything she took for granted with it. Ronson Bramford's DNA contained traits considered even more dreaded and inferior than having white skin.
One of his ancestors had been an albino, a fatal secret that
Bramford had gone to great lengths to conceal.

In fact, she doubted if he had ever felt superior to her at
all. For Earth's sake, the proud and mighty Coal must have
been as self-conscious as she, if not more so. Both of them
had hidden their true identities.

How alike they were, after all. And yet how little Eden
had understood him.

"Are you all right, Daught?" her father said, his voice
shaky.

Even now, as his energy drained away, he only showed
concern for her. For once the dreaded nickname comforted
Eden.

"I'm fine." And it was true until jealousy bit her. "But
how could Bramford have mated with Rebecca? He really
must have loved her to risk a Cotton child."

"I suspect he never knew about the mother's inferiority,"
her father said. "My hypothesis: she had her genome falsi-
fied. She must have paid a heavy price to some rogue genetic
marketer."

The story Bramford had told her while under the influ-
ence of the *bejuco de oro* began to weave together. *The FFP
used you to get to me.*

"Or else," Eden said, "the FFP discovered the truth about
Bramford and set him up with Rebecca in order to guarantee
an albino offspring."

She could live with that scenario despite the racial profile:

seduced by a backstabbing Pearl. At least undying love hadn't
caused such a supreme sacrifice.

"Still, how could any mother agree to have an albino?"

"Perhaps Rebecca didn't know about Bramford's genome
either," her father said. "It's logical to assume the FFP tricked
both of them."

"Yes, that fits." *What were the odds?*

Eden imagined the parents' shock when they first laid eyes
on their son and realized the truth about each other. Bramford and Rebecca became victims of their own lies, which in
turn, branded Logan.

To his credit, Bramford had tried to save the child by hiding him in the jungle. But did pride or love drive him? If the
truth came out, it would topple his empire. Naked fear fisted
around Eden's heart as she considered the consequences of
having signaled Shen. Surely, Bramford's half-brother would
protect the boy.

"There are so few secrets left in the world," her father
said. "I didn't know the truth about Bramford until the night
of the experiment. Of course, he understood that I needed
the correct genome. You can't imagine how it threw off my
calculations."

Not the fire?

"Father, are you saying that your miscalculations advanced Bramford's adaptation?"

"It's quite possible. I made what corrections I could in
the limited time. We argued about the disproportionate risk.
Bramford said he had no choice."

The final piece slammed into place as Eden recalled Bramford's confession. *I'd give my life for him.* When he managed

to hide Logan away, along with the evidence of his inferior genetics, the FFP set their sights on a new goal—her father's work.

Thanks to my big mouth. Eden was not entirely off the hook.

Only, they hadn't figured Bramford would use himself as a guinea pig. She understood he had risked his life in the hopes of saving his son. Even if the FFP stole the technology, Bramford's adaptation would provide her father with necessary samples. And if Logan also could evolve, he might be safe from The Heat, as well as from those who would destroy him.

Eden pressed a trembling hand to her chest. Paternal love, not greed, had been Bramford's primary motivation.

Sweet Earth, how wrong she had been about this incredible man.

A woman's cry pierced the air, and Eden caught her breath. She hurried to the porch, afraid of what she might find.

"What is it, Daught?" her father called out.

"A dead jaguar."

Bramford's third and final donor.

Slumped near the fire pit, its feline head hung at a grotesque angle. Across the compound, Eden saw Maria and Lucy walking towards it. The sadness in their eyes terrified her. She took the steps two at a time, pressing a hand to her injured side.

"Bramford?" she said.

"No sé." Maria didn't know his fate.

Theirs was the deep sorrow of solastalgia, Eden realized.

She watched them huddle over the slain animal with bowed heads, like supplicants in bygone churches who came on bended knee to ask for forgiveness. Long ago, God had died, and nature soon would follow.

Eden stared at the jaguar's pitch-black coat, realizing yet another part of Bramford's plan. Just like the original donor, this animal had melanism, the opposite of albinism. Bramford hadn't chosen the trait for vanity's sake, after all. He had sought to counter the extreme effects of his defective genome, for Logan's benefit. All along, the fiercely protective father had danced one step ahead of disaster.

Flies buzzed round the jaguar carcass. Its flank, matted with blood, told of a vicious battle. A cold knot twisted Eden's stomach. What if Bramford hadn't survived?

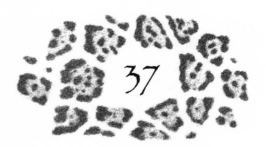

37

IKE STEEL KNIVES, the morning light angled into the center of the compound and burned Eden's skin. Sweat trickled down her chest, draining her energy. But she hardly noticed her discomfort or the blinding glare, as she scanned the area for a sign of her Jaguar Man. What if he had hidden in the nearby bush like a wounded animal on the verge of dying? He might leave this earth and never know how she felt about him.

"Bramford?" Eden cried, running towards the rim of the forest. "Where are you?"

She stopped, straining to listen for a moan or whispered response. But there was none. She moved further down the ring of trees, her anxiety ratcheting higher with each step.

"Hello? Ronson Bramford!"

She ignored the dull pain in her side and the Huaorani women's puzzled looks. Carmen and Etelvina raced out of their hut and skipped behind her. As if it were a game. The Indians might not care if Bramford met the Great Snake in the Sky, but Eden couldn't bear the thought.

"Bramford, can you hear me?"

The broiling heat hobbled her walk, turning her feet to bricks of clay. She clumsily skirted the vegetable path and tripped over a stray potato root. Tangled there among the plants, she noticed several bright red patches on her arms and legs. The words formed in her mind with inexplicable terror: *Sunburn. The Heat.*

Then a shadow fell over her. Bramford's deep voice quickened her heartbeat.

"What are you doing?" he said.

Eden looked up to find dull, bloodshot eyes staring back at her. Bright red slashes ripped across his chest. Wild hair tangled around a battle-weary face. Relief swept through her and, on its heels, indignation. She struggled to stand, sputtering with rage.

"For Earth's sake, why didn't you answer me? I've been screaming your name. Don't tell me you didn't hear me!"

Bramford glanced over at the slain jaguar. Eden felt like small fry in comparison. In fact, she detected a great shift in him. The uneasy alliance between man and beast, which had swung back and forth, now settled in favor of his savage side with solemn gravity.

Still, that didn't excuse his rudeness.

"Well?" Eden said.

"You didn't answer my question," Bramford said, without great interest.

Inches away, his scent rushed over her and left her lightheaded. His indifferent gaze traveled from her shorn locks to the short hem of her dress. She felt naked before him, excitedly so. And ready for the compliments she expected.

Instead, he asked, "Why did you cut your hair? Your neck will burn."

"What do you care?"

"If you don't, I don't know why anyone else would."

He swaggered past her towards the main hut. Furious, Eden stamped after him. "Obviously, you don't care, Bramford. My father might live if you hadn't gone away."

"What are you talking about, woman?"

"Maria says there's a plant that will save his life. It's in the mountains—Heaven's Gate. We should leave right now."

Bramford hesitated on the top step. He looked down at her over his shoulder, an eyebrow lifted. "We?"

"That's right."

"And why is that?"

For a second Eden got lost in his penetrating stare. She struggled to explain, though she couldn't understand it herself. "Um, because Maria believes if we both go, he'll get better."

Bramford's eyes clouded with suspicion, then he turned away. She followed him inside and, as she reached the hammock, saw the shock on his face. Her father lay sleeping, his rapid state of decline plain to see.

"Now do you understand?" Eden said.

"Doctor Newman?" Bramford said softly.

"What?" Her father mumbled something about percentages and ratios.

"I brought the jaguar. How long before you'll be ready?"

Her father continued talking in a nonsensical way. Eden pressed a hand to his burning forehead.

"His fever has spiked," she said, holding back her tears.

Bramford stared out the back window. Eden wondered if he regretted involving her father in his story—another victim of his lies.

"Let's go," he said, turning to her.

"Wait a minute," she said, hurrying to her room.

Eden dug out the Life-Band and tucked it inside her bindings. She had to get rid of it and hopefully, confuse the signal. Their salvation must come from the natural world, she decided. Catalog and reverie—it had to work.

Using her finely developed researcher's skills, she memorized the leaf Maria had given her, which was too brittle to survive the arduous trip. Then, as if it were a sacred object, she kissed the leaf and offered a prayer. *Please Mother Earth, heal Father.*

On her way back, Eden gave the Jaguar Man statue a playful slap. Bramford watched her approach, a shadow of a smile tugging at his lips.

"Come," he said, already moving out the doorway.

She whispered in her father's ear. "I'll be back soon."

"Lily?" he mumbled.

"Please, hang on, Father."

Outside, Eden caught Bramford gazing towards Logan's hut. She wanted to tell him that she understood, that she was sorry for everything, but she didn't know how.

Before she reached the bottom step, he gathered her into his arms and set her on his shoulders. An electric current ran through her at his touch. Eden leaned her hips against the back of his head, thrilled to be back on her special perch. She dug her hands into his silky hair, holding steady, as they flew across the compound.

Past the gate, Bramford pointed towards the mountaintop, which wore a halo of clouds.

"Heaven's Gate," he said.

"It's dangerous," Eden said, recalling Maria's warning. "I guess that explains the name."

"It's called Heaven's Gate because you have to die to get there."

Eden gasped audibly. Bramford roared with laughter and she laughed along with him. As long as she was with him she had nothing to fear except for her small-minded self. The New Eden was eager to meet the world with an open and fearless heart. She wondered how such a giving place could have once terrified her.

A morpho butterfly with iridescent blue, foot-long wings that shimmered in the sunlight brushed her skin, delighting her. Overhead, a group of Wied's marmosets with eerie human-like faces peered down like gatekeepers of an ancient land. Excited birdcalls announced their arrival, *the King* and *the Queen of the Jungle cometh.*

Bramford slowed to an even trot as the mountain slope grew steeper. His low pant blended with the lively hum of the jungle's denizens. After a while, they entered an area so pristine that even the trees seemed surprised by their presence.

Once again Eden suspected that someone was watching them. She bent over to whisper in Bramford's ear.

"I think someone is spying on us."

"That's true," he said.

"But who?"

"Nature."

"Nature?"

Eden sensed something more—a hidden layer of life that she still couldn't grasp. Or could she? *Open your mind, Eden.*

Through the passing miles, she studied Bramford's signals. The quick dart of his head directed her to a harpy eagle that flew in the upper canopy. She understood that he gathered information from its trajectory, probably the location of water or small prey.

She spotted the myopic bee following the dark veins of a *Cattleya* orchid towards the inner yellow track of pollen. An iguana hid on a shadowy branch, camouflaged. A slight shift in the wind pressed upon her skin. By the location of the sun, she estimated their northwesterly direction.

The rhythm of her breath began flowing naturally as she relaxed. *Animals breathe that way.* So that was what her mother had meant, Eden realized. Her cares slipped away. There was only the present moment, and then the next.

She wasn't surprised when Bramford reached up to shift her weight just as she registered a backache. She recognized a silent communication that took place between them. They were in tune, as easily as the jungle life that seemed to play a never-ending song.

"Thank you, Ronson," Eden said, claiming that intimacy for her own.

His hands slipped down her sides, lingering on her thighs. Warm, tingling sensations flowed through her. She fisted her hands in his hair and heard him rumble.

The forest sounds dropped away, replaced by the rapid pounding of her heart. Eden forgot the passing scenery and their destination. Only the hot press of his hands on her bare skin, the tilt of his head brushing her inner leg, and her burning ache consumed her. The more pleasure she experienced, the bolder his touch grew. Now his hand trailed up and down the whole of her leg.

She dared to test the boundaries of their body language and flexed her thighs around his neck. Unbelievably, his gait slowed. A feverish thrill shot through Eden. She could guide Bramford with a mere squeeze.

Did she dare push him further? She couldn't resist the wild urge to flick her hips against his shoulders. At once he picked up speed. She almost squealed—his raw animal power was at her command.

Eden pressed her body against the back of Bramford's powerful head, rocking to the rhythm of his quick pace. A gush of pleasure swept through her. *Like fire and ice. Like sweet, dripping honey.*

Again, she pushed her hips, harder now, and waited breathlessly. He tightened his hold on her legs, the heat from his fingers burning into her as he sped faster.

Eden laughed though she hardly recognized the lush, throaty sounds. In response, Bramford let loose an amorous growl that echoed in the trees and rained down on her delirium. She felt melded to him, no longer a mismatched, centaur-like creature, but a single being. There was no question in her mind that he also felt their deep connection.

Sweet Earth, Aunt Emily's words rang true at last.

He touched me, so I live to know
That such a day, permitted so,
I groped upon his breast.
It was a boundless place to me,
And silenced, as the awful sea
Puts minor streams to rest.

And now, I'm different from before,
As if I breathed superior air,
   Or brushed a royal gown;
My feet, too, that had wandered so,
My gypsy face transfigured now
   To tenderer renown.

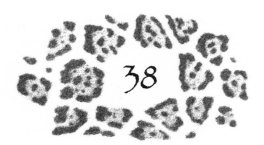

38

EDEN LISTENED in suspense to a loud rumbling ahead that deepened as Bramford carried her towards the edge of the forest. When he stepped into the open, she was stunned to see a tremendous waterfall that plunged thousands of feet below with a deafening roar. A thick mist blew past them, cool and refreshing. A delicate rainbow arced high in the glistening air like a stairway to heaven.

Bramford set her on the ground and stood behind her, his hands lingering at her waist. His warm breath fell on her like feathery blows. Eden drank in the majestic view and the delicious feel of his hold on her. Giddy, she turned and smiled at him. When he smiled back, she thought it was the happiest moment of her life.

It was impossible to be heard over the raging torrent. Bramford jerked his head towards the lip of the fall. *Come.* She let him lead her by the hand, but balked when they reached a narrow ledge, hidden behind the curtain of water.

The path consisted of wide, flat stones, which curved around the face of the mountain. Their uniformity seemed odd, as if cut by some giant hand. The slabs were only deep enough for one person, and probably slippery, besides. The earthen ceiling hung too low for her to sit on Bramford's

270 SAVE THE PEARLS

shoulders. If he carried her in his arms, she would hang over the edge in thin air, which she couldn't stomach. Only one option remained, she realized with a sinking feeling. She would have to walk alone across the ledge.

One slip from that terrifying height—Eden shuddered to think of it. Would she really have to die to reach Heaven's Gate?

Bramford pointed across to the opposite side of the waterfall, making his intention clear. He offered a reassuring squeeze of his hand, a calm look. *Trust me, Eden.*

She shook her head firmly.

She hated to see his disappointment. She really wanted to be his she-cat. But even she-cats had their limits, didn't they?

Bramford held up his hands, resigned. *Wait, here.*

Then Maria's warning came to her. *El Tigre no comprende.* Bramford wouldn't understand the plant's delicacy? Whatever the wise woman had meant, Eden knew she had to accompany him.

She swallowed hard. A quick nod. *Fine, I'll go.*

His face lit up. He cupped her chin, meeting her gaze. *It'll be all right.*

Her eyes strayed to the frightening passage, but he brought her attention back to him. *Just trust me.*

Eden nodded again. *Okay, let's go.*

Bramford pointed at her eyes, then to the water below. He wagged a finger. *Don't look there.* Then he stepped side-to-side and pointed down. *Watch my feet.*

The image of the girl wandering in the jungle beside the jaguar floated into her mind. This was her chance. *Be like her, Eden.*

She sucked in her breath as Bramford edged his weight onto the first rock. He pressed one hand to the side for balance and reached for her. She clasped his hand tight. While taking a small sideways step, he fixed his eyes on her. Eden scraped her back against the sodden wall of earth, sliding onto the footing.

Her heart drummed in her ears, as if pounded by the waterfall. She felt as weightless as the droplets that floated in the air. But she couldn't think about that now.

Barely an arm's length ahead, the water cascaded in front of them. It soaked Eden in seconds. The ledge was as slippery as she feared. Uneven edges between the boulders forced her to raise her feet over the joints or risk tripping. After each one, she had to carefully recalibrate her balance.

They progressed at a snail's pace. She knew Bramford could have sprinted across. And yet, he adjusted his speed to hers, the grip of his hand always encouraging

So different than the man she once knew.

Eden congratulated herself as they rounded the middle bend, halfway across. But for some reason Bramford hesitated. She tilted her head forward and understood why.

Several boulders had torn away from the path, leaving a yawning gap. The frayed earth crumbled on either side of a hole that spanned at least three feet across. Easy enough for Bramford to straddle the distance. But Eden would have to leap across. She looked at him with panic.

Bramford jerked his head back to the starting point and arched his brow. *Go back?* He nodded towards her. *You decide.*

She stared into a small window of space just over his

shoulder. Was this where her reveries had led her? Did she really think she could outwit her fate as a lowly Pearl and become a brave she-cat just because she went natural and cut off her hair?

Serves you right, Eden.

And yet, she had come so far. If she gave into her fears now, she might never again feel the warm press of his hand or see the tender look in his glistening, green eyes.

And that would be a fate worse than death.

Eden gave a small nod, rewarded by the most beautiful smile she had ever seen. Bramford unlaced his fingers, releasing her. Immediately, she felt faint with fear. She dug into the moldy earth behind her, frantic, as it loosened in her hands.

He leapt across the gaping hole, just as she knew he would. At the same time, she knew she would never make it.

Frozen, Eden stared at the scene before her—Bramford mouthing words, his hand outstretched over the broken ledge. She told herself that it had nothing to do with her. She should turn back. Then a memory surfaced of her mother's last breath. Eden had tried so hard to deny her feelings that she also had forgotten about love.

I'm a stone in a cool, dark cave?

It wasn't enough, anymore, to hover outside of her life, numb and full of despair. Eden wanted to be a part of it, all of it, the sadness and the joy.

Bramford's bold eyes beckoned. *Come to me.*

I'm coming.

Eden jumped into the air, her scream lost in the roar of the waterfall. Her feet skimmed the crumbling ledge and slid backwards. A small, clear thought floated through her head. *I'm falling.*

In a flash Bramford caught the bindings around her chest and yanked her onto the ledge. Eden grabbed hold of his legs, shaking badly, on her knees. Gently, he drew her beside him. She was safe with him. *Just like the jungle girl.*

Eden nodded. *I'm okay.*

She shuffled after him until they reached the end. Bramford jumped to the ground several feet below and Eden fell into his waiting arms. He held her tight against his chest, her desire as strong as the rush of water. Couldn't he see how much she wanted him?

"I'm proud of you, Eden," he said.

"Thanks," she said softly. "I couldn't have done it without you."

"But you did it. You'll be a she-cat, yet."

Did he really think so? Maybe even adapted, like him? But he couldn't have meant that. Or could he? He stared at her intently. Once again, she sensed he had more to say. Then confusion seemed to wash over him, and he set her down.

He led her by the hand through a grove of kapok trees. The long, quiet shadows that hovered in dark rows reminded her of reverent monks in contemplation. She could almost hear a distant prayer whispered in the air.

An eerie feeling came over her as they reached a shaded, grassy plateau. Her skin prickled with goose bumps. At the far end of the slope a cliff sailed into the brilliant blue sky, as far as the eye could see. Pillow-soft clouds stepped across it like ladders into infinity.

"Oh!" Eden exclaimed, struck by its familiarity.

"What?" Bramford said.

"I feel like I've been here before but…"

Then she recalled her recurring dream. How could she have dreamt of Heaven's Gate?

She thought of the gentle wind that her mother had believed connected everything in life, even love. Perhaps it had touched Eden, after all.

"Believe it or not," she said. "I was here with you."

Bramford smiled mischievously. "I bet we had fun."

He tumbled Eden onto the dewy grass just as she'd dreamed. *Like playful kittens.* Even the feeling of exquisite happiness was the same.

Side by side, they stretched out on their backs. The steady drone of the waterfall filtered through the thick grove, shielding them from the rest of the world. Purplish periwinkles, blue-crowned passionflowers and white and gold daisies were sprinkled like jewels at their feet. Above their heads, fuzzy, mimosa-like shoots of pink shower trees laced the sky. Eden gazed at the misted light, glimmering through the pretty network, and let go of a dreamy sigh.

A breeze rustled through the trees, filling her head with Bramford's scent. Aching, she turned and saw her desire mirrored in his eyes.

"This *is* heaven," she said.

Bramford draped an arm round her waist, pulling her close. "Yes, Eden. We're in heaven now."

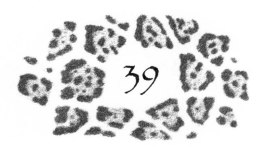

39

THERE, AT Heaven's Gate, Eden nestled into Bramford's embrace with fire-pitch excitement as well as languorous ease. He leaned over her, hesitating. The questioning look in his eyes reminded her of all the secrets that lay between them.

Why didn't he just kiss her?

He sounded serious as he began. "Eden…"

"Yes?"

Then, in response to some mysterious signal, Bramford jerked his head towards the hillside behind them. Eden followed his gaze and, as she stared into the shadows, spied ancient, fortress-like stone terraces, partially hidden by drapes of fuchsia and red bougainvillea vines. In some sections the boulders rose to a man's height. In fact, the masonry reminded her of the ledge under the waterfall.

Taking her cue from Bramford's alert posture, Eden kept her voice low. "Who do you think built that?"

"The Aztecs," he said.

"Then it's thousands of years old. I wish my father could see it."

"They don't like visitors."

She assumed Bramford meant it in a mythical sense, as the Huaorani might.

"So their spirits still guard the place?" she asked.

"A distant branch, actually." His voice dropped a notch. "They're very much alive and watching us now."

"Have they watched us before?"

"Yes."

So that must explain the unseen presence she often had felt in the forest.

Eden scanned the terraced area again but saw no one. "Why aren't they excited to see you like the Huaorani?"

"Because you're here." Bramford gave her a wry smile. "You're *cowode*."

"Non-human, right?"

"I can smell their fear. It's your skin."

Imagining a poisoned blow dart landing in her chest, Eden flattened herself against the ground.

"Are they like you then?" she said.

"Not quite. But more like me than you."

"So you've seen them?"

"Yes. Deep in the jungle."

Bramford's head twitched. Eden caught a flash on the hill where tissue-thin bougainvillea leaves fluttered. She stifled the impulse to run when his calm hand restrained her.

"Let's move," he said, pulling her to her feet.

Her back stiffened as they headed downhill. *An easy target.* Bramford gave her a sidelong glance.

"Just relax, Eden."

He led her to a promontory that jutted out over a glistening lake fed by the waterfall. In the distance an endless river twisted and turned like a silvery ribbon that trailed deep into the Amazon. Shimmering rays of sunlight streaked behind billowy clouds that cabled across the sky.

They stopped among a patch of drab, gray plants near the edge of the cliff. He held her hand in his, as they silently took in the wondrous view.

Eden felt as insignificant as a dust mote, but not unhappily so. She believed that she and Bramford always were meant to be there because the world revolved around them. If only she could express her feelings to him. A kiss would do, she thought, recalling the crush of his lips on hers.

She turned expectantly just as he squatted down to examine the dreary foliage, which appeared out of place in that wonderland.

"Oh, that's it." Eden recognized it as the hoped-for cure.

Bramford nodded and she wondered how he had discovered it.

"Be glad it's unknown," he said, yanking out a plant with a flick of his wrist. "Or man also would have ruined this place by now."

"But if Maria is right, it could save many lives." Eden realized that her father probably would be the first non-native to take its medicine. "We could call it Newman's Cure," she said, hopefully.

Bramford added another root to a growing pile, then looked up at her, radiating intensity. His broad chest and shoulders formed an irresistible triangle above the slim hips.

"The Indians also believe it has power over death," he said. "What if you could have that, Eden? Would you stay as you are, or risk change?"

She wanted to stay forever with Bramford at Heaven's Gate. Nothing else mattered but this deep, simple happiness. She held his intent gaze as the answer teased the tip of her tongue. But old fears crowded in on her. What did he mean by change? Did he think she needed to improve?

"I guess it's the proverbial Fountain of Youth," Eden said, breezily.

He turned back to his task with what sounded like a dissatisfied grunt. She suspected she had missed something, as if a lock had turned, but the door remained hidden. She dropped to her knees beside him, wanting another chance.

"Do you think it's possible, Ronson? To have whatever you want?"

"I don't know," he said, yanking out another plant. "I didn't think so before. But now, I'd like to believe it." He paused and looked at her again. "Did you ever wonder why I put you on probation instead of Ashina?"

Eden decided to forgive the small injustice. "You wanted to keep the peace at the lab," she said plainly.

"No, I tried to protect you. I expected something to happen that night and wanted to keep you out of harm's way."

"I swear I didn't know about Jamal."

"I believe you, now."

Eden sighed with relief. Still, she had to confess the worst of her crimes, even if Bramford already knew, even if she lost him now.

She looked him in the eye and said, "You were right. I let things slip—Jamal used me to learn about my father's plans. I guess I was showing off. Stupid to think..." She shook her head. "I'm sorry. I was wrong."

"We all make mistakes," Bramford said. "And yet, being

here with you makes me think that maybe things were supposed to happen the way they did. Do you understand?"

Eden nodded, though she wondered exactly what he meant.

"I just wish a beautiful girl like you hadn't gotten mixed up in such a mess," he added.

Me? She stared blankly at him.

He laughed. "Don't tell me you don't know how beautiful you are, Eden?"

"I'm a Pearl."

"So was my mate."

Stunned, she searched his eyes for the lie but only detected a warm glow. But was he really thinking of her?

Eden began, haltingly. "You said Rebecca didn't trust you. When you drank the *bejuco de oro.*"

"She was weak," Bramford said, with a trace of disgust. "It started one unguarded, drunken night. When Rebecca got pregnant, I decided to commit myself, for the child's sake. It was time to mate, anyway."

He seemed tentative, as he went on. "I wanted you to be strong. From the beginning, I wanted you to be different."

"Because I look like her?"

"At first the resemblance both attracted and irritated me. It wasn't easy to be around you. I feared you'd betray me like she had...if I loved you."

Unsteady, she sat back on the ground. She could hardly believe he cared.

"You are different," Bramford continued. "When I took the medicine, you stayed by me. And you want to learn, don't you?"

"Very much." *About love mostly.*

"What else happened in the jungle?" he asked.

Eden felt her skin flush at the memory of their stolen passion, the burning kiss.

"You mistook me for Rebecca and kissed me, or rather, her," she said, too sharply.

"Yes, I remember that. Did our kiss frighten you?" Bramford waved a hand over his body. "Did this?"

"No." Eden's voice hitched. "I liked it."

He scooped her into his arms. "And now?"

"I like it," she repeated, hugging him.

"That's because you're my she-cat."

Bramford nuzzled her neck then traced a line up to her lips. With soft licks he parted her mouth. Heat blazed like wildfire through her body. Her mind went blank as he kissed her, deeply.

Eden closed her eyes, giving in to his hungry demands. Their limbs intertwined until her body molded to his. She sank into a river of bliss that swept her outside of time, outside of any barriers—real or imagined—and into a place where she thought anything was possible. Even a future together. When he released her, she knew she would never be the same.

"We should leave before we wear out our welcome," Bramford said, hoarsely. "I'll cut vines to carry the roots."

Breathless, Eden watched him walk back up the slope. Her path never had been clearer. She wormed her fingers into her bandages and pulled out the Life-Band. She heard Bramford working inside a grove of trees that hid him from view. *Do it now, Eden.*

She hurried to the edge of the cliff, praying that the river would carry the device far away so no one would ever find them. But as she reached back to throw it, something caught her hand and violently spun her around. She stood face to face with Bramford, who must have moved like the wind.

"What's this?" he said, snatching the wristband from her.

"It's not what you think," Eden said.

His jaw twitched, the impenetrable mask returned. "Did you use it? There's no point lying now to protect your lover."

"I thought you believed me."

"Tell me the truth." His fingernails cut into her skin. "Did you send a signal? This isn't about us anymore, Eden."

"Only to Shen—he's coming. You told me he's your half-brother. I thought I could trust him."

He looked stricken. "Good Earth, there's no time."

He flung the Life-Band high into the air. Eden watched it sail out over the cliff and twirl like a ballet dancer before it dropped fast as a stone. She sank to the ground, defeated.

Bramford bound the plant roots to his chest, wrapping the vines as tightly as he held his anger.

"I should leave you here," he said.

Eden muttered. "Go ahead."

"I already have enough crimes to pay for."

He hefted her onto his shoulders and sprinted across the plateau. She longed to command him again with her body movements, but the subtle communication between them had slipped away.

How fleeting her happiness had been. Silent tears streamed down her cheeks as they left paradise behind. And yet, despite the pain, Eden didn't regret loving Bramford. Not for one second.

Only Aunt Emily had understood this exquisite burden.

Proud of my broken heart since thou didst break it,
Proud of the pain I did not feel till thee,
Proud of my night since thou with moons dost slake it,
Not to partake thy passion, my humility.

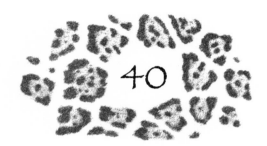

40

FOR ONCE Maria wasn't there to greet Eden and Bramford when they arrived at the quiet, moonlit compound. Eden imagined the worst. *Father?*

Bramford pulled her from his shoulders as soon as they reached the main hut. They hadn't spoken a word since they had left Heaven's Gate. How on Blessed Earth would Eden ever win him back?

She hurried inside and found her father asleep in the hammock, his open mouth loudly sucking in air. Maria kept a vigil beside him, her face drawn. She looked past Eden and brightened when she saw Bramford enter with the plant roots. With a definitive nod, she seemed to tell Eden there was a chance. Then she hurried from the room, moving faster than Eden thought possible.

Eden brushed a hand against her father's fevered check. "I'm here, Father."

"Eden," he whispered, slowly opening his eyes.

"We found the medicine you need."

"We?"

"Bramford and I."

Bramford came up beside her, but she couldn't bring herself to look at him.

"Hello, doctor," he said.

Her father glanced from Eden to Bramford and back again with a knowing look. "You were gone a long time," he said, with great effort.

She quickly shook her head, trying to discourage him. "It was far, that's all. Please, you've got to hold on."

"For some things, you cannot wait."

Bramford knelt down beside the hammock and spoke to him in a firm but gentle voice. "By this time tomorrow, you'll be stronger. How long before the procedure is ready?"

A glimmer of light sparked in her father's eyes. "Another day to complete the sequences, I estimate."

"We've run out of time, doctor." Bramford shot Eden an angry look. "I'll give you an hour once you're on your feet."

"Too much risk—"

"Just be ready. For two, that is. There'll be two of us this time."

Her father looked at Eden in surprise. "Is it true?"

"No," Bramford said sharply. "My son Logan and I will adapt."

"What?" she said, squaring off with him. "You can't do that."

His chest swelled. "I'm his father; I have the right."

"He's only a child. He can't decide for himself."

"I know what's best for him."

"Do you, Bramford? Forcing him to live like an animal?"

"At least he'll survive."

"But at what cost? Go ahead, run away if you want, but leave Logan here. We'll care for him." Eden was surprised to say it, and yet relieved. "I'll take care of him."

Bramford's temper evened. "You would do that?"

"Yes, as if he were my own son."

He studied her, hope flickering in his eyes. Then he shook his head. "It can't be."

"Why?" Eden said, trying to sound reasonable. "Because he's an albino?"

Shock lit Bramford's face. She knew she had crossed a line. But for the love of Earth, why had he put her in such a difficult position?

Icy calm flattened his voice. "I'll bring you my son's genome disk, doctor." Then he strode out of the room.

Eden stared through the window at the moonlight that laddered across the waterhole. She would never love anyone but Bramford. She simply couldn't live without him. Only one choice remained, whether he wanted it or not. If necessary, she would spend the rest of her life convincing him.

"Please, Father," she said, turning to him. "Adjust your calculations for three."

"No," he said flatly.

"But I want to adapt like Bramford."

He looked at her under his eyebrows, the owlish eyes begging for restraint. "That is categorically impossible."

Poor Father. He just had to listen.

"Why?" she said. "I know what's in store for me."

"Eden, I realize that it may not be readily apparent, however, you are my first priority." He started to tremble as he went on. "My deepest regret is that I did not take better care of your mother. I won't make the same mistake with you."

"Don't you understand? I have to be with Bramford."

Her father shook his head, his eyes fluttering closed. She

knew he would never agree. And maybe she didn't mind that he cared, after all. But, now that she had declared her heart's desire, she refused to let it go.

Maria clattered up the steps, carrying a gourd full of a foul-smelling paste. Some Fountain of Youth, Eden thought. With its drab appearance and repellent odor, nature had disguised the plant well.

She drifted to the porch, hoping to find Bramford, but he was gone. The fast knocking sounds of a spectacled owl reverberated in the air, echoing her burning question. *What to do, what to do?* Eden spotted the *Pulsatrix perspicillata* in the crook of a guava tree. The owl swiveled its domed head, studying her, the white markings around its eyes giving it a scholarly air.

Haven't you learned anything, Eden?

Yes, she understood what Aunt Emily had tried to teach her. *That love is all there is.*

"I'll be back soon, Father," she called, hurrying down the steps.

He would forgive her, eventually. And if he never did, well, he had done enough.

Eden slipped inside the laboratory, steeling her resolve. Moonlight streamed through the solar roof, bathing the room with a soft, waxy glow. She gripped a stool, poised to throw it, when she considered Bramford's wrath. He just might kill her. Then the frightening image of his final adaptation popped into her head. He also needed to understand.

She heaved the stool at her father's console and it hit with a loud crack. Glass splintered in the air; electric wires fizzled like live snakes. Eden slipped on the debris as she ran forward. She used her hand to break her fall and cut it on a shard of glass. Overwhelmed by the rush of emotions, she barely felt the sting. She struggled to her feet and charged forward again with a fierce yell.

She was her own damn she-cat!

Even Bramford's furious roar couldn't stop her. He tackled her to the ground with a flying leap. Snarling, he cuffed her wrists over her head.

"Once a traitor, always a traitor," he said, panting hard.

Eden bucked against his weight. "You don't understand."

"That you would get us killed?"

"That I love you, you bastard."

Bramford grew still, his eyes locked onto hers. His voice had a cutting edge. "Who do you think you love? I'm not the same man. There's nothing left for me now but to protect my son."

"I want to adapt with you," Eden said.

His eyes widened in surprise. He started to speak, but suspicion crowded out hope. He jerked his head at the havoc she had wreaked. "I suppose that's why you ruined the lab?"

"My father refuses to give me the procedure. He left me no choice."

"You're lying," Bramford said, yanking her to her feet. "You're just buying time until your mate arrives."

Eden slapped his cheek. "You're my mate."

"But you're too beautiful to change."

She threw herself at him and he grabbed her tight. His mouth crushed against hers. She softly moaned his name, as his lips traced the length of her throat.

"Ronson. You and I. We'll be a family, with Logan, in the jungle—"

"This is wrong," he said, pulling away.

Eden clung to him. "Please, you have to believe me."

Bramford threw her over his shoulder, ignoring her desperate pleas. He sprinted down the path and rounded the bend. Towards the prison again, she realized.

"No, wait!"

He set her down inside the hut. "I should have left you here from the beginning. Then none of this would have happened."

Eden grabbed his arm. "But you can't deny that it did."

"I don't deny it. But I have a choice. This time I'm making the right one. They'll free you after we're gone." He gave her a cold look. "And Eden, it would be foolish to try and find me. I might not recognize you."

He spun away and locked her in. She heard a low, frustrated growl as he left.

"Bramford! Let me out!"

Eden banged her shoulder against the door until it burned with pain. Her voice grew hoarse from yelling. She knew no one would dare respond.

Exhausted, she curled into a ball on the ground with her head pillowed on top of her hands. Tears slid across her face, forming a puddle under her cheek. It could all be so simple.

What on Blessed Earth would it take for Bramford to trust her?

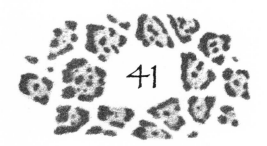

A HIGH, THIN WAIL woke Eden from where she lay sleeping in the prison hut. She couldn't place the sound, but it chilled her to the bone. She stumbled to her feet and stood on tiptoe under the window, listening. Heavy footsteps and men's gruff voices filtered in. Gray fingers of light seeped over the edge. Barely dawn, she thought, her mind racing.

Again, the heartbreaking cries filled the air. The sisters, Eden realized with a start.

"Careful," a deep voice said from the other side of her door. "He said not to hurt her."

"Not yet," a squeaky voice said, and let out a cruel laugh.

Eden would recognize those two anywhere. She steeled herself, as the door burst open. Just as she feared, her repulsive dance partner and his sleazy sidekick stood there, machetes hanging from their belts.

"Yum, Pearly," Giant said, grabbing her.

Eden thrashed against him, caught like an insect pinched in his fingers. He zeroed in for a kiss, his lips puckered. Nobody kisses a she-cat without her permission, she decided, kneeing him hard in the groin.

His eyeballs rolled back in his head, as he slumped to the

ground, groaning. Eden darted outside, but stopped short, her heart in her throat. Jamal was coming towards her. She took in the damage she had inflicted, feeling both horrified and vindicated.

He walked with a hitch, dragging one leg. Hideous scar tissue crisscrossed the warrior tattoo, which now resembled a terrified old man. The grin Eden once admired angled down one side of his face, making him look crazy. Finally, Jamal looked as ugly as he was on the inside. At least he wouldn't be able to trade on his looks in order to dupe the next girl.

"Hello, Little Bunny," Jamal said, giving her a cool appraisal.

"I'm not your bunny," Eden said.

The nasty grin faded. "We'll see about that. I had my doubts about you. But you've proven to be enormously helpful to the cause. We never would have found this place without your message."

"What did you do to Shen?"

"He has needs. Everyone does." Jamal made a disapproving *tsk, tsk* sound. "His mate is a Pearl, didn't you know?"

Poor Shen probably had been forced to choose between saving his brother or his mate. Eden now could imagine why he chose the latter.

"He must love her," she said.

"You've been in the jungle too long. But we'll see about that, too."

"You're too late, Jamal. Bramford already left. You'll never find him." Eden only hoped it was true.

The face in the tattoo seemed to gasp for air as Jamal

frowned. "Even if that's true," he said. "He'll come back for the boy."

Mother Earth. The FFP knew that Logan was there.

Jamal passed her to Squeaky. "Bring her."

Squeaky dragged Eden into the clearing, following behind his leader. The sight of the Huaorani women and children huddled near the fire pit, an armed guard on watch, infuriated her. Her father lay crumpled on a log, his sad eyes following her. For once she wished he couldn't see her.

Jamal gave a jaunty wave as they turned into the gated hut. "Hello, again, Doctor Newman." Over his shoulder, he commanded Squeaky. "Wait here."

Eden watched him walk towards the back of the hut, dreading what might come. He skirted a blanket of leaves that lay on the ground. She assumed he tried to avoid whatever animals might hide beneath. The guard stationed there caught her watching, his eyes shifting nervously.

Logan's pained cry knifed into her. Her blood boiled to a fever pitch, as Jamal dragged the frightened boy into the open. Bewildered pinkish eyes stared through the slits in the bat mask, which sat at a rakish angle on his face. Along with his usual long clothing, it hid his condition. For now, Eden thought.

"Look what I've got," Jamal said. "A little bat."

He reached for the mask, when an angry roar distracted him. *The Jaguar Man was coming.*

Just then Eden glimpsed a young soldier, no more than thirteen-years-old, peeking out from behind a nearby tree. His light brown skin puzzled her. How had a Coal of such obvious mixed race been accepted into the FFP? She saw his pointed look at the carpet of leaves. Too late, she grasped its significance and yelled at Bramford, who leapt towards the hut.

"Stop! It's a trap!"

A net curled up through the leaves as soon as he touched down. He tumbled into it with a nasty growl. The young soldier stepped out from the shadows, holding a rope that had triggered the net and caught the prize. Beaming, he tied the rope around a tree.

"Good job, Kevon," Jamal told him. "At last, the whole freakish Bramford family."

In vain Bramford struggled to escape his roped cage. Eden simply wanted to die when his blistering glance landed on her.

Jamal yanked her beside him. "You see, Eden. You underestimated me."

"You'll never make it out of here alive," she said, though she wondered what could stop him now.

"Wrong again. With your father's technology, I can command the FFP. I can have whatever I want. Including you."

"You don't want me."

Jamal traced the crooked scar down his cheek. "Thanks to you my mate-rate has plummeted. Even Ashina changed her mind. I figure you owe it to me to be my mate. You'll still come out ahead—your child will inherit half my genetics."

Mated to Jamal? Eden's blood ran cold. She could think of no worse fate. But she deserved none better.

"Look," he added, pointing to the compound gate. "I brought you a peace offering."

He whistled and a soldier entered with a muzzled dog, straining at its leash.

Her heart leapt. "Austin!"

At Jamal's nod, the handler released the eager animal. It bounded forward and jumped up on her shoulders. Eden took off his muzzle, and short, sharp barks told her he had missed her. She snuggled into his ruff.

"Me, too, buddy."

"Happy?" Jamal said. "He was well taken care of."

Eden commanded Austin to sit by her side, gathering her wits about her.

"I'm grateful," she said plainly, her emotions in check.

"Good. That's how I want things between us, again, Little Bunny."

She recoiled as he caressed her cheek. Austin growled low, the hair on his back rising. The handler snapped up the leash again.

"Now where were we?" Jamal said, leering at her. "Oh, yes, mates."

"I'll go with you under one condition," Eden said.

"You're in no position to bargain, pet."

She pretended more confidence than she felt. "Let the boy go and I'll do whatever you want."

Jamal laughed. "Do you know how much I can get for an albino? Especially, the Cotton son of the Great Bramford?" He approached the netted cage. "Or maybe I'll keep the boy a secret in exchange for the keys to Bramford Industries."

Bramford raged against the ropes.

"Shut up," Jamal said, giving him a swift kick.

"No!" Eden cried.

He wheeled on her. "Don't tell me you've fallen under his spell?"

"I love him," she said, her eyes on Bramford.

Jamal slapped her face. "Pearl bitch!"

She reeled back with a scream. Austin strained against the leash, growling. Bramford also growled, which, however futile, offered Eden some comfort. She glared at the sickening man she once hoped to mate.

"At least I know how it feels to love," Eden said. "Something you'll never know. You're the beast, Jamal."

He ripped away Logan's mask. "How can you love a man that produced a Cotton?"

The boy moved to cover his face, but Jamal pinned down his arms. Bramford tore at the ropes, which bled into him. A hush fell over the soldiers. The sight of the Cotton child had caught even these hardened men off guard, Eden realized. She eyed Squeaky's machete.

Do something, Eden.

She gave him a swift kick in the knees and he collapsed. But as she reached for his weapon, something whizzed by in the air. The soldier guarding Logan's hut fell forward, a dart lodged in his neck. *Whoosh!* Another well-aimed dart felled the man who guarded the women and children. Then Austin's handler slumped to the ground. In a panic, the young soldier retreated behind the roped tree.

Jamal pulled out his laser, swinging it in confusion.

"Get him, Austin!" Eden yelled, pointing at her ex.

The dog flew through the air and clamped his jaws on Jamal's arm. He dropped the laser and cried out.

"Help!"

Squeaky stumbled to his feet, cutting the air with his machete, as if fighting a ghost. Eden didn't even hear the whistling dart that got him. Blood spurted from his mouth, as he keeled over and dropped the big knife.

But Jamal had the last laugh. With his free hand, he reached for the laser and pointed it at Austin's head.

"Call him off, Eden, or I'll kill him," he said.

Austin's life for those she loved? In the end it was an easy decision. Eden took one last look at Bramford, begging quiet forgiveness.

Then she yelled at Jamal. "Take me instead!"

She heard Bramford's cry, as she jumped towards the laser. "No, Eden!"

A sickening whine followed the weapon's blinding flash. She rolled to the ground, stunned to be alive. Something had gone wrong. She lifted her head to find Austin sprawled on top of Jamal's face. Blessed Mother Earth, he had knocked her out of the weapon's deadly path and taken the hit in her place. His eyes rolled towards her, a deep shudder running through him.

"Austin!" Eden cried, scrambling towards him.

Jamal struggled to lift the dog off of him. Just then Logan made a heartbreaking sound.

"No, son!" Bramford called.

The boy brought Squeaky's machete down onto Jamal's chest with a sickening thump. The woulded leader fell back, his death rattle filling the stunned silence. And brave, young Logan stood by, trembling.

A breeze rustled over the compound and, even before Eden saw the men who had aided them, she realized who they were. The Aztec warriors stepped into the light as silent as the trees from which they took their camouflage of bark and leaves. In their hard-set expressions, Eden detected wisdom and, to her surprise, deep compassion.

A high-pitched scream came from behind Logan's hut. The net loosened and Bramford tumbled to the ground. An unseen hand pushed the confused teenage soldier before them. A boy playing at a man's game, Eden thought.

Two more of the Aztecs appeared with Giant between them. Although he towered over them, it was clear who was in charge. Then the warriors vanished without a trace, and the big man, too. Eden hadn't even seen them move. But why had they left the young soldier behind?

She ran her hand down Austin's heaving flank. Her tears spilled onto his bloodied fur. The women tried to lift him, but Eden refused to let go. She didn't want him to meet *Coatli-cue*. She desperately wanted to keep him.

Please, Mother Earth, don't take him.

Eden thought she heard her father's voice, but he only stared in silence. Too weak to call out, she realized. Still, the meaning in his expression reached her. *Wait and see.*

With a painful cry, she released Austin and let the women carry him away. In a solemn line, Logan and the children followed them inside one of the huts.

Eden had never felt more alone. The steady hum of the jungle and its dazzling beauty seemed far away. Numb to the world, she hardly felt the brush of Bramford's body against hers.

But there he was, folding her into his warm arms. She buried her face against his chest, sobbing.

"Austin…" Eden sputtered.

Bramford held her tight until the storm inside her passed.

She knuckled her eyes dry, wondering how he could be so an-
noying at times and then as irresistible as moonlight.

"I love you, Eden Newman," Bramford whispered in her
ear.

Then he drew her into a deep kiss.

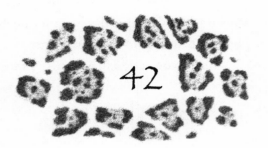

42

EDEN STOOD UP, rubbing the small of her back. She had been digging up vegetables for hours, though the time had passed easily. She enjoyed the rich, earthy smell of the dirt; even more, being part of Mother Earth's nurturing cycle. It also felt good to be of use to the Huaorani who had given her so much. Now that their location had been discovered, they needed to relocate.

Eden wrapped the vegetables in hemp sacks and carried them to the center of the compound where the women made tidy piles of herbs and their few belongings. She tried to imagine saying goodbye to them, but the effort only produced a dull ache in her chest.

At least her father would remain with the tribe. The eponymous cure had worked its magic, and just might allow him to outlive the expected life span of a Pearl. It even had healed the cut on her hand and her broken ribs.

The next day Bramford and Logan would undergo the adaptation and leave forever. Eden would just die if her father continued to stand in the way of her happiness. He had been too consumed with work to talk to her—back to his old tricks.

But time was running out; frenetic birdcalls announced

the end of the day. Eden couldn't wait another minute to settle her future.

She deposited the sacks and ran straight to the lab. Determined, she marched up to her father, who was hunched over
his console.

"We have to talk," Eden said.

"What? Yes, I'm coming," he said, though he made no
effort to move.

Bramford swept in, carrying ropes of vines. He gave Eden
a warm, seductive smile that set her heart aflame. Weak at the
knees, she watched him cross the lab.

She desperately wanted to spend her life with him. It
might not be the life she had imagined, but in her heart, she
felt it was her destiny.

The young soldier, whom the Aztecs had spared, waved
to her with an infectious smile. "Hi, Eden!"

She smiled back. "Hello, Kevon."

Beside him, Lorenzo and Charlie, who had returned soon
after Jamal's defeat, hammered together a makeshift operating bed. The Huaorani practically had adopted Kevon as
an honorary tribe member. Already, he wore the distinctive
bowl-shaped haircut and thin rope around his groin.

Eden could see that his playful spirit had not been tainted
by the FFP. Perhaps that explained the Aztecs' decision to
spare him. She only hoped his dubious past would not threat-
en her friends' future or her own.

"Please, come now, Father," Eden said.

He looked at her and sighed. "Yes, of course."

They walked outside into the gathering dusk, the quick
tapping of his crutch on the ground like the rat-a-tat-tat of

a woodpecker. Eden marveled at how quickly his strength
had returned. If only Mother had taken Newman's Cure, she
thought wistfully.

And yet, the sound of Austin's hearty bark puncturing the
air eased her regret. Thanks to the miraculous plant, he, too,
was healed. As they rounded the bend, she saw him chasing
the pet macaw. Back and forth, the bird followed a ball of
twine that the sisters and Logan tossed between them.

Logan missed a high lob from Carmen and ran after it.
He seemed eager to please his new friends, and the older sister clearly relished her role as teacher.

"He called me Mama this morning," Eden said, recalling
the warm feelings and laughter she and Logan had shared.

They had sat like royalty upon a hill strewn with a purple carpet of jacaranda petals. It had been his turn to be the
teacher, as he'd patiently instructed Eden how to paint the
rolling landscape below.

"I see," her father said, uneasily.

Still, Eden sensed his resistance. "Please tell me you've
changed your mind."

"Just as I suspected, the pheromone signals between you
and Bramford are now quite evident."

"Then you should understand."

"Indeed, I do. However, it is my responsibility to weigh
the consequences since the increased flow of hormonal activity in your brain prevents you from having an objective view."

In silence, they made their way up the stairs to the main
hut. Her father fell into the hammock with a weary sigh.
How could Eden get through to him?

"You know," she said, pulling up a stool beside him. "I
promised Mother I would take care of you."

"What? Why did Lily worry?"

"Oh, in case you sacrificed your health for some crazy, scientific quest and ended up almost dying in a remote jungle. No Life-Band, only plants for food and medicine." She laughed loudly. "Kind of funny, now, isn't it?"

"Yes, well, your mother would have been pleased to see how you've grown, but I doubt she would have approved of your proposition."

"You're wrong. Don't you remember?" Eden repeated the tender words her mother had loved. "'That Love is all there is, / Is all we know of Love.'"

Her father fell silent, staring into space. "I'd forgotten," he whispered. "I had to."

He'd loved her mother deeply, Eden realized. Then how could he deny her this chance?

He looked at her, his face awash with emotion. "Is this really what you want?"

"Yes, it is."

"The evolution of Eden?" He mused. Then his eyes brightened. "Now, do you understand—wait and see? Consider the unexpected trajectory that has brought us to this incredible possibility and the valuable research to be discovered. Eden Newman, mother of a newly adapted race. And others might join you one day. From one couple, a family, then perhaps a group or a colony, slowly taking back the land."

Yes, Eden thought, a large group of adapted people would be wonderful. Perhaps, even, to save all of the remaining Pearls. But she couldn't think about that right now. First, she needed to secure her own future.

"So, do you agree, Father?"

He stared at her intently, as if he really saw her. "Your

mother didn't mind being a Pearl as much as she disliked that absurd label. She regretted what our coloring did to other people and so she covered. Perhaps she would have admired your choice after all."

He paused, and in the stillness that settled over them, Eden felt closer to her father than ever before.

"I will allow you to adapt on one condition," he added, with an enigmatic smile.

"What?" Eden said breathlessly.

"Help me take this ridiculous coating off my face."

She grinned. "Yes, Father."

He reached for her hand. "I'm proud of you, Eden."

That was all she needed.

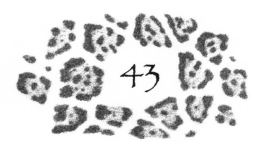

43

TOO EXCITED for sleep, Eden lay in bed, tingling with anticipation for the big day. In just a few hours, she would undergo the adaptation with Bramford and Logan. They would form a family, and perhaps one day—did she dare hope—there would be more children. She and her mate would, well, mate.

Anything was possible, Eden. Anything but sleep.

She slipped out of bed and leaned against the window, breathing in the beauty of a full moon pinned on the velvet sky. Up until now she hadn't fully imagined how she would look as a real she-cat. She angled the hand mirror to catch the silvery light and studied herself, trying to picture the dramatic transformation. Definitely nobody's pet anymore, she thought with glee.

But would panic seize her the next morning when she groggily rubbed her face and felt unusual features? Suppose she didn't like the way she looked?

She and Bramford would be two of a kind, a pair—that was all that mattered. Yes, but here was the bigger question: would he still be attracted to her? Eden simply had to know.

She hurried to the main room and found her father sleeping peacefully. At least they would see each other again in the

304 SAVE THE PEARLS

future. Ironically, by gathering data on Eden and her beastly little family, he would pay closer attention to her than she might like.

A familiar, warm vibration in her belly told Eden that Bramford was near. Her eyes flicked to the window just as he strode into view. He sat down on a boulder by the water hole, his broad back to her.

Possibly, the same question worried him.

She flew outside and, rounding the hut, found him swimming. He turned and smiled at her, which gave her a dewy feeling. The water lapped at his wide shoulders. Wet hair tangled around the rugged, chiseled face that she loved. Soft moonlight haloed his head. *My Jaguar Man.*

"Come, join me," Bramford said. "It'll be your last chance before we leave."

Eden leaned against the boulder, still warm from his body, and pondered his choice of words. By 'last chance,' did he mean she should consider changing her mind? Or even worse, had he changed his?

As if to confirm her fears, he added, "Tell me, Eden. Are you scared?"

She smiled shyly. "A little."

"I wouldn't believe it if you'd said no. Come here," he repeated, flexing a finger at her.

"Ronson?" She just didn't know how to say it.

"What's wrong?"

An indirect approach was best, she decided. "Do you like Logan's portrait of me?"

"Very much," Bramford said. "Though it doesn't quite capture your beauty."

"You really think so?"

He gave her a sultry look. "Do you want me to tell you again? You're very beautiful, Eden Newman."

Though it pleased her to hear him say it, the problem only loomed larger in her mind.

"The shade of your hair was difficult for him to capture," he continued. "At first he painted it white like his. I only helped a little." At her puzzled look, he shrugged. "I taught him to paint."

Not Rebecca? The artist's initials R.B. stood for Ronson Bramford?

Eden recalled her arrogant opinion with chagrin. *Bramford is no artist.* How wrong she had been about him, once again. She shook her head.

"Now what?" he said.

"Nothing, really. I just wished I'd known you better."

"We have time now, don't we?"

This time Eden couldn't deny the hesitation in his voice. The question in her mind begged to be asked.

"What if someone painted my portrait after today?" she said. "How would it look then?"

Bramford gave her a vacant look, then, as understanding seemed to flood his face, he laughed. "Will I still find you beautiful after the adaptation? Is that it?" Before she could respond, he added, "Then you are worried about it."

"I haven't changed my mind," she said quickly.

"You don't have to sacrifice your beauty for me, Eden," he said, though the trace of regret in his voice worried her.

"Please, tell me the truth, Ronson."

"I've changed my mind," he said abruptly.

"What?"

Eden watched in agony as he waded towards her, his expression serious. Water streamed in rivulets off his dark, glistening body, which carved the pearly light. She hadn't come this far, only to lose everything.

"You and Logan only will adapt to my current stage," Bramford said. "I'll wait for you to adjust—however long it takes. When you're ready, we'll proceed together to the final stage. Okay?"

Until he said it, Eden didn't know how relieved she would be. "Okay, that would be easier," she replied, and slowly exhaled. However, the question remained unanswered. "Or are you simply afraid of how I'll look fully adapted?"

He put his arms around her, the wet heat of his body making her shiver.

"Don't you understand?" he said. "You'll be even more beautiful to me because you'll be mine."

"Oh," Eden said, melting into his embrace.

No one had ever loved like this, she thought. Except, maybe dear Aunt Emily.

It's all I have to bring to-day,
  This, and my heart beside,
This, and my heart, and all the fields,
  And all the meadows wide.

Bramford suddenly picked up Eden and carried her, squealing, into the water.

"Stop, Ronson! You know I can't swim."

"I'm right here with you," he said quietly.

Yes, he was. He always had been.

He sank down into the water, cradling her in his arms. As she looked up, a shooting star skated across the glass-black sky like a whispered promise.

"Better?" Bramford said.

Eden smiled at him. "Better than I ever dreamt."

He began to swing her like a lazy pendulum, back and forth, in the soft water. It slipped under her dress, playing over her body. Her limbs felt as pliant and free as an animal's. *Why even bother to catalog a particular species?*

The last residue of tension floated away, leaving her buoyant and calm. Bramford seemed to register the shift in her with a seductive smile. He curled her tight against him, growling lustily.

"It's time," he said.

Her eyes widened. "For what?"

"Jaguars love to swim. And I'm going to teach you how. Let's begin with a kiss." He teased her lips with his, then whispered. "Are you ready, Eden?"

"Yes, I'm ready."

Hoover Public Library

www.hooverlibrary.org (205) 444-7800

02/16/2019

Items checked out to

RIVERA, MARLENE D

ILL- Revealing Eden : a novel
Due Date: *03-11-19*

Join the online campaign to Save the Pearls at

SaveThePearls.com

See Eden Newman's mate-rate video profile,
or add your own!

Visit SandDollarPress.com
for updates on the gripping sequel to *Revealing Eden*—

SAVE THE PEARLS PART TWO

Adapting Eden

BY VICTORIA FOYT

When the past catches up with Eden Newman and her
beastly clan, she must fight to save those she loves
against impossible odds, testing herself beyond
her limits—in love and physical strength—
while the countdown to humanity's
extinction begins.

SAND DOLLAR PRESS, INC.
www.SandDollarPress.com